The Courier

Holly studied PPE at New College, Oxford, and later became a solicitor. She began writing as a hobby at law school, along with hot yoga and marathon running; only the writing has continued. In 2016, Holly undertook a writing course at City University. She is married to James and they have two young children, Cleo and Delilah - Delilah being the exact same age as *The Courier* since she was born the same week as the first word was written. They live in north London.

THE COURIER

HOLLY DOWN

HODDER &
STOUGHTON

First published in Great Britain in 2021 by Hodder & Stoughton
An Hachette UK company

This paperback edition published in 2021

1

A CIP catalogue record for this title is available from the British Library

Paperback ISBN 978 1 529 36295 4
eBook ISBN 978 1 529 36297 8

Typeset in Plantin by Manipal Technologies Limited

Printed and bound in Great Britain by Clays Ltd, Elcograf S.p.A.

Hodder & Stoughton policy is to use papers that are natural, renewable
and recyclable products and made from wood grown in sustainable
forests. The logging and manufacturing processes are expected to
conform to the environmental regulations of the country of origin.

Hodder & Stoughton Ltd
Carmelite House
50 Victoria Embankment
London EC4Y 0DZ

www.hodder.co.uk

For Jodie

Chapter One

I always wait until I pick up the packages from the depot to choose my playlist. I match the music to my mood, like a boxer making their entrance before a big fight. This morning there were two parcels for Paradise Found, my favourite street. A day for *Power Ballad Classics*.

I save those deliveries till the end of my route, to give me something to look forward to. Delivering parcels isn't the most exciting job in the world but it gives me a chance to get to know new people. A fresh start on every doorstep is how I like to think of it.

Tina Turner is in full flow as I pull up to the gate at Paradise Found. I'm tapping my fingers on the steering wheel, feeling all-powerful from the height of the van's front seat that's like sitting on a throne. It's one of those perfect bright, cold days and I'm belting out the chorus as I pull the handbrake. I wait until the track dies away before switching off the music and entering the key code through the window. The moss-green gate glides open, revealing the row of five imposing houses. I let the van roll inside, taking care not to rev the engine and disturb the peace.

At other deliveries, I aim to execute as quickly as possible: I've got it down to thirty seconds when the recipient is at home, two minutes when they're out. Here, though,

I dawdle. There's something about this street that I've fallen in love with, though I wouldn't like to admit that out loud, and it's not just the obvious wealth. Of course, it's *nice* that the residents take care of their properties – the crocuses in the Bateses' window boxes are already coming through and the Cohens have had their guttering painted over the weekend – but it's more than that. It feels like a home.

I hop down from the van and open the back doors. The wire racks are empty apart from the bottom one where I store the Paradise Found deliveries; there's less chance of something falling and getting damaged down there. There's a department store box for number one and number five's monthly contact lens delivery. I've been getting to know the inner workings of the households in the six months I've been coming here. Deliveries say a lot about you: when your birthday is, roughly when and how much you get paid, what you like to eat and drink, when you get ill and for how long. It's almost like being part of the family.

I walk to the end of the row first, along the stretch of pavement that runs in front of the small patch of front lawn. The houses are identical – white-painted fronts with glossy black railings – but there are subtle differences that provide character. Evelyn at number two is of the generation that appreciates quality. Her curtains are a luxurious heavy brocade, if a little dated for my taste. The Addo-Smyth family at number three are on a constant hand-me-down cycle as the kids outgrow things. There's often a bed frame or a table-tennis table left disassembled outside, awaiting council collection. Number four is the Cohens and there are small signs of Bryce's style everywhere – the rich purple front door, the gold knocker. His husband Harry is more of an antiques man, but I bet inside is fabulous.

I reach number five and take a moment to compose myself. The Bateses are older than my parents and have lived on the street the longest. They bought the house well before London's property market got silly; it's amazing the details you can find online. They're only recent converts to online shopping, so I like to make sure they have a good experience. I hope they close the door and say to each other *what a nice young lady*, despite me turning forty this year, and tell their friends that they must try home delivery – there's nothing impersonal about it.

I press the doorbell once and wait. They're slow movers – their record is almost five minutes between the ring and the door opening – but I don't like to hustle them. People forget that older people haven't grown up with online shopping and it does require a degree of trust. You are opening your door to a stranger after all. I strain my ears and hear soft footfalls inside before the sound of the door being unlocked. The top deadbolt seems a little stiff, but that could be the fingers turning it, and when the door opens I'm surprised to see Mrs Bates's face in the crack; it's usually her husband at this time of day. She leaves the chain on.

'Delivery, Mrs Bates,' I say brightly and loudly. 'I'm going to need a signature.'

'Of course. Is that you Laurel?'

'That's me.' I feel a fizz of pleasure that she's remembered. It's shocking how many people can open and close

3

their door without actually seeing me, without recognising that another person is there.

I hear the rattle of her undoing the chain and keep smiling while I wait. The door opens another couple of inches. In the tiny gap I can see that the hallway is decorated in an ornate wallpaper with a dark green shag-pile carpet underfoot – nothing I haven't seen before. Mrs Bates is wearing her lambswool slippers. I shift position, moving from foot to foot in a way I hope isn't obvious, but the angle isn't wide enough to see beyond the wall.

'Here's your parcel.' I hand her the narrow box of prescription lenses. 'All I need now is your signature.'

She takes the plastic stylus – her knuckles are swollen and red and I wonder if it's arthritis – and reproduces her signature in copperplate lettering on the screen. Young people barely bother with a squiggle, usually without looking up from their phone. Once the transaction is over and the door begins to close, I feel a sudden desperation to prolong it. The day has been a brisk one and there haven't been many opportunities to chat.

'Lovely flowers,' I say. 'Nice to see a bit of colour already.'

The door wavers. A slight frown crosses her face but it softens when she sees my look of admiration. 'Thank you. It has been a mild winter hasn't it?'

She doesn't wait for me to reply and there's a click as the door shuts and then the rattle of the chain and the turning of locks. The Bateses are probably not planning on venturing out again this evening and I don't blame them; it's starting to get cold. I stare at the purple buds emerging from the planter for another few seconds, wondering if they'll survive the February chill, before striding back along the row to number one.

I don't like to play favourites, but Patrick Williams is the resident who intrigues me the most. Ten years ago his novel was a smash hit. Back when I got the tube to and from work every day, I remember every other person devouring the words between its distinctive yellow cover. I've read the rave reviews. The film was a flop but he must have made a pretty penny: a year later he spent £1.8 million on this house, another titbit I found online. Not a sniff of a sequel as far as I can see and he's always home; even the Bateses miss a delivery more often than he does. I wonder what he does to keep busy in there, living alone.

His is the shabbiest house. There are little signs of neglect, like the three strands of cobweb in the top-left corner of the front window and the tub of Halloween sweets that has been on the inside sill since October. None of the others would allow that to linger. Patrick always answers quickly. He must have his writing desk on the ground floor. Perhaps he's typing his next novel as I stand outside. Maybe I'll feature. I smile at this thought as I press the bell though there's nothing worth writing about me – nothing good anyway.

I don't need to look at my watch to know Patrick is taking longer than usual. I hesitate, unsure whether to ring again or keep waiting. I push the bell. I wait a while. I know it's silly but I'm worried. He's only mid-forties so there's unlikely to be anything wrong with him, but this is out of character. Company policy is not to interfere but I like to keep an eye on my regulars so I take out my phone, wondering who I can call. It's only after another couple of minutes that I think to check whether he's listed a safe space. I tap through the details and find he has: *Take side path. Leave inside green bin.*

I feel a frisson of excitement at the change in routine. I've never seen anything other than the front of the row before as the others have always selected '*leave with a neighbour*' as their delivery instruction when they've been out. As the end-of-terrace, Patrick's house has a narrow path alongside it, barred by a wrought-iron gate that I've always assumed was locked, but the latch opens easily. Why haven't I tried it before when I must have been here close to a hundred times? *Because that would be prying,* I tell myself.

Patrick's bins are stored against the wall and at the end is another gate. I run my fingertips along the smooth painted wall as I walk to the end. My hands are getting stiff with cold so I push them deep into my pockets. The second gate is locked with a padlock but through the bars I see an overgrown lawn, a rusty barbecue, and the other side of the fence that backs onto the footpath I'm familiar with. The garden is entirely ordinary and this side of the house doesn't even have windows. I'm disappointed but I tell myself not to be silly. Paradise Found is just another street, after all. And really, it's none of my business.

I return to the bins and unclip the lid of the green one. It's empty. I place the package inside and complete the details on my phone so that Patrick receives the instant delivery notification. Once I'm done, I feel deflated. The chill in the air makes me shiver in my thin company-branded fleece and I hug myself, trying to rub some warmth back into my skin.

I know I should leave but my eyes fall on the second bin, and I feel my brain start whirring. It's gone four. Soon it will be dark but the light hasn't disappeared yet and the passage isn't overlooked. I could take a quick peek. It's amazing the things people throw out these days. It can tell you a lot about them and I would like to get to know Patrick a little better. I do see a lot of him.

I look around me to check I'm alone before lifting the lid and pulling out the first black bag. This isn't something I make a habit of but I tell myself it's only rubbish; things that have been discarded, like I have been. I promise myself I'll only do it this once as I make quick work of the knot. The sulphurous smell of rotten egg makes me gag. On top are several broken shells and a gooey mass of what might have been cake mix. I didn't have Patrick down as a baker but it just goes to show, you should never judge a book by its cover. I go to close the bag up again but then I spot a sheaf of papers further down, and my pulse quickens. It could be a manuscript. Perhaps I'll uncover Patrick's second bestseller that he's cast aside too hastily. I picture him thanking me profusely for rescuing it, telling me he'll dedicate it to me – and then catch myself and shake my head at my own silliness.

I scrape the goo to one side and extract the top piece of paper. It's a letter from a solicitor with a fancy header and a date at the top from 2016. Patrick must have been having a clear-out. I scan the text but it's just a standard fee quote setting out the hourly rates and disbursement charges. I have several of these in my own files only from a different type of lawyer. This must be from his divorce. His book was dedicated to '*My darling Maria*' and there's no darling Maria living at number one, Paradise Found.

I drop the letter back in and flick through the next few sheets. It's all correspondence – invoices from plumbers and letters from estate agents asking if he wants to sell – nothing of interest. I delve deeper. Beneath the paper, a bathroom bin has clearly been emptied. There's a squashed bottle of Listerine, a couple of cardboard loo rolls as well as – my fingers fumble – a slippery used condom and—

'What the hell are you doing?'

I stand up so fast my neck cricks. My face is on fire and that sickeningly familiar feeling of shame I hate so much is spreading across my chest. Patrick is inside the gate with a pile of shopping bags at his feet. His face is twisted in anger and his rimless glasses are steamed up from the exertion. I know I need to act quickly, and my mind races in search of an explanation. What can I say? It's risky but all I can think of is to lift my hand and tug the silver moon-shaped earring from its hole.

'I'm sorry. I lost my earring.' I rub the empty hole with the earring pressed into my palm, praying he won't spot it. 'I was leaving your parcel in the safe space and I just popped a crisp packet in your bin when I realised it was missing.'

His expression is a mix of incredulity and disgust. I force myself to hold his gaze and try to convey that this isn't me, it's not who I really am. I edge back from the gaping bin bag to distance myself further from my own actions. Patrick is a handsome man – my 'type', as they say – the perfect combination of scatter-brained academic and square-jawed aftershave model and I've allowed myself to daydream about him on more than one occasion. Needless to say, my daydreams don't contain moments like this.

He still hasn't spoken so I go on, my words coming out in a rush. 'I thought I felt it come out when I bent down and it has sentimental value. It was a gift from my husband, my ex – well, he died so . . .' It's always hard to find the right words.

Patrick pushes his hand through his thick, salt-and-pepper hair and pushes his glasses up his nose. The intensity of his stare makes me shift uncomfortably and there's a moment where I see I'm in the balance – my job, *everything*, is in his hands – then his expression lifts and I feel a swoop of relief. 'I'm sorry, gosh. Can I help you look?'

I dump the bag back into the bin and let my earring fall inside. 'Don't worry. Maybe it came out in the van.'

It's cold enough now to see our breath, and it's time to go home. My body feels wrung out from the tension. I open the recycling bin and lift out Patrick's package, trying to hide the tremors in my hands. 'I can bring this to the door if you need a hand?'

He picks up his shopping bags and tries to figure out a way to carry the box too before nodding and saying stiffly, 'That would be helpful.'

For ten seconds it feels like we could be an ordinary couple, returning home from a trip to the supermarket. Perhaps we've bought steaks and a bottle of red, maybe a cheesecake for dessert – my favourite, but they're always too big for one. The silly fantasy warms me and the panicky feeling fades. I watch as Patrick unlocks the deadbolt first, then the Yale. There's no alarm. He steps into the dark hallway and deposits the plastic bags inside before returning for the package but I don't leave right away. I need to make him understand.

'I'm sorry about before. I would never have done that if it hadn't been so important to me.' My hand returns to my lobe and I rub some heat into the bare skin.

'I understand,' Patrick says, and he meets my gaze. 'I really do.'

As his eyes bore into mine it's as though he's trying to communicate something to me, and we share a moment that makes me think that Patrick knows loss intimately, in the same way I do. But then the moment is over; he doesn't invite me in or even turn on the light. I've only seen a glimpse of the hallway and now his back garden. It's the kitchen I'd like to see, and the bedroom: the heart and soul of the home respectively. But I know they will have to remain the stuff of my daydreams.

'Thank you,' he says.

I give him a bright, fake smile, walk back to the van and haul myself into the driver's seat but I don't turn on the music. I look down at my hands and realise that I'm still shaking. What was I thinking? That was too close. What must he think of me? I glance back and see that Patrick's lights are still off. Perhaps he's behind the curtain, one finger hooked around the edge to make an eye-sized gap, watching me.

Chapter Two

The spell cast by Paradise Found is soon broken when I join back-to-back traffic just beyond the gate. My visit is the one moment of calm and light in my day, but the feeling never lasts long. Rush hour in London starts early and finishes late, and 'hour' doesn't quite cut it. Tension quickly returns to my shoulders. A moped cuts in front of me and I jam the horn. I'm in no rush but you learn not to show weakness on the roads or you become a victim. That's a lesson I learned the hard way.

It's less than a mile as the crow flies to the low-rise estate in Whitechapel where I live, but it takes forty minutes in the traffic. Patience is something I've learned in the five years since I became a delivery driver, that and being able to sit alone with my thoughts. My old job in banking didn't allow for much self-reflection, but nowadays I have too much time for it.

By the time I reach my parking space in the alleyway behind the estate, I've already been over the incident with Patrick several times in my head, my thoughts buzzing with the implications and insinuations. It wasn't so bad, I tell myself. He seemed to accept my story and maybe it will give us something to bond over and laugh about next time. *I can't believe you thought I was snooping in your bins – how funny!* I test it out a few times aloud, adding a false laugh at the end that I work on so it sounds authentic.

I park up and as I walk to the entrance my feet crunch on broken glass, sending empty laughing gas canisters skittering. This area is an odd mix of young people looking to party and families. I'm here because it's cheap since all the money I earned is long gone. Legal representation is expensive. Another lesson I learned the hard way.

My flat is on the fourth floor and the estate is teeming with life as I make my way up. There are people shouting, a baby crying, and someone is playing hip-hop too loudly. I step over kids tapping on phones on the stairs and breathe in the aromatic smell of dinner that wafts through the building at this time of day. I like being so close to everyday family rituals. It's easy to feel like I'm part of them and I can fool myself into thinking I'm not so alone.

When I first moved in, the noise took some time to get used to. Our old flat was on the top floor of a new glass building that felt as if it had been hermetically sealed. None of the windows opened and I can remember the stillness of the air and the sound of footsteps echoing on the hardwood floors. Sometimes it felt hard to breathe in there.

This block is an ugly seventies building made from dirty grey bricks with small rooms and tiny windows, and it's bursting at the seams. It's not much to look at but each floor has a walkway that runs the length of the building with quite a view over the city. There's an unbroken sight line to the dome of St Paul's but I don't like to look out for long – the city holds too many bad memories for me.

The walkway is used as an extension to people's living spaces and is always cluttered with drying racks, stacks of bikes and weedy potted tomato plants. Next door, Ramzan is out on his deckchair, wearing a shiny red puffa jacket and smoking a cigarette. His hair is parted in sleek curtains that he has a habit of smoothing onto his high forehead and his nose pokes through the middle like a blade. He gestures to the pack of Embassy on the arm-rest with a flick of his skinny wrist.

'Thanks,' I say and he tosses me the packet.

I light a cigarette and breathe deeply. I don't often smoke but after what just happened, I feel like I need one. It takes a minute for the nicotine to circulate but soon I feel it tingling in my fingers and toes.

'Rough day?' he asks.

I shrug. Ramzan drives an Uber so he gets it.

'You?'

He cocks one eyebrow and I can tell that he's got a story. One of us usually does given that working in our jobs you see the worst of humanity. He takes a long drag of his cigarette before launching into it. 'I had this one lady right, picked her up on Oxford Street and drove her all the way to Holland Park. She only went and left her shopping in the back and then she calls me wanting me to drop it round right away only I'm already on a job to Gatwick.'

I nod along but Ramzan needs little encouragement. We act as a form of therapy for one another, taking a minute out on the walkway to vent before entering our own flats and dealing with our own shit. I consider him a friend, perhaps my only one, but I'd never tell him that. 'So I must be, what, an hour away, and she says—'

He's interrupted by a squeal and a thump from inside his flat followed by a loud wail. Ramzan is only twenty-four but he's married with two kids already. He opens the door and yells something in Bengali. The noise stops. He takes out another cigarette and lights it from the tail end of the first, smoking faster as though aware our time is coming to an end.

'Where was I? Gatwick, right. So I cancel the job and get back to her house an hour later with her shopping and guess what?'

'What?'

'She's only gone out. I ring her and she says to come back tomorrow. I'm tempted to get her stuff up on eBay.'

We both laugh but I know he'll be driving across London again tomorrow. He can't risk his rating. We smoke in silence for a minute. I lean with my back against the railing, elbows on the metal guard rail, and think of Patrick.

'What?' Ramzan says.

I realise I'm frowning as I go over again in my head what happened with Patrick. Ramzan might not understand so I just give my head a little shake and force a smile.

'I actually had a nice one today,' I say.

'Why am I not surprised? You always get the good ones. A guy was it?'

I nod.

'Bet he wanted a piece of the Laurel pie.'

I give a strangled-sounding laugh, not wanting to let on how much I wish this was true, which Ramzan interprets as me agreeing. He whoops and flicks his hand so the fingers clack together.

'I knew it. Come on, don't leave me hanging. What was he like?'

'Just a guy,' I say quickly.

'Age?'

'Forties.'

'Peng?'

'What?'

'Come on, man. Nice-looking? You know, fit.'

I think of Patrick's scruffy charm and try to see him through Ramzan's eyes. Today he was wearing chinos and a blazer with orange patches on the elbows and he looked like he hadn't brushed his hair in days. A far cry from Ramzan's carefully cultivated look of designer labels and lots of hair gel. 'He has a certain appeal,' I settle on.

Ramzan's face twitches as if he's unimpressed.

'What about his crib?'

I hesitate. 'It's big.'

Ramzan flicks his hand again, twice this time. 'That's what I like to hear. You want to focus, girl. He could be your ticket out of here. Get yourself installed in some mansion and Uncle Ramzan can come for afternoon tea. Hey, I'll be your driver. You pay well?'

'Of course.' We're both laughing as Ramzan drinks from an imaginary teacup, his pinkie finger sticking up into the air. I don't tell him that I've already been on the other side and lived that life. My last bonus from the bank was probably more than he gets paid in three years.

There's a loud crash from inside Ramzan's flat and he jumps up.

'That better not have been the telly.'

He opens the door and shouts again but his wife calls back in strained tones. It sounds like he's needed.

'Bloody kids. Don't have any.' He says this with a smile and we both know he's joking. His kids are his world. I laugh along and try to suppress the flicker of jealousy. A normal family life isn't an option for me.

'I better go,' he says and grinds his cigarette on the bricks beneath his kitchen window. He goes inside, telling off his children to a chorus of noisy tears that I hear as if I'm in the room with them. The insulation here is dreadful, but I'll happily take the noise if it means I can enjoy our chats. It's rare that I have any other conversations that go beyond '*delivery for you*' these days.

I savour my cigarette before unlocking my front door. Inside smells of damp and the noise of the tantrum from next door is barely muffled. There's nothing inviting or homely about the place but I haven't made much effort. I've moved four times in the past five years and never really put down roots. What's the point when it's just me?

It's not much warmer inside than out and I switch on the bare bulb overhead, going straight through into the main living space – a single room with kitchen units on one side that look out onto the walkway. My only furniture is a desk that used to be my dad's before he retired, a crappy sofa that I got from Gumtree that looks worse in reality than it did in the photos, and an ergonomic desk chair – a large leather monstrosity that has a rest for every part of my body, some days I sleep in it.

My notebooks take up a lot of the rest of the space. They're piled on the desk and there are stacks behind the sofa that have grown to almost waist-height. Older ones are filed in the boxes in the bedroom and it's clear from the pungent smell of damp in that room that some have got wet, only I can never find the right box and I've grown used to it now.

It may look like a mess but I have a system. It started as a way to fill my evenings after I'd finished my deliveries. I'd record little details about my day – nice things people had said or funny things I'd seen – but I know it's got a little out of hand. I keep finding streets where I want to keep a record of everything I learn. Places like Paradise Found with the perfect combination of luxury and comfort; the polar opposite of here. It's just a hobby, I reason, whenever I start to feel like it's going too far. There's no harm in looking, as they say.

The wall above the desk is dedicated to Sophie. There are my favourite photos from when she was a baby blown up to A4 size. A newborn Sophie, pink and wrinkled like a baby mouse. Her first day of nursery, with her hair in two plaits, hugging her llama blanket to her cheek – she never let it out of her sight. The last picture I have of her is in the centre of the wall. She's just turned two; her baby fat is already disappearing and her brown eyes are serious like mine – it's the straight eyebrows that do it.

My notes are on Post-its scattered around the photos of her. Different colours for different theories. Some days I add to them, my adrenaline pumping as I have a new idea, and other days I tear them down in disgust. Today, I don't have the energy; it hurts to even think of her, so I don't. I've become an expert at controlling my thoughts since otherwise I wouldn't be able to get out of bed.

I open the kitchen cupboard and take out the bottle of Johnnie Walker and a glass. I pour it with shaking hands and slam a couple of inches back. It's tempting to keep going at that pace but I've promised myself I'll slow down. Much like the notebooks, my drinking started as a small escape, but it's even harder to keep it under control when it's one of the few pleasures I have left.

I pour a second, my hands steady this time, and take it over to the desk where my Paradise Found notebooks are displayed in pride of place. It's only been six months but the blue covers are already getting tatty. I slide out 'number one' and open it to the next blank page. I write: *Yale + deadbolt + no alarm*. Next, I draw a diagram of the side passage and mark the location of the bins. Not that I can check them again for a while; I've already drawn too much attention to myself. *And not that I would want to*, I remind myself. Today was just a one-off.

The whisky begins to soften the edges of my thoughts and I rest my head back. It was a close call today, but I realise I don't regret it. Since I began visiting I've felt a certain sort of kinship with Patrick. We both live alone, both pursue solitary careers, and we were both married once. Perhaps we're both lonely? I haven't really dared believe it before but despite what happened, it felt like a breakthrough. At the very least, I've made an impression now where before he probably never even noticed my existence. That's something.

My eyes grow heavy and I let them close. Next time I'll ask him a question. Something beyond '*How are you today?*' An opener. I never was brilliant with men but I wasn't a total disaster. I managed to marry Dominic, after all. It wasn't all plain sailing but there were some good years, back when my life was on track. Perhaps Ramzan may be right, I think as I drift off to sleep: Patrick could be my way back. But of course, it could never be the same, not without Sophie.

Chapter Three

At the depot the next morning I open the Zippi app and put the barcode under the entry scanner. The gate whirs open. A collection point number flashes up on the screen and I drive to the correct bay. My parcels are already stacked in a precise order in a trolley, which I heave over to the van. As I load them into the wire racks installed in the back of the van, the delivery log pops up on my phone. I like working for a start-up – everything is streamlined and electronic, and there's no need to deal with colleagues.

Finding Zippi was a godsend really. I'd already done a stint with a few other delivery companies and was on the lookout for a new employer when the company seemed to rise up from nowhere. It was only founded two years ago but managed to secure a couple of premium partnerships delivering for John Lewis and Boots and it really took off. It's a tech unicorn apparently, valued at over a billion dollars, but all I know is it keeps me busy and I like it that way.

I check the delivery log. There are no packages for Paradise Found today but I don't let it get me down. You can't win the jackpot every time you play. I listen to Coldplay as I drive my route. It's a slow day. More people are out than usual, and as the day goes on I feel

20

a familiar, rising frustration. Why do people order things when they know they're not going to be home? It's plain bad manners. I know it's not personal but it's hard not to feel that way when I'm filling in my fifth '*sorry we missed you*' form in a row.

My final delivery takes me further afield than usual, as far as Archway where I get snarled up in a backlog caused by a set of temporary lights. It's been an overcast day with low, hazy clouds that have never cleared, and I flick on my lights earlier than usual as I crawl back south. Soon I'm running late and my frustration flicks over into annoyance. When the car in front stalls at a red light I lean on my horn but it doesn't make me feel better. It's just my luck that the one day I have plans I'm held up.

I arrive at my group after the start. The church hall is draughty so I zip up my fleece to the chin as I slip inside. The usual half-dozen sad women sit on plastic chairs in a circle, cradling styrofoam cups of tea. The urn is on a table by the door and hisses and spits as the water boils again, providing the soundtrack to our sessions. Sharon, our newest member, is already speaking, so I take the empty seat closest to the door.

'It was right after Christmas, and that time of year is hard enough.' She has a strong north London accent that makes her sound tough but there's a tissue primed in her fingers and her voice wavers.

Everyone is nodding. They dread the festive period but for me it's the best time of year. People order so much more – there's no time to think about what might have been – and there's always a ready excuse for a drink. *It's*

Christmas, have another! No need to feel guilty. We even have wine at group.

Sharon goes on and there's a hush of anticipation in the room. 'We'd been rowing, but what family doesn't? Over silly stuff like what to watch on the telly but also she'd got this new fella. I'll say straight off that I didn't like him. A wrong sort. Been in trouble with the police more times than he'd been in school. And he didn't have a job. No means to support her.'

A few people nod and exchange glances. We all know the type. I keep watching Sharon as she presses her lips together with a wince of regret. We don't look anything alike but occasionally I catch glimpses of myself in her. I think it might be that we both blame ourselves. Sharon can't be much older than me but she doesn't look after herself. Overweight, claggy make-up, and a bad dye job. She always smells of sweet perfume with a strong undertone of fags and as soon as she gets outside after we finish she always lights one up. Not that I blame her – I'm usually desperate for one after a group session too.

'So I said he couldn't come round for Christmas dinner and she took the hump and said she'd go to her dad's then, and I thought fair enough, let her dad deal with the drama for once. But she never turned up.'

Sharon's voice cracks and turns into a hacking cough. She doesn't sound healthy. We all shuffle in our seats and exchange uneasy glances as we wait for her to stop. I wonder if she's had that cough checked out. She finally manages to get it under control and dabs at her eyes with the tissue.

'I thought she was with him and he thought she was with me. Took us a few days to realise that they were gone. Only sixteen she was.'

We take that in, knowing how hard it is to get anyone to show interest at that age.

'That was three years ago and I haven't seen her since. He's from one of those big families with people all over the country. I get news she's in one place and by the time I try to reach her, they've moved on. All I want is to tell her she's welcome home any time. I heard she had a baby, a boy. I haven't even met him. My own grandson.'

Sharon can't go on. She presses the tissue to her face. Audrey reaches out from the next seat and squeezes her hand, making me think of two chubby baseball mitts stuck together. I feel sorry for Sharon but a part of me is hardened against her story. Runaways don't hold much sway with me because there's always a chance they'll run right back. Some of the women in this room have much heavier crosses to bear.

'Let's leave it there for now, Sharon,' Denise says delicately. 'Thanks for sharing. That's what we're all about – sharing our pain, along with our coping strategies. It helps to know what each other is going through.'

Denise is the mother hen of the group and our unofficial leader. A bookish woman called Elaine organises the sessions and takes care of the admin but it's Denise we look up to. We all know her story: her Dion went to school one morning in the nineties and never came back. Murdered is the presumption, but no one has been charged. Denise has fought the longest and the hardest of anyone here.

She peers over the top of her red glasses. It's one of her trademark looks. I've seen it printed in the paper. Everyone looks at their feet except me.

'Laurel,' she says, 'we haven't heard from you for a while.'

I start at my name and regret not looking down. My heart thuds and I feel my face growing hot.

'How are you?' Denise asks gently.

I know it's not really her fault, but Denise makes me feel like I'm back at school. Actually, scratch that – I always did well at school. She takes me back to my job in banking, where expectations were so high it was easy to fall short. Or back to my marriage. I was always disappointing Dominic.

Group isn't a place where you can brush off questions with a stock response so I don't answer right away. Sharon blows her nose. Everyone waits. I wonder what's safe to tell them. I can't tell them what happened with Patrick because I don't want to get into trouble. Everyone gets online deliveries and never for one second considers that the person at their door might be going through their own issues, that they're human too. I don't want to shatter that illusion in case it gets back to Zippi. It wouldn't be the first job I've lost for that reason.

'I've been having these dreams.' My voice sounds odd when I'm not speaking in my perky courier tones. It's been a few days since the last dream, but they feel so real and linger with me for days. 'I wake up terrified. Like it's happening all over again.'

'I think we all get those.' Denise's voice is warm. I see others nodding. 'Do you want to tell us about them?'

I close my eyes and see the window with the suction handle stuck to it and the spiderweb of cracks. I never knew they could be removed in one piece but I've watched it done on YouTube many times since. It can be done in under ten seconds – there's a knack to it. My dreams don't usually get much beyond that image. It haunts me, popping into my mind at unwelcome moments. I've got better at controlling it when I'm awake, but what can you do about your subconscious?

My eyes flick open and I see everyone is watching me. I'm sweating. I tug at the zipper of my fleece and pull it down a few inches. I don't need to look to know that an angry red rash will be climbing my neck.

'I'm sorry. I don't feel up to sharing today.'

Audrey rushes in. 'Of course you are going to relive it. What an awful day. I can't even begin to imagine—'

'Thank you,' I say stiffly, cutting her off. I don't need Audrey to tell me how bad it was. It was the worst day of my life. The day when I split in two: before and after. I think that's how everyone feels who has lost a child. We talk about it here in those terms.

There's an unofficial divide in Missing Mums between those of us whose children were taken and those whose went of their own accord. Denise and I have always banded together. I've felt her support even when she hasn't spoken. She is silent now and I can't read the look she is giving me. I try a small smile but she doesn't even nod. Perhaps my case isn't high-profile enough to hold her interest. Sophie hasn't been on the front page of every paper like Dion.

'Let's take a break,' Denise says.

Most people get up and cluster around the trestle table where the biscuits are laid out on paper plates. Sharon and another woman go outside for a cigarette. I stay seated. I find the chit-chat awkward when we know such intimate details about each other. I've never felt able to debate the merits of chocolate Hobnobs versus plain after the things we've said.

'Mind if I join you?' Denise sits next to me and pulls her chair in close. She always looks well put together with her long braids piled on top of her head and statement earrings. Today's pair has orange feathers that brush her shoulders. I'm in my work uniform, all black – trousers, flat shoes, fleece but no cap and the contrast makes me feel embarrassed. I should take better care of myself.

Denise clears her throat. 'Thanks for sharing. It helps us all to know others are going through the same things.'

I nod but I think of Sharon. I don't want to be uncharitable but she and I are not in the same boat. Her situation doesn't help me.

'Has there been any progress with your case?' Denise asks.

I shake my head and drop my gaze as I feel the prickle of tears. If I'm honest, my search for Sophie has dried up to a trickle. I no longer spend hours trawling the internet for photos of children her age or driving around new areas of London with one eye on the road and the other scanning the pavement. The notion that I'm giving up is too painful to admit, let alone say aloud. A lump that feels like the size of a mango is stuck in my throat.

'Keep going.' Denise squeezes my shoulder as if hearing my thoughts and her kindness makes tears leak into my eyes, but I blink them away. 'I'll tell you what, let me take it up with my contacts at the Met. See if there's any way we can get new lifeblood into it.'

'No.' The word bursts from my mouth before I can stop it and Denise's eyebrows knit together. I didn't mean it to come out with so much force but when she gets something in her head she's like a terrier with the scent of a squirrel. I know she means well but Sophie is my daughter and her disappearance is my loss. What to do about it is my decision.

I rearrange my face into what I hope is a grateful smile.

'Really, there's no need.' Thankfully my voice comes out softer, more controlled. 'I speak to them regularly and they're doing their best.'

The little line between Denise's eyes doesn't go away. She speaks again and I think I hear a note of incredulity lifting her voice. 'After the inquiry I have contacts right the way to the top. Are you sure you don't want me to give them a nudge?'

'I'm sure.' I think quickly and come up with a reason Denise might accept. 'I don't want my detective to think I've gone over his head. You understand that?'

Denise nods. 'Who is your detective?'

A worm of anger wriggles its way under my skin. Why won't she leave me alone? Group isn't about pushing people. It's a safe space.

'Can we just leave it?' I demand.

Denise looks startled. She pulls at one of her earrings and the lobe stretches. My insides are whirring. I glance at the door. The desire to flee is almost overwhelming but Denise puts her hand on my arm. 'Of course. It's your case and it's up to you how it's handled. Let's get a biscuit, shall we.'

She releases my arm and leads the way; I don't have any choice but to follow her over to the table where the others are chatting. We hover on the edge of the group and I try to catch the gist of the conversation. Audrey is talking about an American dating programme where the contestants fall in love without seeing each other. She thinks it's a romantic concept but it sounds ludicrous to me. I try to join in but as I don't own a TV it's a bit awkward. Denise returns to my side with a couple of digestives. She's still frowning and she stands close so she's speaking almost in my ear.

'You do have support, don't you?'

I guess she means beyond group. I nod. She waits, and I see that hasn't satisfied her.

'I've just met someone actually,' I find myself saying.

Finally, she smiles.

'A writer.'

Audrey stops talking and turns her sizable body towards me like an oil tanker turning. I sense a few others listening too.

'How did you meet him?' Denise asks, a new bounce in her voice.

I have no choice but to press on with the lie. 'Through work.' Her eyes dart to the logo on my fleece and I carry on quickly. 'I don't usually chat much to people but we just hit it off.'

'It sounds like the plot of a film,' gushes Audrey.

I smile as she begins to outline a possible future for Patrick and me. She finishes with, 'And then, of course, he'd bury you under the patio.'

We all laugh, and she shrugs.

'Romance doesn't sell,' she says.

The conversation moves on and I'm grateful that the attention is off me. I edge over to the urn and make myself a cup of tea, just for something to do with my hands. It's been a tense evening and I'm sweaty beneath my fleece despite the chill in the room. Denise's eyes follow me; it's like I can see the cogs turning in her head, trying to work me out.

When it's time to go, I slip out ahead of the others to avoid any goodbyes. I cross the road to where I parked the van and hop up onto the front seat, just sitting for a moment and enjoying the quiet. My van is my kingdom. It may be a second-hand transit but it's clean and there's a heady scent of strawberry from the air freshener dangling from the mirror that I find strangely moreish. I dig my fingers into the foam seat, resisting for as long as I can before reaching across to the passenger side and opening the glove compartment, where I keep my flask. It's handy that these days reusable plastic water bottles have gone out of fashion – metal is so much more discreet.

Chapter Four

I arrive at the depot the next morning with a hangover, my mind still whirring. Who does Denise think she is? I know she meant well but her questions sent me into a downwards spiral, bringing up memories of Sophie that I had to drink to suppress. As my stomach roils, I hate myself for being so weak. Driving for a living means I should control my alcohol intake, I know that.

I scan the delivery log. There's nothing for Paradise Found. Again. I'm beginning to feel anxious. I know that the residents don't need me exactly, but I don't want them to forget about me. I'm part of the community. And what about Patrick? Now we've had a conversation, I might be able to get to know him better. Who knows where it might go? It could be one of those moments we recount to our kids. *The first time we met, Daddy thought Mummy was a strange lady!*

Without a trip to Paradise Found, the day passes in a blur of slammed doors and fast fashion bags. People think they're original but I see the same size and shape parcels again and again. I'm not in the mood to chat so I finish my deliveries early and the evening stretches ahead of me, empty. It's been a long time since I had any plans other than group and that's over for a week. Usually I settle in with a drink and my notebooks but today I have a restless energy. I start for home but on the way I change my mind. I drive against the traffic instead, taking the familiar route to Paradise Found. I won't go inside, of course. The entry code is for professional use only. That's a company rule and I do try to follow them, when I can. But sometimes, just being close makes me feel better.

I've been listening to whining guitar music but I switch over to love songs as I make my way there. What I like best about Paradise Found is the way that it's so unexpected. One moment you're driving past a Carphone Warehouse, the next you're inside the gated street – an enclave in a brash part of central London, only two streets back from Tottenham Court Road. It's a mews but with grand houses built to look detached even though they're terraced and with little gardens front and back, not the cramped living most Londoners are used to. Even the penthouse apartment we lived in was small, or 'compact' as the estate agent described it.

I park the van a short distance away from the gate in a pay-and-display spot. Parking has become one of my biggest outgoings, after premium liquor. It's getting dark and there's a bite to the air so I pull my company cap low over my eyes and make for the back fence of the properties that's accessed by a narrow footpath between two busy roads.

It's nice to be outside after a day cooped up in the van. My ponytail swings as I walk and I'm humming Celine Dion as I reach the corner. The fence is eight feet tall and the panels are solid wood and greying from the weather. At regular intervals is a sticker that reads: *Beware, this area is monitored by CCTV,* though I've never seen a camera. There's no way to see over but it's fun to guess what is going on behind the thin planks of wood, so close that in the late summer days, when I began coming here, I could sometimes smell what they were having for dinner.

The Bateses must employ a gardener – neither is supple enough for all that bending – so I imagine that their garden is neat and well-planned. There's probably a row of daffodils waiting to emerge. Bryce Cohen seems like the water-feature type – one of those cheeky cherubs weeing into the pond – and the Addo-Smyths have a trampoline, I've heard the springs pinging. Evelyn is an old-fashioned enthusiast; she probably has flowers for every season and knows all their Latin names.

I dawdle behind Patrick's house. There are streetlights but they're widely spaced so the arcs of light are interspersed with shadow, and Patrick's fence happens to be a gloomy spot. I've already seen his garden but there's a chance that he could be outside at this very moment, pacing the lawn for inspiration or smoking a cigarette on the terrace. I sniff the air and run my fingers against the wood until I feel the sharp nip of a splinter. My hand goes to my mouth, and that's when I spot it: the small hole in the centre of a knot in the wood. It's almost the perfect height. I'd only need to stretch onto my tiptoes to peep through.

I glance up and down the pavement to check there's no one around. My pulse quickens and before I can wonder whether it's really a good idea, I take one last look and step up to the fence. But the hole is higher than I first thought and it's a terrible angle. All I can see is a small section of the white-painted wall and the corner of a window. What room is that? The lights are off so the glass is dark. I haven't seen the floor plan of Patrick's house but most of the others have their dining room at the back. It might be his study. Imagine, if the light was on, I'd have a clear view inside.

A man clears his throat from behind me. It feels like my heart stops for a moment and as I move away quickly, it restarts at double-speed.

'Hey,' he calls out, 'just a second . . .'

I don't want to run – running would look like I've done something wrong – but I walk faster.

'Hey!' he yells, sounding angry now.

I reach the end of the footpath and turn onto the busy street, feeling immediately safer with more people around. I whip off my cap so that I look like someone else, but I'm not sure if he's behind me. I consider ducking inside the off-licence but then I'd be cornered. My heart is still thudding and I'm casting about for somewhere to hide when I spot a gap in the traffic and dart across. Someone slams their horn but I reach the other side and crouch behind the back wheel of a parked Range Rover, resting my hands on my knees and sucking in as much air as I can. I peer across the road and make out the shape of a man in a long overcoat standing on the pavement with a dog at his heels. I recognise the brown fluff-ball – it's Harry Cohen's Cockapoo.

Harry looks around but soon the dog begins straining on the lead, wanting his walk. My legs ache from holding a crouching position. I don't have the muscle tone I once did; I spend too much time sitting in the van. Harry shrugs his shoulders theatrically – he's a man who likes his temper to be known – and lets the dog pull him up the street. I wait until they're out of view before I stand and stretch out my knees.

My thoughts are coming too fast. What have I done? How much did he see? What if he says something to Patrick? I'm hyperventilating and I have to concentrate to keep my breathing under control. It's the second close call in a week, and for what? I could lose my access to Paradise Found with a single email. All it would take is one customer complaint and I'd be allocated a new route, or worse, Zippi could decide I'm too much of a liability and fire me. I wish I could say it hasn't happened before but delivery companies operate such strict rules and there's never any discretion applied. What was I thinking?

I take the long way round to return to the van, avoiding the footpath in case Harry comes that way. It's a relief to get back inside and a gulp from my flask settles me before I set off for home. But I can't relax. One swig won't cut it. The steering wheel grows slippery in my grip. I jab the button and switch off the music. Could Harry have spotted me? He only saw my back but he might have recognised me given that I've handed him a hundred packages, at least.

Back at my flat, I go straight to my desk, opening a bottle of red that I keep in a box underneath, filling an empty whisky glass to the brim and glugging it back. I take out my Paradise Found notebook labelled 'number four' and begin reading from the first page. It's strange to think that my first delivery to the Cohens was six whole months ago. A case of wine. 'Rosé', Bryce had said. 'Simply divine in the sunshine.' And he'd laughed at his little rhyme. I'd liked him right away. I flick forward until I land on the day I met Harry – older and stockier, a silver fox with his grey, combed hair and neat moustache. A month later and the weather must have turned. Harry signed for a new weighty duvet without a word.

Next, there are pages filled with what I discovered online. Not much on Bryce beyond his social media accounts that display his magpie tendencies for anything sparkly. Harry, on the other hand, has a reputation as a prominent antiques dealer to maintain. He appears at events, writes articles, and provides titillating information for magazine profiles. There was even a spread of photos from his last home, before he married Bryce.

I've always felt wary of Harry. There's a steel core beneath that three-piece suit – you can tell from the way he holds himself – and he's pernickety about his deliveries. He often barks at me to keep things upright and insists I use the parcel trolley even for lighter pieces. I'm sure he won't go down without a fight. I pour another glass of red and keep turning the pages of my notebook. I don't know exactly what I'm looking for, but I'll know it when I find it. I always do. It doesn't need to be something big and obvious. The smaller things are often cleaner.

My mind is starting to whir in the way it does when I drink. My brain connections fizz, taking me in all sorts of directions. I open my laptop and visit Harry's website where he buys and sells antiques. His impressive credentials fill the screen. I return to my notes and go through each delivery, every individual item. It's gone 4am when I push my chair back, exhausted but triumphant.

Gotcha.

Chapter Five

The next morning there are two packages for Paradise Found: one for Mrs Addo-Smyth at number three and the other for Bryce Cohen. I'm apprehensive about delivering to the Cohens so soon but I put on Oasis and turn the volume up high. When you're not in a good mood, 'fake it till you make it' is my motto.

It rains hard most of the day and I seem to get caught in a shower at every stop. Drivers typically dash out and let the cardboard get wet but I take the time to put up my branded umbrella as we're meant to, adding a minute to each delivery, so I'm later than usual when I arrive at the electronic green gate and needles of rain glimmer in my headlights.

Patrick's house is dark. There's no inviting porch light or warmth from the window. I'd like to knock on the door and pick up where we left off, picturing us as two lost souls drifting at sea, deciding to share the same boat. I consider pretending I've misread the address on one of the parcels but I dismiss the idea quickly. Two close calls is dangerous; three would be suicidal.

I do, however, walk slowly, stepping over puddles and peering through the black glass of his front window from behind my umbrella. With no light inside, the glass is like a piece of black mirror, reflecting only my bedraggled self. Perhaps I should be grateful I don't have anything for Patrick today: my hair needs a wash and the late night has left my skin pale and even more visibly lined. There's nowhere to hide at forty.

At the Addo-Smyths' house, I push the bell and there's an immediate stomp of feet coming down the stairs. The door flies open and one of the children appears, the youngest, a girl named Issy who's only nine or ten but is already transfixed by the mobile phone in her hand.

'Mum!' she yells over her shoulder. 'Door!'

I stare at her – she's striking with her dad's freckles and her mum's dark skin – and I will her to look at me, just once, but she turns and tramps back upstairs without any acknowledgement. Part of me feels sorry for her. No one is teaching this generation how to interact, how to love. The other part wants to scream just to get her attention. I shake my head as another set of footsteps approaches and Mrs Addo-Smyth opens the door wider, revealing a couple of bikes stacked in the hallway. This family is always on the move.

'Oh, it's just a delivery.' She's wearing a blue-striped apron over her expensive exercise gear and is drying her hands on the front. She is the type of woman Dominic should have chosen. Attractive, but understated with it. Her black hair is usually in a sleek ponytail – she must take the time to get it straightened – and with that bone structure she doesn't need make-up. She likes to keep fit but not at the expense of homemaking. And of course, she doesn't work. I often wonder, if I'd made different decisions, would my life be more like hers?

'Awful weather,' I say conversationally as she signs and accepts the box.

She's completing the transaction on autopilot, returning my phone and closing the door with her toe, but I see her frown and open her mouth to reply just as the door bangs shut. I don't blame her; this time of day is always hectic at their house, she probably doesn't have time to stand around and chat. The kids are home from school and Mr Addo-Smyth will still be at the office. He's a partner at a law firm and works long hours. A specialist in tax structuring according to the firm's website. *Yawn.* It always surprises me that Mrs Addo-Smyth is so cold. You'd think she'd be happy for a friendly face, someone to share a wry smile with, given that she spends most of her day alone.

I contemplate the state of the Addo-Smyths' marriage as I walk along to the Cohens'. They never seem that happy, unlike Harry and Bryce. Without kids, their deliveries are often frivolous and fun – a bunch of flowers for Bryce, a pair of tennis rackets, a crate of wine, and that's just the last couple of weeks. Rain drums on the umbrella and I compose myself before I knock. If Harry answers, it's crucial not to overplay my hand. There's an art to it. Conversations like these are not something I relish but sometimes they're necessary. I take a deep breath and rap twice with the knocker.

There's a silence before I hear a heavy tread that I recognise as Harry's before the door opens. I feel a hit of nerves but really I'm pleased. It's best to get this sort of thing over with. The door opens and there's Harry in a pale blue shirt with a burgundy waistcoat, looking very sharp. When I'm at home I usually wear mismatched items that Dominic left behind.

I smile and say with gusto, 'Delivery for you.'

He looks in my general direction but his eyes don't seem to focus on my face as he takes my phone and scribbles on the screen with the stylus.

Determined to get his attention, I raise my voice another notch. 'It's a big one. Would you like me to put it inside for you?'

A scornful look crosses his face and he reaches for the box, but when he actually clocks me his expression changes. He smooths his moustache with his fingers nervously and a question glints in his eyes – enough to convince me that I'm doing the right thing – before he goes to shut the door. I put my hand out and stop it. It's hardly an aggressive gesture but Harry leaps back as if I've slapped him.

'A lamp, is it?' I ask innocently.

Harry stares at me, clearly baffled at my omniscience, but it's hardly rocket science since there's a sticker on the side that says 'The Lighting Company'.

'I'm doing up my flat and I saw your website online. There's some lovely stuff on there.'

He narrows his eyes as if he's doing the maths on my salary. His antiques go for a small fortune.

'It's great for ideas.' This makes him nod; that adds up. 'It's amazing how some antiques look just like things you can find at high-street stores.' I meet his gaze. '*Uncannily* alike, in some cases.'

It was a side table that gave him away. Delivered by John Lewis in its own packaging so I'd known exactly which one and lo, three months later he posted an identical '*1960s Danish teak table*' for two grand when the retail price was £150.

He stares at me, frowning, until I see the moment, the flash of realisation and the slow diffusion of blood through his cheeks.

'What do you want?' he asks warily.

I hold up my hands and smile, showing both rows of teeth, to let him know that I mean no harm.

'I don't want anything, Harry.'

He sputters as if I've said something preposterous but he doesn't seem to be able to form words.

'I just don't like gossip. There are some things that it's best to keep to oneself. Do you agree?'

His face goes from red to purple and I begin to worry he may keel over but then he gives a small nod.

'Glad we understand each other, and thank you for the inspiration.' I drop my hand and let him bang the door closed in my face. I may be out in the cold but I feel a slow burn of satisfaction. I'm not proud of myself, but at least Harry Cohen won't be a problem for me. I couldn't bear it if one little mistake cost me my access to Paradise Found, not when I've already lost so much.

I let out a sigh of relief as I climb into the van's front seat and close the umbrella. It's over and, for once, all I want to do is get home and sleep. I go to start the engine but I see a plastic bag has caught on the windscreen wiper and is sagging and bagging in the wind, obscuring my view. Bugger. Rain blows in when I open the door and I have to battle the wind but I don't bother with the umbrella this time. I rush to the front and tug the bag free, rain running down my neck and sticking my hair flat to my scalp. I look around for a bin to discard the wet bag but then I notice there looks to be something inside. It's probably the remains of someone's lunch but I'm curious now. I hold it between two fingers and climb back into the dry and turn on the interior light.

Inside is a small square of white paper. My pulse raises when I realise it's an envelope, which turns soggy in my wet hands as I lift it out. It's not sealed and when I unfold the top I see a glint of metal in the bottom. My mind is running through possibilities as I try to work out what it is but then I recognise it. The slender moon attached to a silver hook is my earring. The one I dropped into Patrick's bin. I run my fingers inside the envelope but that's all there is. No note.

I squeeze the earring in my fist feeling a mix of wonder and disbelief. Patrick must have emptied the bin, just for me. I picture him in yellow marigolds, sorting through the detritus, and feel a rush of happiness. I take out the stud I'm wearing and slide the earring into place.

Chapter Six

I stop off on the way home and pick up a bottle of chilled champagne – just a run-of-the-mill brand, but fizz always feels like a celebration, and why not? It's not like I have much to celebrate these days.

Back when I worked in the city, champagne always was my drink of choice. Bubbles were acceptable at all times of day – client breakfasts, long lunches with colleagues, and of course, after-work drinks – no one ever batted an eyelid and I discovered that a glass or two always makes everything somehow sparklier.

The sky is black when I get home and the wind is whipping the rain in all directions, but Ramzan is outside, huddled in his deckchair. I waggle the bottle, glad to have someone to share it with, and he grins but I catch the slight lift of his eyebrow. He probably thinks of me as his crazy neighbour. At least I don't have any cats.

'What are we celebrating?' he asks.

'I found my earring.' I point to the dangling moon and Ramzan peers at it curiously.

'Are they bling, then?' As he eyes up the flimsy metal, my cheeks grow warm. Ramzan knows his jewellery. He wears two gold chains and a diamond thumb ring; he's not going to be fooled by a curve of dirty nickel.

'Do you remember that nice customer I had?'

He smiles in a knowing way and I carry on quickly, not wanting to give the wrong impression. 'I lost the earring on his delivery and he returned it.'

He slaps his knee. 'I *knew* he wanted some Laurel loving.'

'He was just doing the decent thing. No point going overboard.' I remember the champagne just as I say this. Oh well. 'I'll just get some glasses,' I say, glad to have an excuse to halt the conversation.

I nip into my flat for a couple of tumblers since the flutes that came from my wedding gift list went to the charity shop, along with almost everything else from my old life. I search the cupboards for something I can put into a bowl but all I have is half a packet of stale digestives and some instant noodles and neither qualifies as nibbles. Giving up, I return to the walkway with the glasses, popping the cork and sloshing in the champagne so foam spills over onto the cement floor, before topping them up and handing one to Ramzan. He lifts it into the air and says with mock seriousness, 'To love.'

I roll my eyes but I'm smiling. 'Just drink it.'

The bubbles make my nose tingle and I knock back more than I intended to, emptying the glass in one go, but Ramzan is staring out at the halos of light from the office blocks and doesn't seem to notice. The light outside my flat flickers – I really should get that fixed.

'When was the last time you went on a date?' Ramzan asks.

I've just taken another big gulp and this time it goes down the wrong way. My eyes water and I cough.

'You must be out of practice. I keep telling you to get on the dating apps. There are ones for all different types, not just young people.'

I let this one go.

'What are you going to say when he asks you out?'

'He's not going to.'

'Maybe you should ask him.'

The thought makes my skin prickle and I turn to look out over the balcony and get a face full of rain.

'I can't,' I say. 'He's a customer.'

'There's no law against it.'

'It's against company rules.' The word they use is *fraternising* – 'no fraternising with clients' – as if drivers are a separate species that need to be kept apart.

'Who cares?' Ramzan says dismissively. 'They're never going to find out. You won't say anything and it's not like your guy will be reporting it.'

'He's not *my guy.*'

'Whatever.' Ramzan shrugs but he's smiling. He really believes that something could happen between Patrick and me; that a man who lives in a big house would date the delivery driver. I want to believe it too but really I know that Paradise Found is a fantasy. When I pull through those gates it's pure escapism, imagining living there, being part of it, with Patrick by my side. Silly really.

I busy myself with topping up our glasses.

'How did you meet Rashida?' I ask.

'My parents arranged it but it wasn't like there was no choice. You know, we met and got talking and that was it.'

It almost feels like a chat with girlfriends. There's wine. We're discussing relationships. I used to enjoy that type of thing. Once a week we'd sit in a wine bar comparing the failings of our husbands but not anymore, of course. Alice, Katie, Jo – they kept away after it happened, and that suited me just fine. It's easier with Ramzan. He doesn't judge.

'You heard about the virus?' Ramzan says, interrupting my train of thought.

'Virus?' My mind drifts back to Patrick again.

'It's been all over Facebook. You must have seen it.'

I only use social media for investigative purposes but I did see a headline in one of the free papers. 'I saw some people are getting sick in China.'

'They say they're bringing it over here now, people flying in from Wuhan. Wherever that is.'

I nod but I'm barely listening. It really was kind of Patrick to find my earring. I'm not going to ask him out but I feel I should do something to thank him.

Ramzan isn't deterred by my silence. 'How can there be a city that's bigger than London that I've never heard of?'

I have an idea. When he breaks off, I say, 'Ramzan, if someone were to buy you a present, what would you want?'

He grins. 'Now we're talking. What are you getting me?'

'I'm not. I just want a man's opinion.'

'Nintendo Switch no question, with a Mario Kart games bundle.'

'Ri-ight.' Perhaps Ramzan isn't the best person to ask. He and Patrick must be twenty years apart in age and I can't see Patrick playing computer games.

Ramzan's just getting into his stride. 'Or the new iPhone. The camera is meant to be banging.' He stops and slaps his forehead. 'Wait, if this is for your guy you want to get something romantic to show him you're interested. Maybe that David Gandy aftershave that's on all the posters.'

'I was thinking of a book.'

He grimaces. 'No way, man. What about trainers?'

I glance at Ramzan's feet. The soles of his shoes are thick pieces of white rubber that look like they could be inflatable while Patrick always wears brown leather slip-on deck shoes.

'What about—'

I'm saved from hearing his next suggestion by the sound of his front door opening. We look up and see a pair of dark eyes in the gap at low level. Ramzan barks what sounds like a reprimand but there's a flash of white teeth as the boy grins and lets out a high-pitched giggle before the door swings and he runs outside stark naked in a blur of brown, skinny limbs. Ramzan yells as his son jumps and jigs out of his reach and attempts to run the length of the walkway, shrieking with laughter. It's hard not to join in and I use my glass to hide my mouth.

'Don't encourage him,' Ramzan says, but I can see he's holding back a grin too.

He grabs the boy's skinny arm and drags him inside. The smile dies on my lips as I wonder if Sophie would be thin like that or if she'd have filled out. At two she was solid and squishy, perfect for cuddles though I never got enough. If I could hold her right now, I'd never let go.

'I'd better help Rashida with bath time,' he says. 'Thanks for the drink.'

'No problem.'

He leaves his glass on the windowsill with an inch of straw-coloured liquid left in the bottom, and it's only then I realise that somehow the bottle is nearly empty. Did I drink all of the rest? I pour the dregs into my glass and let myself into my flat, going straight to the desk and opening my laptop. A thank you gift is the perfect next step with Patrick, but it needs to be just the right thing.

I think back to all the presents I gave Dominic. Running gear was my fail-safe – he was a personal trainer so that was all he wore – but there was also the Cartier watch for our wedding, framed photos of the two of us on beaches around the world, and Cuban cigars when Sophie was born. We lit one just for the smell and it felt deliciously decadent.

What would Patrick like? I search 'gifts for men' and several list ideas come up. The *Telegraph* suggests vintage port and monogrammed stationery. Wired is all electronics that Ramzan would like. My Google adverts point me to surveillance equipment, but I think they must have been tainted by my recent searches: I had all sorts of strange ideas when I was worried about Harry Cohen.

An hour passes but it's impossible online – there's too much choice and it's hard to translate the items from the screen to reality. I want to weigh things in my hands and feel the quality so I decide to book a day off. Typically, I work seven days a week. The shift booking system is on the app so it's easy to make myself available each day just by checking a box. Occasionally I receive an email

47

letting me know I need to take a break to comply with the Zippi road rules, and on such occasions I stock up on wine for a few days at home, but otherwise work gives me purpose.

I log in and uncheck the box so I can take Sunday off.

Chapter Seven

On Sunday I wake to bright sunshine, feeling like it's Christmas morning. I always loved shopping, and spent years amassing my old wardrobe. Each item hung the right way or clung to the right places and I had heels for every occasion but after what happened, the whole lot went to a charity shop. I discovered it's impossible to be vain when you hate yourself.

I dress in jeans and a T-shirt that came in a pack of three from the supermarket, with my Zippi fleece for warmth. I don't often look in the mirror anymore but before I leave, I stand in my dingy bathroom and check my reflection. My face is thinner than it once was and my skin is pale against my dark hair. Very vampiric. I run my fingers through the tangles in an attempt at a style and try not to notice the silver threads running through the black, before pinching my cheeks to get some colour. In the bottom of my make-up bag I find a lip balm that survived the purge and apply liberally. Two minutes of effort isn't much, but it's an improvement.

The sun's out and the sound of children playing rings around the estate. I take the tube to Covent Garden so I don't have to worry about parking and enjoy people-watching as I stroll along the pavement and take the stairs down to the platform. It's crowded and I squeeze onto the next train, standing holding on to a strap in the vestibule, squeezing closer and closer to a teenager with huge headphones over his ears until I'm pressed against him and I feel the hard nub of his erection on my thigh. Shifting away only makes my leg rub against his so I stand stiffly, counting down the stops. Each time he exhales there's a waft of Red Bull. It's easily the closest I've been to another person in years and I can tell from the redness of his face, he is as mortified as I am.

An announcement tells us that the next stop is Covent Garden, and there's a flurry of people picking up their bags and shifting closer to the doors. When we pull in, the whole carriage surges out and along the tunnel to the lift. I'm funnelled into a spot against the wall with my hip at an odd angle to accommodate the person behind. There must be thirty of us inside a space no bigger than my bedroom, recycling each other's air, but no one mutters a word or makes eye contact. The only noise is a tinny beat escaping from my teenage friend's headphones. I remember now why I despised commuting.

The lift rises and finally the doors open and we stream out and through the barriers, straight onto the street where everyone tips back their head and takes a grateful lungful of air. I blink into the light. A fresh breeze whips along the street but I keep my fleece open, enjoying the cooling wafts, and set off at a good pace with a spring in my step.

I'm on a crowded high street with the usual brands – Zara, M&S, a Gap – but Patrick's taste is surely more eclectic. I cut through into the back streets and walk on the cobbles to Charing Cross Road. My first stop is the flagship Foyles halfway up because a book does seem like the natural choice since Patrick is a writer. I wander the shelves, picking things up, browsing the backs, and wondering whether Patrick likes sci-fi or spy novels or perhaps something more literary. He buys a lot of books but I never see what's inside the packaging. His own novel was horror and the ending was rather gruesome.

Giving up on my gift search for now, I find my way to general fiction, the 'W' section where there is one yellow spine that bears the name 'Patrick Williams'. I slide it out and run my finger over the raised lettering. Inside is the dedication to his wife that I smudge my finger over as if I can rub it out. Next time, maybe it will be to *my darling Laurel* – that's rather a nice thought. I flip to the back to the author photo. It's a black and white shot of Patrick in front of a bookcase, head turned to the camera but unsmiling. His hair is unruly and I begin to wonder if it's a look he's cultivating, to try to give himself a bit of edge.

Beneath the picture is the author bio. *Growing up with three older sisters, Patrick spent his formative years being dressed up and called 'Patrice', perhaps inspiring his love of storytelling. He toughened up on the rugby pitches of Winchester College, before reading English Literature at Warwick University. A failed lawyer, Patrick spends his time writing, drinking black coffee and eating steak with his Argentinian wife, Maria.*

My smile fades as I snap the book shut but I tell myself it's over now, she's out of the picture, and I take the copy to the till and join the queue. When I reach the front, the woman at the desk with heavy black eye make-up and purple hair takes the book to ring it up and flips the book around so she can see the title.

'Ooh I remember this,' she says. 'I won't give it away but it's excellent – very creepy and a great ending – I didn't see it coming at all. The author is either a genius or a madman.'

I feel a surge of pride and want to blurt out that I know him but I manage to hold back and just smile and nod.

'Shame about the film though.' She pulls a face. 'Did you see it? What a hack job.'

My smile fades and I narrow my eyes. Surely that's just a matter of taste.

'I liked it,' I say primly.

She gives me a pitying smile and returns to scanning the book. We conduct the rest of the transaction in silence and I leave with the bag hooked over my elbow. The film *was* god-awful but it would feel disloyal to Patrick to say so.

I return to the winding roads around Covent Garden and window-shop. There's a brightly lit watch shop that could be an option but everything looks too shiny and new for Patrick. Next door is a sock shop and I study the rows of stripes and spots and different shades of pink. I almost go inside but decide it's too novelty. I want something more meaningful that he won't just shove in a drawer and forget about.

It's getting busier so I wander away from the main drag onto a quieter street where there's a short row of antiques shops. When I peer through the window of the first shop, I see it's full of elegant, quirky items and a buzz of excitement surges through me – it's the perfect place. Inside has the exalted hush of a library and I wander the shelves, picking up a glass paperweight that feels like it could do some damage. I put it back down and examine a set of old-fashioned scales that are perfect for a baker but when I turn over the price tag and see that they are £800, I nearly burst out laughing.

I hastily leave that shop and try the next in the row but it's not until the final shop that I get a hit. It's an antique map shop and as soon as I step inside, I know it's the place. It smells just as I imagine Patrick's house will smell – of thick, creamy paper with a sharp note of ink. I browse the old maps of London, intrigued by the changing landscape of my usual delivery route. Parts of it would have been farmland a century ago.

'Can I help you?' The man behind the desk spots me and gets up. He's exactly the type of man you imagine working in a shop like this: older, with a white beard and gold-framed glasses that he wears on the end of his nose, and a very jazzy waistcoat. 'If it's Islington you're interested in, there's a whole box in the back.'

I hesitate before launching in. 'Actually, I'm looking for Fitzrovia. There's a gated street – you probably don't know it – just behind Tottenham Court Road. Paradise Found, it's called.'

'Oh yes.' He looks rather excited. 'Interesting little place. One of those names that sticks with you. Used to be quite an ordinary mews but the developers really got their teeth into it – they call it a super mews, I'm told. Let me just dig something out.'

He goes behind a short curtain and I see him rifling through a cardboard box.

'The name wasn't always so quirky, you know?' He calls out. 'It was Milton Court before war damage left it in need of development. The moniker began as a little marketing ploy by the developers but it stuck.'

He pulls out a sheet of cardboard in a plastic cover. 'Ah yes, here we are. Very interesting.'

His eyes rake over me as he returns. 'Are you local or just a passing interest?'

Nosy parker.

'It's for a friend.'

This seems to satisfy him. Clearly I'm not the sort who would be living there.

'Lovely print from the thirties. Hand-drawn. Limited edition, of course.'

It's a beautiful sketch of the facades of the previous homes. They're similar in style to those that replaced them, only not so large. Where there's now the turning circle where I park my van is a gas streetlamp. In the bottom corner is a smaller inset map showing the location and on the top corner of the plastic is a small sticker with £350 written in pencil. It's the perfect thing but much more than I wanted to spend.

I hand it back. 'I think I'll keep looking.'

'There were only fifty prints made. It really is a special piece, a collector's item. I'm sure your friend would be absolutely thrilled.'

The only other idea I've had is socks. I picture Patrick's face as he opens it, the surprise and then delight that he'd surely feel. My stomach churns but I look up and nod.

'I'll take it.'

'Excellent choice.'

I try not to calculate how many days' wages it is as the man takes it to the desk and folds a sheet of tissue paper around it. I leave the shop feeling high and cross to the sunny side of the street where there's a line outside a trendy coffee shop. I used to think nothing of buying a daily flat white at three pounds a pop but I've got out of the habit. While I'm feeling reckless, I join the back of the queue, excited about the hit of caffeine. Maybe I'll get a croissant too.

'Laurel?' A woman's voice comes from behind me.

I go cold all over despite the sun on my face. There are very few people from my past I relish seeing. I turn slowly and see Priya a few feet away with an uncertain smile on her face. Cuddled to her chest is a tiny baby. Its arms and legs dangle limply from a carrier and its dark hair gleams in the sunlight. The sudden longing I feel almost floors me. I never felt that way about children before Sophie.

'Hi.' My throat feels tight and I cough gently to clear it. 'How are you? Congratulations are in order, I see.'

Priya wraps her arms around the baby's back and I can't help but think she's trying to shield it from me. She's still smiling but I see a flicker of horror in her brown eyes. We worked six feet apart for seven years after Priya made the move across from a rival bank. She was on the trading team and had a reputation as a ball-breaker, a headset permanently clamped to her ear, barking orders from behind a block of screens. I was in sales, not quite as revered but generally thought to have more charm, which was essential since it was my job to convince clients to buy complex bond products that they didn't understand. The trick was to make them think that everyone else did.

'Thanks.' Her hands move rhythmically up and down the baby's back. 'Never thought I'd have a kid but here I am, loving it.' She catches herself and her eyes seem to glimmer with tears. 'Oh God, Laurel, I'm sorry.'

I rush on to cover her awkwardness. 'No, don't worry. Of course you are. You should be. Loving it, I mean.' I can't take my eyes from the baby. I'd kill to feel its weight in my arms, to press my nose into its soft hair and sniff that new baby smell. I catch myself staring and drag my eyes back to Priya's.

'Boy or girl?' I say.

'Boy. Hugo.' She bends forwards and turns him a fraction so I glimpse his tiny sleeping face. The pink-shelled eyelids are closed and his eyelashes are surprisingly long.

'Beautiful,' I murmur.

'And you? How are you, Laurel?' The emphasis she uses makes it sound like she truly cares but Priya wasn't someone I went for drinks with or even chatted to in the ladies'. Then again, I haven't seen or heard from any of those people since the day I left.

'I'm great.' My voice is too high and sounds false. 'Busy with work so no change there.'

Her eyes flicker to the logo on my fleece.

'I joined Zippi around six months ago.'

'Good for you. It's so difficult to get out of finance and make the leap to the start-up world. Are you on the operational side?'

'Delivery.' I say it breezily but I see it register. She gapes at me and her cheeks flush. I'd like her to leave but she's not finished. She moves closer and lays her hand on my arm.

'I just wanted to say how sorry I am about your daughter. It must have been—'

'Thank you,' I cut in.

'I think it's scandalous that the bank didn't support you more.'

'I did resign.'

'But still.'

The heat from her palm feels like it is burning through my fleece. Priya looks like she wants to say more but I take control. 'Well, it's been lovely to see you,' I say brightly, stepping out of the line. I'm not hungry anymore.

'You too. We should get a coffee sometime?' Her voice lifts almost hopefully but I can't imagine that Priya would really want to meet. We have nothing in common and no one from the bank has stayed in touch. Why would she be any different?

'Yes, we must.' I say the words but of course I don't mean them. My face is starting to hurt from smiling as I stride away, giving her a wave before crossing onto the shadowy pavement and hurrying away.

I take the first turning I come to – down a narrow, cobbled street – and I spot a pub. One of those huge tourist traps that's like a rabbit warren inside with lots of dark wood and sticky floors. I veer in, taking a flight of stairs up to the first floor where there's no queue at the bar and order two double gin and tonics. Once I have the glasses, still warm from the dishwasher, I find myself a table at the back, placing one across from me on a second coaster as if I'm waiting for someone. The first sip steadies me and I realise just how worked up I am. I avoid people who knew me back then for a reason. I can't bear to see the judgement in their eyes, the shock and, in some cases, glee at just how far I've fallen. To Priya's credit, she hid whatever she really felt well. All I saw was her pity and that feels almost worse.

The first glass is soon empty and when I'm finished, I simply swap it with the second. The ice hasn't even melted yet. I move tables for the second round though there are enough people in for a lunchtime drink that I'm not conspicuous. All thoughts of shopping are gone from my mind. All I want to do now is drink myself to oblivion.

Chapter Eight

I wake the next morning with a searing pain in my eye socket as if someone has jammed a screwdriver into my skull.

It takes me a moment to remember – the chance meeting with Priya, a pub, another, and then there's nothing. Blackouts used to panic me but now I just accept them. I've dealt with enough to know it's easier that way. My head swirls and I force myself out of bed and to the fridge. I don't like to drink before work but sometimes it's the only way to function. I keep an emergency cider for these occasions when something sweet and cold is all I can stomach. Leaning against the fridge door, I crack the top and wash down two paracetamol and two ibuprofen before staggering back to bed and crawling under the covers where I curl into the foetal position and wait for them to kick in.

The glistening look of pity in Priya's dark eyes flashes into my mind and I hear myself moan softly. At one time her opinion mattered to me, I wanted her to respect me, but I saw in her eyes how far past that we are, how far I've fallen. I'm furious that I've allowed myself to sink this low again but I try to let it go. The hangover is enough to deal with.

At last the sharp pain fades to a dull throb and I'm able to sit up. The spinning of the room begins to slow. It doesn't matter anymore what Priya thinks of me, I tell myself, I've moved on. As if to prove the point, I get out of bed and go into the bathroom where I turn the shower as hot as it will go and scrub myself until my skin is bright pink.

That's when I remember the gift. Though my panic is dampened by the booze and pills, I feel a dull spike of dismay. Did I bring it home? I try not to think of the money as I get out and wrap a towel around me, leaving a trail of wet footprints on the spongy lino floor as I hurry into the kitchen. Pale sun streams through the kitchen window. Why can't it be cold and grey like February should be?

Sophie seems to be staring right at me from the photos on the wall as I cross the room to my desk and shame joins the mishmash of emotions I'm feeling. I'm hot and cold and still not feeling right. The room spins and I grab the edge of the desk before I lose my balance, sitting heavily on my chair. A lump rises in my throat and I'm close to breaking down but that's when I spot it: in the centre of the green leather is what must be Patrick's present. It's the right size and weight, but it's wrapped in classy brown paper and tied with a ribbon. I turn it over in my hands and underneath there's even a card with his name on the front in my handwriting.

I'm not as surprised as I should be. I always managed to get things done after a heavy night; it was one of my talents. I turn over the card but the envelope is sealed so the contents are like a lucky dip. The risk that I've exposed myself is too great so I crush it into a ball and drop it in the bin, before returning to the dark bedroom and dressing quickly. For a moment it's like I'm seeing the room through Priya's eyes and I feel another burn of shame. The bed is entirely surrounded by cardboard boxes that are filled with my notebooks and the air is stale. The striped sheets are tangled and need a wash. Putting my uniform back on is a relief. I'm not Laurel in these clothes, I'm just the courier.

The hangover now feels like a low-level flu and I'm relieved to get outside into the fresh air. I hurry down to the van and I sit up in the front seat shivering despite blasting the heaters, and set off for the depot. I can't face music today. I cling to the steering wheel and by the time I arrive at the depot, the back of my shirt is soaked with sweat but I'm still cold. Checking in, I discover that there are six parcels for Paradise Found. *Six!* One for Patrick, three for the Addo-Smyths and two for the Bateses. I wonder if Harry Cohen is avoiding me – they haven't ordered from any retailers that use Zippi since our little chat – not that I'd blame him. I sit for a moment and let my head sag, before taking a deep breath and forcing myself to start the engine.

It takes a lot of focus to drive the route today. I'm conscious of every bubble of gas and swirl of stomach acid that occasionally burbles and make its way up into a burp that tastes of gin. I hold my breath at each delivery, keeping my eyes down and praying that no one looks too closely or sniffs for that matter. The sweet, cloying smell of alcohol must be radiating from every pore but, thankfully, no one pays me any attention. Sometimes it's good to be invisible.

As the day goes on the balance of power in my body shifts and I begin to win the war. The feeling that I might vomit on someone's front step passes and I manage to listen to Radiohead on low volume. When there are only the packages for Paradise Found left in the back of the van, I pull over and check my face. Of course, it's a disaster: the whites of my eyes are pink, my face is puffy, and my skin is dry and pale. I do what I can with the situation, finger-combing my hair and rubbing tinted lip balm all over my cheeks in an attempt to liven my skin. If anyone asks, I can tell them I've been ill, which isn't too far from the truth. I pop in a piece of chewing gum and I'm as ready as I can be.

The sun has disappeared behind a low haze of cloud and it looks like the wind has picked up. I roll down the windows to freshen the air, turn up 'Creep', and drive the final stretch to Paradise Found, going through the gate and stopping in the turning circle where I usually unload. It's designated 'no stopping' but there's another van parked at the far end, outside the Bateses' – a large white one with a roller door at the back. I feel my face pucker in confusion. Occasionally there's a car being loaded or an Uber idling, but never another van. Could it be a rival delivery service? The thought makes me sweat even more. Of course it's ridiculous but it feels like I've caught them cheating.

I edge in behind the van and try to make out why it's here but I can't see any branding or other hints from this angle. Going round to the back, I unload my packages slowly but I can't manage them all so I take the two for the Bateses first. The old couple always make me feel better. Their devotion to each other is obvious even at a glance. It gives me hope that one day maybe I'll have that again. We all deserve to be loved, whatever we've done.

As I pass the van, I almost drop the parcels I'm carrying. *Move-rite* is emblazoned on the side in large, red letters. Who could be moving? I turn a slow circle and stare at each house. There haven't been any 'for sale' signs up and my Google search notification hasn't alerted me to anything online. The churn in my stomach returns. Suddenly there's too much saliva in my mouth and I feel a surge of panic that I might be sick.

A flicker of movement at the Addo-Smyths' window makes me swallow hard and the chewing gum goes down too. I'm coughing as I reach the Bateses'. I press the bell and it doesn't take long for the door to open. There's a man in overalls with a clipboard in the hall.

'Afternoon,' he says.

His dirty boots are on the shag-pile. Next to him is a stack of flattened cardboard boxes. I know what I'm seeing but I don't understand. Why is he here?

'Delivery?' He says it slowly and clearly as if I don't speak English.

I manage a nod.

'Vera!' he yells over his shoulder. 'Delivery for you.'

Vera? My head is spinning. I can't process that the Bateses – the sweet, old Bateses who I practically introduced to online shopping – have the movers here. It must be a mistake. Why would they want to leave Paradise

Found? Perhaps they are redecorating. The place could do with an update. That must be it.

'Hello, dear,' Mrs Bates says as she comes to the door.

'What's going on?' I try to keep my tone light but her face still puckers like she's sucking a lemon.

'We're packing up.'

She reaches for her parcels but I take a step back. I'm not ready to relinquish them yet.

'Why?' I ask.

There's a flicker of irritation in her watery blue eyes. She pulls herself up a couple of inches. I know I'm pushing it but I need to know.

'With all this talk of the virus, David and I decided to move to our Cotswolds home permanently. Now come on, dear, I don't have all day.'

I know it's silly, but after all the effort I've put into their deliveries I can't help but feel a little betrayed.

'I can't give you the packages until you've signed,' I say with a hint of admonishment.

I hand over my phone and the stylus and she taps out her signature with more force than usual. There's a frosty air between us. I don't want to leave things like this since it could be my last delivery to her. We swap mobile for packages and I arrange my face into a bright smile.

'When do you go, Mrs Bates?'

She's already turning away and she slams the door as if she hasn't even heard. I stand for a minute, breathing hard. It's almost too much to take today. How did I not know? It must have happened so fast. It's silly but I'm biting back tears as I return to the van to retrieve the three parcels for the Addo-Smyths. I avoid looking at the moving truck like the game Sophie used to play – if I don't look at it, perhaps it will disappear.

The parcels are small enough that I can hold them in one arm and draw myself up as I ring the bell. Mrs Addo-Smyth opens quickly as if she's been waiting for me. Her hair is loose today and she's wearing a beautiful, cream cashmere sweater that looks soft. Her eyes rake over me in the way only another woman's can and I find myself tucking my hair behind my ears and straightening my fleece. Not that there's much to work with, especially today.

'Delivery.' I hand over the packages and offer her my phone. 'Sign here, please.'

She accepts the phone but doesn't sign immediately. The way she's looking at me with her head cocked, I can tell she wants to say something. My mind starts racing. Perhaps she's spoken to Harry Cohen or noticed the state I'm in. I press my lips together so she can't smell my breath and brace myself.

'I heard your music,' she says.

'Oh, I'm sorry, I—'

'No, don't worry. I love that song. I used to listen to it on repeat when I was at university.'

I feel a rush of relief and give her a tentative smile. 'Me too.'

'Those were the days.' She smiles and taps her signature on the phone. As she hands it back to me, our eyes meet.

'Are you okay?' she asks.

'Long day,' I say with a shake of my head.

'I know those.' She gives a little laugh. 'Would you like a glass of water?'

Normally I would jump at the chance to prolong my visit here but today I think it's safest to get on my way. 'I'm fine. Thanks, though.'

Mrs Addo-Smyth gives a small wave and I return to the van to collect the final parcel for Patrick. That was the most she's spoken to me in six months. For some reason I'd always assumed she was haughty since she rarely even cracked a smile but perhaps I've misjudged her. It's nice to think that today hasn't been a total disaster.

My gift for Patrick is on the passenger seat and I go to pick it up, but for a moment I hesitate. Will he think it strange? But no, why shouldn't I give a thank you gift to a customer? Returning my earring was a kind thing to do so it's only good manners. Balancing the slim parcel on top of the box, I turn towards Patrick's house but an ear-splitting screech of metal on metal makes me flinch – the mover has thrown open the back of his van – and my gift slides off the top box onto the floor. I bend to pick it up but a slim hand darts out from behind me and reaches it first.

'Let me get that for you,' Mrs Addo-Smyth says.

I jump. She came from nowhere; I'm really not with it today.

'Is this for Patrick?' she asks.

All I can do is nod and wait as she turns over the parcel and takes in that it has no address label or postage. I see her frown a little, glance at me, and then realisation dawns and she smiles. Heat suffuses my cheeks.

'I can manage,' I say.

'Don't worry, I was on my way over anyway, a letter of his came through our door that I need to drop round.'

She wafts a small, brown envelope and sets off along the path to Patrick's door and presses the bell. I follow slowly, carrying Patrick's parcel, with a heavy feeling of dread in the pit of my stomach and pray he doesn't answer. This is not how I wanted to play it.

The door opens.

'Patrick!' Mrs Addo-Smyth sounds ecstatic and I cringe. My mind goes to the used condom. She wouldn't, would she? And he wouldn't, would he?

Patrick looks at her and me and frowns. 'Stephanie, to what do I owe this pleasure?'

Stephanie.

'This came through our door for you.' She hands over the envelope. 'And this lady had her hands full so I thought I'd help. She's brought you a gift.'

She says the last part with obvious relish and I have a moment of clarity where I see the absurdity of it. I think back to the day when I stood on the opposite side of a doorstep, with Sophie on my hip, and try to imagine how I'd have felt if a delivery driver had brought me a present. It's such an obvious misstep that I can't believe I haven't realised before now. Clearly I've got carried away, making more of Patrick returning my earring than there was. I'd laugh if it wasn't so tragic.

I clear my throat and try to work out what to say. I have to say something. 'I just wanted to thank you for returning my earring.' I gesture at the gift in Stephanie's hands. 'And you got that.' I push the box into his hands, trying to wrestle back control of the situation.

'Sign here please.'

I hold out my phone and he jabs at the screen before taking the box and placing it at his feet. Next he takes the wrapped parcel from Stephanie and holds it tentatively with his fingertips.

'Aren't you going to open it?' Stephanie demands. She's smiling widely, clearly intrigued by the situation.

Patrick looks from her to me and back again before gently sliding his finger under the paper and opening the flaps.

'It's just a token,' I say desperately.

The paper comes away and we all look at the sketch in Patrick's hands. I wish I'd gone with aftershave or a box of chocolates, something impersonal that would have looked like I didn't give it a second thought. The map is a long way from that. Patrick brings it closer to his face and there's a flash of what looks like astonishment before he grins.

'Wow. This really is fantastic. Wherever did you find it?'

Stephanie peers over his shoulder at the drawing.

'It's here,' she says dumbly. 'Does that date say 1933?'

'1935,' Patrick says swiftly. 'Before the houses were re-built. What a gem.' He sounds genuinely excited. 'The novel I'm working on is set here in the thirties. I've been looking online, trying to find something from the period that's similar but Paradise Found is unique.'

I nod; we agree on that at least.

Patrick meets my eye. 'Laurel, thank you so much. This is a real treat.'

I feel myself blushing and quickly look away. Stephanie is hovering and we're an awkward trio but it hasn't gone as badly as I feared.

'What a lovely thought,' Stephanie says. 'I wish Oliver was half as thoughtful. The last gift he gave me was a six-pack of sports socks.'

We all laugh and I'm grateful to her for breaking the tension. The front door at the Bateses' opens and the mover wheels out a loaded trolley. My van is blocking the rear where his door is open.

'I'd better go,' I say.

Stephanie smiles. 'Me too. Supper time!'

We watch her bouncy stride – it's amazing how Lycra makes everything look so pert – and I realise I need to actually move. I jerk into action but Patrick's voice stops me.

'Laurel?'

Turning back, I see Patrick carefully folding the paper back around the map.

'I just want to say thank you again. I really appreciate it.'

My face grows warm and we exchange a smile before I walk back to the van feeling as light as air. The mover doesn't seem to want to make eye contact with me and busies himself with his clipboard as I pass him and get into the driver's seat. I take a deep, shaky breath trying to release some nervous energy. Today hasn't gone exactly as planned but perhaps it's gone even better. Patrick seemed thrilled and Stephanie was almost kind – is it too much to hope that I've made a new friend?

Chapter Nine

Guilt is something I've learnt to live with, along with shame, helplessness and all those other negative emotions that threaten to suck me under day after day.

People say working mothers suffer from it – that it's impossible to 'have it all' – but that was never a problem for me. Dominic and I found an equilibrium that suited us. I was the breadwinner and he took the lion's share of the childcare. I never questioned our arrangement but it's when you've lost a child that you really come to know guilt. It's that constant feeling of being sick to your stomach while a voice in your head screams your inadequacies. The only time I can forget is when I drink, but the kicker is that when I sober up, the voice is even louder.

I wake the day after giving Patrick my gift, knowing I pushed my body too far. I'm still shaky and the booze lingers in my system two full days after I saw Priya and went on the bender. The headache, dry mouth and sour taste at the back of my throat remain and there's a new tightness in my chest when I think of my visit to Paradise Found. I risked everything going in that state. Any one of Patrick, Stephanie or the Bateses could have noticed my condition and reported me to Zippi. Two-day hangovers are a message from above saying: *You're too old for this.*

Getting out of bed, I move with purpose to throw open the half-length curtains in the bedroom for the first time in weeks. Not that it makes much difference; the thin nylon bleeds light anyway but at least it shows my intent. The bed sheets go into the washing machine and I go to straighten the copy of Patrick's novel I left on my bedside table but end up reading a couple of chapters before tearing myself away from a chilling scene with a shudder. I decide that one day soon I will have a spring clean and get rid of some but for now it's enough to open the windows and door and freshen the stale air in the flat. Outside, Ramzan's kids are playing on the walkway with toy cars. I listen to the brum-brum noises they make until one of them starts wailing.

As I get ready for work, I play the radio through my phone so I have something to keep my mind occupied. I need to block out my worries about what Patrick might think of me, not to mention Stephanie. I know it seemed like it went as well as it could have done but I can't help worrying that they were faking gratitude and have already contacted Zippi to report me. My actions certainly breached at least three of their rules.

Nerves build as I leave the flat and go down to the van. What if my app doesn't work at the entry scanner or someone comes down to speak to me as I load up my parcels? I tell myself I'm being ridiculous but when my trip to the depot goes off without incident I feel a rush of relief. There are no deliveries for Paradise Found but, for once, I'm grateful. I've drawn too much attention to myself recently and I don't think I could face Patrick or Stephanie again so soon.

On my route I notice pale pink blossoms have sprouted on some of the trees. It's still only mid-February but the weather's gone haywire. I give the rest of my clients the care they deserve. Everyone gets a full two minutes to answer the door and if they're not home, I complete all of the fields on the 'sorry we missed you' form on the app. And when a woman in a smart blazer answers the door and screams at me for not having the blouse she ordered next-day-delivery, I simply listen and apologise.

By the time I finish my deliveries and make my way to my group meeting, I feel desperate to see the others and be among people who understand. It's been a bad couple of days and I don't want to slip up. I can't go back to how things were before, back when it happened. I've fought hard to get back on track, if you can call my way of life that.

I'm early for group and Elaine is setting out the biscuits on a paper plate, arranging Party Rings in a heart. She glances up and gives me a nervous smile before turning back to the biscuits. I notice her close-set eyes are a little pink, like she's got a cold or has only just been crying. Elaine has been coming to Missing Mums since long before me. She didn't tell her son he was adopted and it blew up in her face when he found out. They haven't spoken since.

'Hi, Elaine, how are you?' I say. 'Can I help?'

'Hi, Laurel.' She never raises her voice above a whisper. 'If you could put out the chairs that would be a great help.'

I arrange the plastic chairs in a circle – we're never more than ten and usually only six so I put out eight as a compromise – while others start arriving. I'm glad to have a job so I don't have to stand around chatting about how my week has been or the virus, which seems to be the hot topic of conversation as I listen in. Just before the start, Denise sweeps in dressed in a turquoise silk shirt and matching head wrap with gold hoop earrings. She goes straight to the tea urn and I wait to see where she sits before taking a chair as far from her as possible, but not opposite. We are seven tonight. I notice Sharon hasn't returned.

Elaine gives a little cough to begin and stands, wringing her hands together.

'I have an announcement,' she says, giving a small smile. 'It's fantastic to be able to share some good news for once. After last week, Sharon managed to get a message to her daughter through a family member and her daughter came home yesterday.'

There's a beat where we all take this in before a little round of applause breaks out and Audrey lets out a cheer, only I don't join in. I feel a surge of irrational anger towards Sharon. It makes me wonder how hard she can have tried when a week was all it took for her daughter to come home. Did she not understand that this isn't a knitting circle? It's for mothers who've lost – *really* lost – not just a place to air family disagreements in front of an audience.

I see Denise is watching me and realise I'm biting the inside of my mouth and I'm the only one not clapping. The frown line between her eyes is back. I smile and clap a couple of times but it's too late. She's already formed a judgement about me.

Denise raises her hand and the clapping stops. 'How wonderful for us to get a positive outcome,' she says. 'It's a reminder for us all that there's hope. Perhaps not always for resolution – for some of us that's not possible – but for a future that's not so bleak.'

I sense she's speaking directly to me and I slump down into my seat, wishing I had just clapped along with everyone else.

'Why don't we all share what a positive next step would be for us? I'll go first.' Denise leaves us with little choice. 'I've already accepted that Dion isn't coming home. What I'd like is to continue to use his disappearance as a force for change. That's why my work with the Met is so important.'

She sounds a little smug and I struggle not to roll my eyes.

'Laurel, what would you like to happen next in your situation?'

Everything goes still. The tea urn begins to chug as the water boils. I know I need to speak but I'm still biting the inside of my cheek, rolling the flesh between my teeth and wondering what exactly to say.

I settle on the truth and say in a small voice, 'What I'd like is my daughter back.'

Denise nods her head but she doesn't leave it at that. 'Can you explain to everyone what that means please. I'm not sure we all know the details of your case.'

A few heads in the circle nod. *Traitors*. I open my mouth to speak but I find I don't have the words. I came here for support. That's what this is, a *support* group. I'm not here to be interviewed or to justify my every move.

I drop my voice so they can't hear my anger. 'It's pretty simple. Five years ago she was taken and I want her back.'

Denise lowers her head so that she's peering over the top of her glasses. She'd make an excellent teacher.

'Do you think there's something else you can do to take control of the situation? Perhaps accepting your role in losing her?'

I jump up and my chair scrapes on the floor causing a horrible screech. I want her to shut up but most of all I want to be outside and away from all of their stares.

'Laurel, please sit,' Elaine says gently, giving Denise a stern look. 'No one has to talk if they don't want to. I'll go.'

There's a tense silence as I consider marching out into the night but I know there's only a bottle of red waiting for me at home. Denise keeps quiet as I slip back into my seat and Elaine starts on her hoped-for next step.

'I'd like to keep working with adoption charities to get the message out that silence is not the answer.'

They continue around the circle, trying to pull positivity out of black holes, but I'm too angry to focus. How dare Denise challenge me? I've been coming here for years and there are rules. We listen, not question. Why is she bringing up a history she knows nothing about and making accusations in front of the entire group?

We reach the break and everyone gets up and gravitates towards the biscuits. It's been a hard session and it's not only me who looks a little fragile. I go outside. It's dark now and I stand in the churchyard looking out onto Upper Street, which is busy with cars and buses and people walking home. I miss Sharon. If she were here I'd bum a cigarette. My desire for nicotine is so strong I can almost taste it. The door opens behind me and Denise comes out.

'Laurel, can we talk?'

She hasn't brought her coat and there's a cold wind so she folds her arms across her chest. My teeth squeak as I grind them at the front by moving my jaw from side to side but I don't move. Instead I incline my head to allow her to go on.

'I've noticed you're struggling.'

'I'm not struggling.' It comes out defensive but of course she's right.

'We all have rough patches,' she says.

The wind blasts and Denise tightens her arms. I'm tensed, waiting for her to try to tell me what to do but she softens her voice. 'How can I help you?'

Her kindness brings tears to my eyes but I stare into the wind and shake my head. 'I don't need help.'

Denise has great skin despite all she's been through. There are tiny creases at the corners of her eyes but she looks good for late fifties. It's only when she purses her lips in annoyance that I see the deeper lines around her lips. I can tell she's used to people falling apart and her being the strong one, holding things together, but I've been through worse.

Denise doesn't give up. 'You've been coming here for what, three, four years?'

'Five.'

'Gosh, time flies,' she says with a sigh and a shake of her head. 'And in all that time, has your situation changed?'

I clamp my lips together and we both know my silence is her answer.

She puts her hand on my arm. 'Maybe it's time to try something new. Open up to us. Tell us what you're going through and maybe we can help you find a way forward.'

I try to picture sitting in that circle and reliving that day. Talking about Sophie, how I strapped her into her car seat and—

Squeezing my eyes shut, I see the suction handle and the plate of cracked glass on the floor. It's all I can do to clench my jaw and stop myself from crying out or bursting into tears.

'If you want to help,' I say, 'then leave me alone.'

I hurry out of the churchyard and join the throng on the street but when I glance back, Denise is still outside, watching me.

Chapter Ten

Instead of going home, I drive around aimlessly, taking junctions at random until I find I'm zeroing in on Paradise Found and I force myself to turn around and head for home.

Halfway there, I realise I'm studying every person I pass, taking my eyes from the road to check their faces in my mirror. Not exactly careful driving. Most children are indoors at this time of night but when I see a little girl with dark hair I slow right down and crawl alongside until I get a good look at her face. But it's not her. It never is.

It's late when I get back to my flat and I go straight to bed but I can't sleep. I turn, thump my pillows and shake out the duvet – all those things that everyone tries but never work. I can't stop thinking of what Denise said at group, that I should consider *my role* in what happened. But that would require me to go over the events of that day, and that's not going to happen. I'm struggling to stay sane as it is.

Through a gap in the curtains I watch a small sliver of sky. When it lightens from inky blue to a velvet mauve, I allow myself to get up and go through into the living room. After boiling the kettle, I make myself a cup of tea and sit at the desk to check my emails. There are two beyond the usual junk. It's cold inside and I wrap my fingers around the hot mug. Opening the first email, I see it's from Zippi. Most of my interactions with them are through the app and email usually signals a change in the rules or a reprimand, though I've only received one of those and that was a misunderstanding. My fingers tighten around the mug and I sit up straighter but I tell myself there's no need to be nervous as I scan the text.

It starts with '*Hey Laurel*' – the usual jaunty tone that sets my teeth on edge. As part of their recent efficiency drive, they've noticed I'm not following the delivery route that's been carefully planned for me by the company's patented algorithm. *Do you know it's the quickest route for you, and the most efficient for our planet?* That's the downside of working for a tech company – they track my every move. I think of Paradise Found and how I save it until the end of my route since I like to visit in the early evening and not be rushed. There's no way around it – that's going to have to change.

The second email is from Priya. I don't open it immediately; instead I stare at her name and wonder how she got my address. It's not like I sent a 'keep in touch' message when I left the bank since it wasn't exactly a friendly goodbye. On the odd occasion an old colleague has tracked me down before, I've simply hit 'delete' and blocked the sender. Those days aren't a time of my life I want to remember. This time, my finger hovers over the trash button but something makes me hesitate. Priya was surprisingly friendly when I saw her and she seemed genuinely pleased to see me. I decide it can't hurt to see what she has to say so I open it. She gets to the point quickly – she wants to meet for that coffee we promised. She has a proposal for me.

The mention of a proposal intrigues me since I have no idea what that could be. Priya is a successful forex trader and that's not my sector, and it's highly unlikely she wants child-rearing tips from me. I laugh aloud at that ridiculous thought. Sipping my tea, I glance at the lightening sky that now has a soft grey hue and allow myself to imagine meeting her for a chat. It would be nice to sit in a coffee shop and catch up like old friends. Maybe she'd bring the baby and I could hold him. The thought gives me a lift. I don't reply but I don't delete the email either. While it's sitting in my inbox, I can always pretend to myself that I'm waiting to respond. Only deep down I know I won't reply. Changing my routine is not good for me.

I get up and shower, humming a little tune under my breath, and when I leave, ready for work, Ramzan is outside having a cigarette in the breezy early morning air. Having not seen him in several days, it's comforting to see his shiny jacket bundled in the chair but when he looks at me I see his eyebrows are knitted together and there are already several cigarette butts in a small heap on the floor by his feet.

'Want one?' He nods to the packet balanced on the chair arm.

I shake my head but I lean against the balcony and look over at the area of scrubland below – you can't call it a garden. From inside his flat we hear cartoons blaring.

'You heard the virus is in London now?' Ramzan demands, sounding worried.

The question takes me by surprise and I shrug. 'London's a big place.'

Ramzan shakes his head and jabs his cigarette in the air when he speaks again. 'You haven't got every fucker coughing all over you from the back seat. I picked up one guy from Heathrow yesterday who must have sneezed ten times. He didn't even put his hands over his mouth, just sprayed it all over the back of my head.'

I wince. 'That does sound bad.' I try to lighten the mood by saying lightly, 'You could get one of those masks? Like Chinese tourists wear on the tube.'

He laughs and slumps back in the chair. 'And look like Darth Vader driving a Prius?'

I laugh too. Ramzan takes a long drag and blows smoke from his nose in two plumes.

'Are you not worried?' he says.

I shake my head. I'm not scared of getting sick and I don't have anyone else to worry about. Not anymore.

He snorts and smoke comes out of his nose. 'Science never was my bag but even I can see we're sitting ducks. Look at all the people crammed in this place. I'm picking people up all over London and the kids are at school. When one of them gets a sniffle, I'm ill for two weeks. How can we not get it?'

He's worried about his family. I reach over and put my hand on his shoulder. What can I say?

'Seriously, Laurel, you want to get out of here. Get yourself back to a life of receiving packages, not delivering them.'

The sky is a hazy stretch of cloudy grey. You can already tell it's going to be a dull day.

'What do you mean?'

He gives me an amused glance. 'Come on. I know you're not from this world. I've been trying to work it out. Rashida is convinced you must be in witness protection.'

'I like it here.'

He looks sideways at me. 'This isn't your place.'

I don't know how to respond and there's a long silence before Ramzan clears his throat and asks, 'You're not, are you?'

I frown. 'Not what?'

'In witness protection.'

I burst out laughing and he joins in. Ramzan's a good kid. He looks after his wife and works all hours for his family. He plans to open an estate agents with his brother, and they're working on building up the capital first. I imagine telling him about Sophie. In one minute that wide-eyed innocence would be gone. He'd never look at me the same again. My smile fades.

'No, I'm not.'

He crunches his cigarette on the floor and kicks the small pile of butts over the edge.

'I'd better go. I've got to get the kids ready for school.'

He goes inside and I head to the van. My footsteps echo on the stone steps as I jog down to the back exit. Whitechapel is quieter in the mornings. The hipster crowd responsible for the late-night noise is sleeping it off and the families keep to themselves.

On the drive to the depot I listen to Aretha Franklin's 'Respect' on repeat to try to keep my spirits up. I know I'll have to return to Paradise Found soon and the thought makes me fidgety. I collect my parcels and there's one for Mr Addo-Smyth and one for Patrick. Just my luck to have to face both Stephanie and Patrick again on the same day, but perhaps it's better to get it over with.

After the email from Zippi this morning, I pay particular attention to the route. Paradise Found is in the middle of my list so I estimate I'll be there around lunchtime, which is a bad time for deliveries as more people are out across that period. I may not see anyone.

That thought makes me take my time on the morning's deliveries, trying to chat with each recipient to eke out the time and delay my arrival at Paradise Found. Most people don't want to talk – they just mumble a reply and shut the door – but I don't give up. I try the weather and the traffic but I find I get the most mileage out of the virus. Like Ramzan, a lot of people seem to be anxious and there are lots of theories. I get twenty minutes out of one old man who tries to convince me to turn off my phone since he says the phone signal can transmit particles into my bloodstream. I nod along, not believing a word but pleased to pass the time.

Despite my best efforts, it's only just after 1pm when I arrive at Paradise Found. Pulling through the gate, I see the 'for sale' sign outside number five and my fragile good mood is crushed. I feel like ripping it out of the ground and shoving it in the back of the van, but that won't help: the Bateses have already gone and the particulars will be up online soon. At least when the listing goes live, I'll get to see their interiors. I often check out houses on my route this way. It crosses my mind that perhaps this time I could even book a viewing and actually walk through their living room, kitchen and bedroom. A shiver runs through me. Why haven't I thought of that before? It makes me feel much better about the whole thing. The Bateses' departure is an opportunity, not just an ending.

I hop down and collect the packages from the back of the van, forming a plan. Estate agents don't actually check your credentials; they just need a believable story. It was only five years ago when I had it all anyway. I'm whistling as I ring the bell at the Addo-Smyths', my apprehension banished, and Stephanie opens the door.

'Delivery,' I say brightly.

She breaks out into a dazzling smile that shows all her pristine teeth, as if she's genuinely pleased to see me. 'Hi. Laurel, isn't it?'

'That's right.'

'Thanks for this.' She takes the box. 'I'm Stephanie, by the way.'

It seems she's thawed after witnessing my gift-giving generosity. It would be nice to have a friend at Paradise Found but I've never really believed that Stephanie and I would get on. She's far too proper to befriend the courier. Or at least, that's what I used to think. She signs for the parcel but she doesn't close the door.

'Busy?' she asks.

I try not to let it show how pleased I am she's continuing the conversation.

'Always,' I say breezily before remembering what she has on her plate. 'But who am I to talk? You're the one with four kids. Honestly, I don't know how you do it.'

She waves her hand to dismiss the compliment, but her eyes glow with pleasure and she leans against the doorframe, crossing her arms as if settling in for a chat.

84

'It's better now they're older. They don't need quite so much looking after. Do you have any children?'

I give only the slightest moment's hesitation before I say, 'One.'

'Is she at school?'

Best to keep my answers factual, I decide. 'She's seven.'

'Such a great age. I only have one left at primary school. My baby. I'd love another but Oliver says it's him or a newborn. Sometimes I'm not sure I'm making the right choice.'

We both laugh.

'Would you like any more?' she asks.

I try to mimic her smile. 'One is enough for me.'

Stephanie grimaces as if it's a crime not to want more kids.

I lean closer and drop my voice. 'To be honest, I barely survived the baby stage.'

Stephanie inclines her head and turns her mouth down as if to say *you poor thing*. 'You get through it though don't you? And they bring you such joy.'

'Don't forget about the misery.' I raise my eyebrows so she understands I'm joking. Again, we laugh. There's a lull but Stephanie doesn't seem to want to close the door and I don't want her to either. It's nice to chat, especially about Sophie. I don't often get the chance and she is my baby, after all. Thinking of her is enough to almost overwhelm me, though, and I clutch at another topic.

'It's a lovely neighbourhood,' I say. 'People seem close.'

Stephanie shrugs. 'It's friendly for sure.' She smiles and I spot a glint in her eye. 'And how are things with Patrick? You two seem to get on well.'

I see where she's going and smile. 'He's been kind. I'd like something . . . Well, maybe . . . We'll have to see.'

Stephanie grins. 'Say no more.'

I don't let her see how pleased I am that we're confiding like friends do. I'd love to stay longer but I don't want to push it.

'I'd better get on.'

'Of course. Take care and see you again.'

The door shuts and I take the few short steps to Patrick's, feeling thrilled about my fledgling friendship with Stephanie. I try out her cheerful gait, letting my hair swish as I walk but I compose myself before I ring the bell. Footsteps come quickly and Patrick appears with a piece of toast between his teeth and a mug in his hand. His lumberjack shirt is untucked and he hasn't shaved – it looks like he just got out of bed.

'Mnngh.' He bites the toast, spraying crumbs everywhere before taking it out of his mouth. 'Sorry, I mean, hello.'

There's an awkward pause where we seem to be both waiting for the other to speak. Then I rush in with, 'Delivery for you.'

'Oh great. It must be my coffee subscription. You hear so many people getting subscriptions these days for all kinds of things so I thought I'd try one.'

'Yes, they do keep me busy,' I say.

I hold out the phone for him to sign. As he juggles the mug and toast to scrawl on the screen I peer over his shoulder but all I can see is the mat by his feet and the bannister behind with his blazer slung over. Patrick returns the phone and cocks his head.

'I don't know if this is allowed but do you have time for a coffee? It's single origin. Guatemalan. If that can't persuade you I don't know what will.'

It takes me a moment to comprehend the question and when it sinks in my heart lifts and soars. The idea that Patrick would actually want to sit down and share a coffee with me is hard to believe but why else would he ask? That little voice in my head whispers, '*Because he doesn't know the real you,*' but I block it out. I deserve this. I open my mouth to say yes, almost tasting the bitter coffee on the tip of my tongue, but then I remember the email from Zippi. My movements are being logged and they warned me about any deviations.

'I'd like that—' I try to convey with my eyes just how much '—but I'm working. I've got to finish my route.'

Colour rises in Patrick's cheeks and he scratches his stubble on his cheek in a way that looks like it might be painful. 'Of course. Silly of me, really.'

This is torture. 'I'm sorry, I wish I could.'

He waves away my apology. 'No, never mind.'

'Another time?' I try to cling on.

'Of course.' He gives me a distant smile as he closes the door and I'm left outside. Alone. It hits me like a physical pain in my chest that I came so close to seeing inside one of the houses here – on a date with Patrick, no less – only to have it snatched from me.

I turn and walk slowly back to the van. Silly really to let myself believe that I belong somewhere like Paradise Found.

Chapter Eleven

Back at home, my disappointment turns to anger. I knock back two glasses of whisky and tear pages from my old notebooks, building a pile of crumpled paper on the floor.

Patrick finally invited me in – it was my chance to see inside a Paradise Found house after all this time, and also to get to know him better. Instead, I had to carry on with my deliveries and take useless crap to people who didn't need it. That's my job now. The media says bankers are materialistic and my old career was despised after the last recession, but at least we were honest. We wanted money and things, but doesn't everyone? As a courier I see the constant stream of things people order that must go way beyond what they actually need.

Sophie watches me from the wall but I can't look at her. I haven't made any progress on finding her in months. Not a single lead. The colourful Post-its with my notes on seem to taunt me. I dig my nails into my palms before letting out a sudden, deafening roar and pulling them down, letting them drift to the floor so it becomes spotted with pink and yellow squares. When I'm done, I slump in the chair, breathing hard, but the buzzing adrenaline isn't gone so I shove the pile of papers into the wire bin and take it outside.

Ramzan's flat is quiet so they must be out. His parents live nearby and they sometimes stay over. I'm glad they're not here. I'm sure they think I'm crazy enough already. I put the bin on the concrete floor and borrow Ramzan's lighter from his windowsill. It takes a few tries but I set the edges alight and they curl into orange flames that burn out as fast as they come. Shards of ash lift and swirl in the cold air like snow, and I feel my pulse slowing. It looks pretty.

I go back inside and log in to my computer. The Bateses' house is up online and I'm grateful to have something else to focus on. I study each photo in turn, poring over their dated decor with china ornaments on every surface. Someone is a big fan of cats. The master bedroom is at the front of the house and I recognise the shape of the big front window, but they have heavy curtains that drown the light. The bed has a tasselled throw and it's stacked with embroidered pillows. It's not to my taste but the room has good proportions and the bed must be king size. I spend some time looking at paint colours and new furniture, allowing myself the luxury of imagining I'm going to be the buyer.

It's late when I'm done and I've polished off half the bottle of whisky but I finally feel calm. Before I shut down my computer I complete the online form with the estate agent. *Yes, there is a property I am interested in. Yes, I would like to view it. No, I don't want to receive any marketing emails.*

Hauling myself into bed, I slip into a fitful, whisky-soaked sleep and when I wake, I check my emails – the estate agent's automated reply tells me they will call soon. The buzz of excitement carries me into the shower and down to the van. I put on some nineties garage and drum on the steering wheel as I drive through the morning traffic.

There are no packages for Paradise Found but I don't allow disappointment to creep in. I can't expect to go there every day. The sky is an ominous smudge of grey but I'm feeling cheerful as I drop off my deliveries. It doesn't even bother me when people don't answer their door and I have to complete the *'sorry we missed you'* forms that take forever. I'm parked in a loading bay at one of my drop-offs when my phone rings and I feel a thrill of anticipation as I answer. It can only be the estate agent because no one else ever calls me.

'Hello?' I say.

There's a pause. I wait for the estate agent's professional tones.

'Hi.' It's a woman. 'Is this Laurel?'

'Yes?' I'm willing her on, sitting up on the edge of my seat.

'Laurel, it's Denise from group.'

Denise? I slump back, disappointed and faintly alarmed. What on earth does she want?

'Are you there?' she asks.

'I'm here.' My voice sounds flat.

'Oh, good. Laurel, I wanted to apologise for cornering you last week.'

My annoyance lifts a fraction. She *should* apologise.

'It wasn't fair of me to push you. It's your journey and it's up to you to come to terms with what happened when you're ready.'

Come to terms? Each word hits me like a pick against a sheet of ice. It's not much of an apology. The phone is tight in my grip and anger is coursing through me. There's a long silence because I can't bring myself to speak.

When Denise talks again her voice is quieter, gentler. 'Laurel, I've spoken to the police.'

Blood pounds in my ears.

'I asked you to stay out of it.'

'I just want to help.'

'Help? You think it's helping sticking your nose in?'

She clears her throat. 'Missing Mums is about supporting each other and making sure other members get what they need.'

'What I *need* is for you to stay out of my business.'

'When my Dion went missing—'

'I don't give a fuck about your Dion.'

I hear Denise gasp and I close my eyes for a moment. That didn't come out quite right.

'I'm sorry, I didn't mean that. It's just not the same situation,' I try again.

'Laurel, please—'

'No, Denise. Just because your son isn't coming back doesn't mean I have to accept the same thing. My daughter is out there and I will never give up hope.'

'But—'

I hang up, tingling with fury. Denise has let the power go to her head. How dare she speak to the police against my wishes? She may think she is doing me a favour but I'm the one in control of the investigation. I'm her mother.

I'm shaking as I drive to the next house. I try to re-store my positivity but I'm drained. I turn off the music. Overhead, the clouds are so dark they're purple in places like a healing bruise. Spots of rain land on the windshield and I turn on the windscreen wipers. They begin squeaking against the glass but before long it's pouring and they're swishing double-time. The phone rings again and I check the number before answering. I can't face Denise again but it's a London area code and Denise called from a mobile. Pulling into a roadside space, I answer the call.

'Hello?' I say, warily this time.

'Laurel Lovejoy?' It's a perky female voice.

'Yes?'

'Hi, Laurel, it's Nicole from Hamiltons. You registered an interest in a property in Fitzrovia.'

Relief washes over me that it's not Denise again but some of my excitement at the prospect of viewing a house at Paradise Found is gone. Damn Denise. I roll my shoulders and try to relax.

'That's right,' I say.

'Can I just take some details?'

'Of course.'

Nicole runs through her initial questions that establish who I am and my budget. I use my old identity, the Laurel Lovejoy who worked in an investment bank. Wife of Dominic; mother of Sophie. That person might have been genuinely interested. Dominic and I would have been looking to move up the housing ladder a rung or two and with a good bonus behind me, we might even have been able to afford it. Perhaps we'd have been growing our family but that thought makes me fall silent, biting my lip and trying desperately not to cry.

'Laurel, are you still there?'

Getting myself back under control I say, 'I'm here.'

'Oh good. Thought I'd lost you for a minute there. How does Friday morning work for a viewing?' Nicole asks.

Friday is three days away.

'Can you do any sooner?'

'I'm fully booked, I'm afraid. Friday 9am?'

I sigh, but there's nothing I can do. 'Fine.'

'I do have to warn you that there's a lot of interest in this house. There's nothing like it on the market at the moment and these tend to get snapped up. We've got a couple from Dubai and a young Russian woman already interested.'

Of course people are interested in Paradise Found. It's the perfect place.

'I'll send a confirmation by email.'

We hang up and I watch the rain pelting the window. It's loud against the glass and the droplets land and slide down in erratic patterns that are quite mesmerising. There are still packages in the back but I don't feel like moving yet. Instead, I imagine walking around the Bateses' house, touching their things, being inside a house on the street for the first time, and find I have goose bumps.

Chapter Twelve

The next day there are no deliveries for Paradise Found and it's early evening when I finish my route. Glimpsing my pale face in the rear-view mirror, I am struck by how haggard I look, how unhealthy. I stop off at Tesco Metro on the way home to stock up. Most nights I eat instant noodles with a handful of veg and, if I'm feeling adventurous, some grilled chicken thrown in. I'm not a bad cook, it's just hard to motivate yourself when you're making a meal for one. I used to enjoy cooking. Most weeknights I worked late so Dominic took charge but sometimes, at the weekend, I would choose a recipe and make something special. Beef Wellington was Dominic's favourite and Sophie liked roast chicken. Well, she liked the mini sausages I made as a side with mashed potato and gravy. I decide to make roast chicken with all the trimmings – and I don't buy booze. I've been drinking too much recently.

When I get back to the estate, the bulging bags strain my arms as I carry them up the stairs. Not for the first time, I curse the fact that the building doesn't have a lift. Puffing hard, I lurch around the corner, and see Ramzan out on the balcony again, sitting on his deckchair.

'Been shopping?' he calls.

'I'm cooking.'

He gives me a bemused look. 'Not like you.'

I shrug, a little put out at how well he knows my routines. Perhaps I should tell him that once, I made individual cheese soufflés for a dinner party of twelve and not a single one failed to rise. There were calls for me to apply for *MasterChef* but that was at the end of the evening after *a lot* of wine had been drunk, but before Dominic and I attempted a tango in the kitchen. I find I'm smiling at the memory.

'You had a visitor,' Ramzan says, raising his eyebrow. 'Some flash geezer in a gilet with a mole right here.' He jabs his finger into the hollow of his cheek.

The smile is wiped from my face and the bags slip from my grip and smack on the floor. A cold horror trickles through me. It sounds like . . . *But how can it be?*

'Jeez, Laurel, you all right?' Ramzan leaps up and picks up the bags but the carton has split and milk leaks across the cold cement.

'I'm fine.' My voice is unusually high. 'Sorry, I'm not sure what happened. Let me wipe this up.'

Ramzan sorts through the bags and removes the offending milk carton while I stand and search my pockets for a tissue. Even as I'm checking I know there isn't one inside but I'm not sure what else to do.

'Laurel, sit.' Ramzan leaves the bags by my front door and steers me into his deckchair. He disappears inside his flat and returns with a kitchen roll, wiping up the mess while I try to hold myself together in the chair. I'm running through all the possibilities, praying I'm wrong, but really there is only one.

'You want a cigarette?'

I nod blankly and he takes one from the packet and lights it for me. 'Here.'

The first drag is harsh on my throat but soon gives me a small lift that returns me to myself. I catch Ramzan watching my face intently.

'Are you going to tell me what's going on?'

I shake my head and shrug at the same time, trying to downplay it. 'Nothing. I just came over a bit funny. Whoever it was, it must have been a mistake.'

Ramzan gives me another long look. 'He was looking for a Laurel. It's quite an unusual name.'

I suddenly feel like I might be sick and turn away to look out at the famous skyline so he can't see my face. The Gherkin, the Walkie-Talkie, the Cheese-Grater, I tick them off as I breathe deeply. The buildings leave me cold but I keep staring until I am back in control.

'Did you get a name?' I ask for Ramzan's benefit, though I know exactly who it was. I can picture him now in the Moncler gilet he lives in with his wraparound sunglasses perched on his head and his blinding white teeth, here to pick over the bones of my old life like a vulture. From the frown on Ramzan's face, I can tell he isn't fooled.

'Nah, never asked. He said he'll come back.'

It's nothing I didn't expect but hearing it aloud makes me shiver violently. Of course he will; he didn't give up last time without a fight. I know that now he knows where I am, I'll never see the back of him. It's a mild day for late February, but suddenly I'm freezing. I stub out the rest of my cigarette on the floor and force myself to stand, though my legs feel shaky.

'I'd better get on. That chicken isn't going to cook it-self.'

I take out my keys but I fumble with the lock. Ramzan watches me struggle then comes over and gently takes them from my hand.

'Listen, Laurel, I don't know what's going on but if you need anything you just have to ask. I know people around here. If you want, I could have his head kicked in for you?'

I almost laugh at the absurdity of it before tears prickle my eyes and I feel ridiculously touched.

'No, but thank you. I appreciate it.'

Ramzan unlocks the door while I gather the shopping bags. My mind teems with thoughts. How did he find me? And why now? After it happened he tried many times but he's gone quiet recently. I thought I'd lost him but now he's undeniably back. What can I do? Perhaps I'll move? There's nothing keeping me here, except I've come to feel comfortable here. There must be thousands of flats like it across London.

'Don't you up and leave us,' Ramzan says, as if reading my mind.

I look into his big brown eyes and smile sadly, but say nothing. I can't promise anything, and I don't want to lie to him. After what happened, I vowed Simon was out of my life forever, and I will do whatever it takes to keep it that way. It was all his fault. Without him, Sophie would still be with me.

The door swings open but I don't switch on the light. I don't want Ramzan to see any more of the inside than absolutely necessary.

'You want help with your bags?'

I picture him going into my flat, looking around at all the mess and squalor. 'No. Thank you.'

I edge inside and shut the door. Going through into the kitchen, I dump the bags in the sink and open my emergency bottle of red. So much for roast chicken; my stomach recoils at the thought. I take the bottle over to my desk and turn off the lights. I need to think.

The estate agent calls the next morning and the sound of my phone drags me from the depths of unconsciousness. I don't think you can call it sleep after I polished off the bottle of red and half a bottle of vodka last night. I'm still in my chair and my neck aches from sleeping with my chin on my chest. The phone continues to buzz and I stare at the screen but I can't bring myself to answer. Paradise Found is a fantasy – what might have been. Simon's visit has reminded me that the dream is already shattered.

The call goes to voicemail and I log in to the Zippi app to let them know that I'm ill. There's no way I can make it today since I don't feel hungover yet and I'm sure the alcohol is still coursing through my system. I've taken enough risks recently. It's the first sick day I've taken in two years and once I've tapped the correct button, the app asks me: *Are you sure you're not well enough to drive?*

I tap *yes*.

We're really sorry to hear that, Laurel. Unfortunately, this means you'll lose your Reliability Bonus this month, as per our Terms & Conditions – are you okay with that?

I tap *yes* again.

Sad times! Your route has been reallocated today. We remind you that after two days we might need to reallocate your route permanently and you may be assigned a new route, subject to availability.

I've heard of drivers being sent to Kent or never getting back on the system. It's only one day but I still feel a tremor of fear as I scroll down for the final message.

Feel better soon, Laurel!

Thanks a bunch, I think, and I toss my phone on the desk. It's the false friendly tone I detest when I know I'm just a number to Zippi, one driver in a pool of so many. My head screams as I stagger to the loo. I avoid the mirror in the cramped bathroom and close my eyes so I don't see the black mould above the shower. It started as a few specks on the tiles but has spread to a thick down across a large portion of the ceiling.

Our old flat had three bathrooms. Mine and Dominic's en suite, the family bathroom, and a small loo that was larger than this whole room. I never had to appreciate the dryness of the tiles or the pristine ceramics, thanks to our regular cleaner. A clean bathroom is something you take for granted until you move somewhere with a cheap bathroom suite that has been battered by previous tenants. Some stains can't be scrubbed off, not that I try.

On my way back to my desk, I take another bottle of vodka from the kitchen cupboard and pour a glass, cradling it in both hands. I long to throw it back – everything gets easier as alcohol circulates – but I force myself to stare at the photos of Sophie and take small sips.

Like many people, I discovered alcohol as a teenager and found it gave me the confidence I lacked. It was in a pub where I met Dominic and I'd never have had the courage to speak to him if it wasn't for the two large glasses of white I'd drunk. But I was never an alcoholic. Mostly, I drank for fun but after Sophie was born, the only opportunity I had was at work. In banking there are always lots of willing partners in crime and Simon was the most willing. I'd meet him for breakfast and we'd say goodbye at four in the morning. Of course, Dominic said he was a bad influence, and that was before everything happened.

The estate agent calls again as the afternoon sun fills the room with a pale yellow light.

'Hello,' I answer.

'Hi, Laurel.' I wonder if she's always so chirpy. 'It's Nicole from Hamiltons. We've got an appointment to view number five Paradise Found tomorrow?'

'Yes.'

'I'm really sorry but I'm afraid the owners have decided to accept an offer so we'll have to cancel.'

I almost drop the phone but manage to hold on to it. It feels like I've been sucker punched. My glass is two-thirds full and I slowly swallow the rest while Nicole is still wittering on. 'It does sometimes happen when there's a lot of interest in a place but we do have similar properties in the area I can show you if—'

'No.' My voice cracks with emotion.

'I'm sorry,' she says again. 'We do have another lovely gated community not too far away if that's what you're—'

I clear my throat. 'No.'

I'm on the verge of tears. How can they have sold so soon? It can only have been on the market a few days.

'Is there any way I can still see the house?' I plead.

'I'm sorry. I did say it was likely to go quickly. There are a quite a number of disappointed parties and we advised the owners to hold out but they already had several bids and there was one couple who really wanted it. It's gone for significantly above asking price and they are chain-free so the sellers are happy.'

I swallow hard. How can I say I don't want to buy it, all I want is for a quick look around? I consider asking again but even I can hear that sounds strange.

'Is it one of the international buyers you mentioned?' I ask, deciding that I may as well find out all I can about my new customers.

'No. A young couple actually, with a child. Dad works in finance.' I can hear she's apologetic, telling me these things to gee me up. It only makes me feel worse since that sounds like us. Me, Dominic and Sophie.

'A banker?'

'That sort of thing. You know the type.' She gives a little laugh.

I manage to join in – I really do.

'It's gone so quickly.' I'm just whingeing now but Nicole's peppiness doesn't slip.

'It is unusual but all parties are desperate to move quickly. The sellers are older so they are keen to get out of London and the buyers want to get in as soon as possible. The lawyers are already instructed.'

'And the new family is going to live there?'

'Yes. A lot of properties like this are bought as invest-ments and sit empty. If it's any consolation, this family is really excited to move into the area.'

At least there'll be a new family to get to know on my route, closer to my age than the Bateses.

'Are they nice people?' I want to keep her talking but there's a pause and I wonder if I've asked one question too many. Estate agents like to talk but I'm sure there are rules about how much they can say. I don't want to give her any cause to worry about my intentions so I add quickly, 'Only it would be easier to think I've lost out to decent folk.'

'From what I saw of them they seemed lovely. The daughter was very excited that there's no traffic on the street. She brought her scooter to one of the viewings to ride up and down.'

'How old is she?'

There's another long silence and when Nicole speaks again her voice is clipped. 'I can't disclose information about the purchasers for confidentiality reasons. I'm sure you understand.'

'Of course.'

'If you're still interested in moving, do let us know.'

She hangs up before I can say goodbye.

Chapter Thirteen

I return to Paradise Found the next day to find an ugly red 'sold' sticker splashed across the 'for sale' sign outside number five. I can't help but feel angry with the Bateses. If they'd simply stayed put, none of this would have happened.

There's only one package, a rare one for Evelyn at number two, and I feel a rush of relief. I can't face any of the others today, not even Patrick. I go to ring her bell but hesitate when I see there's a note sellotaped to the front door.

'*Deliveries – ring bell and leave on step due to virus. No contact please.*'

It's not the first of its kind I've encountered on my route but Zippi has procedures I have to follow. I press the bell and retreat to wait a few extra metres away to try to ease some of her worries but Evelyn doesn't come. I press it again. After a minute or two, the door opens a crack and her narrow face appears with her helmet of steel-grey hair and sour expression. She must only be late sixties, but her deliveries are usually medical.

She takes me in, her eyes narrowed. 'Didn't you see the sign?'

'I'm sorry, Mrs White.' I use the loud, slow voice I re-serve for older people. 'I need a signature.'

She scowls at me worse than ever. 'Can't you do it?'

'No, Mrs White. I'm very sorry but it's company poli-cy that the recipient must acknowledge receipt for insur-ance purposes.'

The door opens another inch but I see her claw-like fingers are gripping hard on the wood, holding it in place, as if I'm about to kick it open and charge inside. Not that I'd dare. Evelyn is frail but she's no pushover. A few months ago one of her deliveries arrived broken and she came out to the van and gave me a dressing-down in the road, waving her fists in the air and yelling for the whole street to hear. Not that it was my fault; they hadn't stuck a 'fragile' sticker across the top. Since then we haven't exactly been on speaking terms.

'Haven't you heard about the virus?' she demands.

I fight the urge to roll my eyes. 'I have, Mrs White, but company policy hasn't changed.'

'It's all over northern Italy now. The old people are dying.'

'I can assure you I haven't been to northern Italy.'

She narrows her eyes further to tiny slits. 'Of course not, silly girl. You're all over London in your van, though, handing things over to every Tom, Dick and Harry.'

'My route is north-east London.' I know this is churl-ish but I'm beginning to lose my cool.

I hold out my phone with the signature screen ready.

'I just need a squiggle. You don't need to take my phone; just use the stylus.' I pray she'll get on with it so I can carry on with my route.

'I've had cancer, you know?'

I did know actually. When I first came to Paradise Found, Evelyn's daughter visited a lot more and she received a lot of prescription drugs. I looked them up online and saw there was an anti-nausea medication that's often used by cancer patients during chemotherapy.

'I'm sorry to hear that.'

'I don't want to risk my life because you need a signature.'

'Would you like me to return the parcel?'

'I just want you to leave it here. Is that too much to ask?'

We stare at each other in a stalemate. There's nothing else I can offer without breaking the Zippi rules.

'Can I get your manager on the phone?'

I sigh but catch myself because Evelyn looks furious. Back at the bank, I was the lead salesperson in my department. All the big clients came through me because they liked my style, and I brought in the biggest trade three years in a row. It was a badge of honour that reflected well in my bonus. In this moment, I fully realise just how far I've fallen.

'I can give you the email address,' I say.

She scowls even harder. 'Ridiculous. Why can't you ever speak to a real human these days? It's always automated lines or email.'

I do have some sympathy for this.

'Excuse me, ladies, can I help?' Patrick's voice carries across from his door. He bounds over in a faded rugby shirt with the collar turned up. I see Evelyn's face soften.

'This silly delivery woman says I need to sign her little device.'

'It's company policy,' I repeat flatly, not meeting Patrick's eye.

'Here, let me.' He sweeps the device from my hand and dashes out his signature.

'Oh, thank you, Patrick. You know with my health, I can't be touching things when I don't know where they've been.'

I ignore the implication as I complete the delivery notification in the app and say as brightly as I can muster, 'Have a nice day.'

Leaving the parcel on the ground, I walk back to the van, holding my head high, aware they are both watching me. I can hear Evelyn muttering to Patrick about customer service these days but I'm soon too far away to hear Patrick's response.

'Laurel?' My breath catches as I hear Patrick coming after me. 'I don't suppose you have time for that coffee?'

I glance back and see Evelyn watching us, the package now in her arms after all that fuss.

The Zippi tracking comes to mind and a polite refusal is on the tip of my tongue, but then a feeling of recklessness overtakes me. 'You know what, that would be great.'

Patrick smiles and pushes his hand through his hair and suddenly my face grows warm and I don't know where to look. He really is very attractive. I follow him along the path to his front door, and glance back to see Evelyn's reaction. Her expression has hardened, and I give her a broad smile, feeling my mood lift further.

He must have left the door ajar when he came out so he strides straight inside, leaving me with no option but to follow and no time to feel excited or nervous or anything else. I go into the hallway as butterflies begin to flutter in my stomach. It's a small space and every inch of wall is cluttered with frames housing photos and posters and the air smells of cinnamon. I want to stop, to savour the moment, but he's already gone through the next door and is shouting, 'Do you take milk?'

I go through into the kitchen and take in the room from the doorway. It runs the full length of the house and at the back is a classy set of folding doors leading onto the garden; the doors are partly open, letting in a cool breeze. The kitchen units are farmhouse style and there's a red Aga oven in the centre with a tray of baking on the top.

'I've had a go at cinnamon buns,' Patrick says, watching the progress of my eyes around the room. 'Not my best effort, but do help yourself.'

It's clear that he lives in the kitchen, and who can blame him? It's light and bright, with more framed pictures on the walls and a scrubbed wooden table that's covered with newspapers and magazines. Patrick's laptop is in front of the middle seat and his coffee cup is next to it. This must be where he writes.

'Chop chop,' he says with a laugh and I realise I haven't moved from the doorway.

I'm not hungry but I pick up a sticky bun from the tray – they're still warm – and perch on one of the dining chairs at the table. It's wonderful to be inside but I'm conscious that I'm sitting here in my Zippi uniform while we smile politely at each other. To even think it could be a date is a stretch.

'Lovely place,' I murmur.

'Thanks. Sorry for the mess. I would say it's usually tidy but that would be a bare-faced lie.'

I laugh. 'You should see my flat.' I think of the stacks of notebooks and the empty bottles lying around and a gentle heat rises up my neck. Our messes are very different. It's cosy in here but I'm grateful for the breeze. Otherwise it would feel like getting into the warm pocket of air in a bed after the other person has just got up.

'What do you think?'

I frown before realising he's talking about the bun. I nibble the edge. It's surprisingly bitter.

'It's good,' I say.

'Liar!'

We laugh and he hands me a plate so I can put it down before returning to the kettle.

'Milk in your coffee?'

I realise I didn't answer him the first time. 'Just black.'

As he pours my coffee, I look around the room, making as many mental notes as I can. He's reading the *Telegraph* – hardly surprising – but there's a copy of *Crime and Punishment* on the table and an anatomical textbook cracked open next to it, which is a curious mix, and my fascination with him grows. There's a small pile of plates next to his seat showing he's eaten all his meals here and the dirty pots from the baking are piled in the sink. Not house proud, then but of course, I can't judge.

He sits beside me with a bun and I sip the coffee. It's strong enough that I can feel the grit in my mouth. He takes a big bite and chews.

'It's a shame the Bateses are moving on,' I say to fill the quiet.

'It might do this street good to get some new folks in. Liven things up a little.'

'I heard it's a young couple and a child moving in.'

Patrick raises both eyebrows. 'You do have your finger on the pulse.'

'Doorstep chat,' I say quickly.

He smiles. 'I suppose you must get sick of talking about the weather.'

'Rain is my specialist subject.'

He laughs again and finishes off his bun, licking sugar off his fingers.

'It's good of you to take an interest in our little street.'

'I wouldn't call it an interest.' It comes out too fast and his frown returns.

It's another moment like when he caught me at the bins. I get the feeling that he senses there's something a little off with me and I try to smile naturally, feeling the weight of his judgement before he nods at the wall. The sketch I gave him is in pride of place in a gold frame.

'I meant your gift. It's beautiful.'

My smile widens. I'm touched that he's bothered to put it up already, and in a place he must look at every day.

'I'm glad you like it, and thank you again for finding my earring.'

I drink my coffee as Patrick wipes sugar off his plate with his finger.

'What did you do to poor old Evelyn?' he asks.

'She was worried about the virus and didn't want me coming near her in case I was contaminated.'

'That dratted thing. It sounds like it could cause all sorts of disruption. People in Wuhan haven't left their homes in a month. Not that it would bother me. I'm a homebody, happy enough with a pot of coffee, a piece of cake and a newspaper. What about you?'

'Same.' I don't say that I'd prefer a nice bottle of scotch and my notebooks.

Patrick has an oversized clock on his kitchen wall. Some of the numbers are big and some small, and the handles are curved and different colours. It looks as if it belongs in *Alice in Wonderland*. Eight minutes have gone by since I sent the confirmation for Evelyn's delivery. I think of the packages in the back of my van. The company logs delivery times and factors in traffic. It will know that I've stopped. Ten minutes could be a loo break but anything more risks another email.

'I'm sorry, but I can't really stay. I'm working.'

'Of course. Me too. Well, I should be. I've promised my editor I will send over a first draft by Easter.' He rubs his hair forward then back. The man doesn't leave it alone. 'Not that it's going well.'

'What are you working on?'

'Another horror.' His eyes light up. 'This one is going to be particularly grisly. I just don't think I've got the heroine quite right. She needs to be complex, sympathetic yet totally deranged.'

I laugh politely but I find it strange picturing him sitting here, conjuring up all sorts of monstrosities. His last book had a husband poisoning his wife – his ex must have found it disturbing. But it is fiction, I tell myself, and who am I to judge the inner workings of someone else's mind? Mine isn't exactly shipshape.

Patrick goes on, 'Listen to me rabbiting on when you've got to go.'

I'd like to stay for longer and just enjoy the smells of his kitchen. I'd be happy sitting in silence with him working on his novel but I don't say this. Instead, I stand.

'Thanks for the coffee.' I mentally kick myself – my conversation skills really are rusty.

'Anytime.' The way he says this sounds like he might genuinely mean it. I try not to get carried away but I feel a flicker of hope as he walks me to the door.

'I don't suppose you would . . .' He stops. 'No, I'm sure.'

My heart soars. 'Yes?'

'Would you like to meet for a drink one evening?'

Our eyes meet. We both smile and turn a little pink. It's been a long time since I felt this way. 'I'd like that.'

'Let me take your number, just a second.' He goes back into the kitchen. I hear him shuffling papers and I force myself to stand still and breathe slowly. Touching my face, my skin feels warm. I hear his footsteps returning as I spot the Halloween sweets in the orange tub on the windowsill. I slip one into my pocket just before he returns with a newspaper and a pen. I dictate my number and he writes it on the blank strip at the edge.

'I'll message you the details.'

'Great, and thanks again for the coffee.'

I'm grinning as he closes the door and I have to force myself to act natural as I walk back to the van, resisting the urge to dance or sing or any of the other silly things I'd like to do. I can't quite believe it. Patrick and I have a date – a real date – and there was no need to see the Bateses' house after all. I pop the toffee in my mouth. Patrick's kitchen was exactly as I'd hoped. Who knows, perhaps next time I'll get to see the bedroom? This thought has me giggling to myself as I drive out of the gate, turning the music to full blast.

Chapter Fourteen

We exchange messages and plan to meet on Friday evening at a wine bar near Paradise Found. As the day approaches, I float through my deliveries, handing packages over with a flourish and greeting every customer with a wide smile. Some people seem to find my chirpiness annoying, but I don't care.

It takes some planning to get ready since I have nothing to wear – my Zippi fleece won't quite cut it, this time – and I've binned all of my make-up. Browsing online fills my evenings and it's a thrill when another Zippi driver delivers one of my parcels. He's a young man with a beard and he's gone for the polo shirt not the fleece. I try to engage him with a knowing smile but he doesn't make eye contact as he taps on his phone and holds it out for signature. I'd like to give him some feedback but I know better than to send an email to Zippi. They view all feedback as a complaint and I don't want to get my comrade into trouble.

When Friday comes around, I get ready carefully and arrive early and sober for the date with Patrick. My mouth feels dry and I'm desperate for a long drink of something alcoholic but I need to be at my best tonight. I want Patrick to think I'm a normal, happy person. Drinking alone is not part of the plan.

The bar is one of those trendy nooks, with a shiny, mirrored bar at the back of the room and half a dozen tables made from upturned wine barrels with tall stools that are already all taken even though we're meeting early. The air is heavy with the smell of wine and warm bodies and the front window is steamed up. Patrick is sitting at the back, closest to the bar, and is speaking loudly in Spanish to the man behind the counter. They seem to know each other well, as if Patrick is a regular. The table closest to ours is a group of five men in suits and shirts. They must have come straight from work and they're already looking dishevelled with their shirtsleeves rolled up and faces flushed.

'Laurel, there you are.' Patrick stands and throws out his arms, looking happy to see me, and kisses me on both cheeks.

I feel self-conscious in my new jeans and black top with the lace on the neckline plus lipstick and mascara. Patrick has only seen me dressed as the courier. Sliding onto the high stool opposite his, I fiddle with my hair. I've worn it up to show off my silver moon earrings as a little reminder of how we came together.

'You look great.' Patrick squeezes my fingers and the moment I feel his warm hand around mine, I relax a little.

I've replaced my fleece with a black leather jacket that I slide off and hang on the back of my chair.

'You look nice, too,' I say and it's true, though he's in his usual chinos and button-down shirt – tonight's is racing green and needs an iron. He's added a cherry-red sweater around his shoulders that clashes horribly but it only adds to Patrick's slightly off-key charm.

'Do you drink red?' he asks.

I suppress a laugh. 'I drink everything.'

'Seb was just saying they have a new Tempranillo on the list.' There's a chalkboard behind the bar with scores of wines written in tiny letters that I don't even attempt to read. 'He says it's dry with a delicate berry flavour. Shall we try a bottle?'

I nod, pleased he's going straight for the bottle.

'And how about some cured meat on the side? They do delicious salami here.'

'Why not?'

Patrick relays this in Spanish across the room. When he turns back to me he says, 'My ex-wife was Argentinian so I speak a little.'

It sounds like more than a little, but I don't want to feed his ego too much so early on in the date.

'Ex?' I wouldn't usually start with previous relationships before a drink but he's brought her up, and I'm glad of the opportunity to probe.

His face clouds over. 'We wanted different things after a while; she was much younger and keen for adventure, I was getting on a bit and ready to settle down. We fought and let's just say it didn't end well.'

'Sorry to hear that,' I mutter, feeling more sorry for bringing it up and killing the mood.

There's an awkward silence and Patrick seems to be lost in thought. I struggle to think of another topic but thankfully at that moment, Seb brings over a bottle of red and pours two glasses. Patrick takes a big gulp. 'This is delicious.'

I follow his lead and knock back half of mine in one go, grateful for the buzz of alcohol as it hits my bloodstream.

'A healthy thirst, now that's what I like to see in a woman.' The room is warm and my face is hot. I tell myself to slow down but Patrick doesn't seem to have any such compulsion, he's racing through his first glass like a dog lapping up water on a scorching summer day. When he puts the glass back on the table, there's only a splash left in the bottom and he seems to be visibly relaxed.

'Now, where were we?' His eyes go to the ceiling, casting about, before they return to my face. 'Ah yes, my ex.'

Hearing the words aloud makes it sound like an interrogation, and I flush again. 'We can talk about something else.'

He shakes his head good-naturedly. 'Good to plunge into the deep end and get the skeletons out of the closet. Or am I mixing my metaphors?'

'You're the writer.' I think of what's inside mine and give what I hope is a breezy laugh. 'The skeletons can stay inside for me.'

'Nonsense. Let's get it all on the table.' He pulls his chair closer to mine so I'm engulfed in a cloud of his cologne. So he *has* made some extra effort for our date. My stomach squirms. Our faces are close enough that I can see the patch of hair by his ear that he missed shaving and I feel the urge to run my finger over the stubble but instead I fold my hands in my lap.

'It's all ancient history now, anyway. Maria left me seven years ago. The excitement of the first novel had waned and she realised that the life of a writer is more libraries than parties.'

'What was it she did?'

'She was a student when we met. Fine art. She made all these crazy sculptures out of her own hair that no one wanted to buy. We settled down for a while but that wasn't the life she wanted. Paradise Found wasn't exciting enough for her, if you can believe it?' He raises his eyebrows and I laugh.

'Surely not?' He thinks I'm joking but part of me wonders how anyone could fail to find Paradise Found fascinating.

'Little did she know, if she'd waited it out just seven more years she would have had a brand-new set of neighbours to spice things up.' Patrick runs his hand through his hair and laughs, rolling his eyes.

I try not to look too interested.

'What are they like?'

'Who? The new neighbours?' He raises his eyebrows.

I try to laugh off my question. 'It's nice to have new faces on my route. A change to the monotony.'

'Quite. I hear that the man is a hot-shot in the city apparently. One can read about him in the *FT*.'

City types don't excite me for obvious reasons. 'And his family?'

Patrick waves his hand dismissively. 'God knows. I haven't met them yet and Bryce Cohen had nothing to report about them but I'm sure we shall find out soon, when they move in. Now enough about them, tell me about your job. It must be fascinating to see inside people's lives like that.'

I try to look unconvinced. 'It's mostly just ordinary deliveries.'

'Mostly?' He raises an eyebrow.

'Well . . . I suppose there are times when I get a glimpse of something I shouldn't.'

'Now we're cooking on gas.' He leans closer. 'Are we talking nudity?'

I laugh and take another sip. 'On occasion.'

'Flashers?'

'It's usually more innocent than that. Someone comes running from the shower and their towel slips, that sort of thing.'

Patrick shudders theatrically. 'How thrilling. What's the most flesh you have actually seen?'

I think of the old man who opened the door nude from the waist down and insisted on calling me Debs. I waited with him until his carer arrived but I don't think that's quite what Patrick has in mind.

'There was a woman last week who came to the door in her pyjamas. She only realised the top was gaping open after she'd signed and taken the package.'

Patrick lets out a loud bark of laughter and the men on the next table turn to stare but Patrick doesn't seem to notice. It must be nice to be so carefree and secure in himself. Seb interrupts with a chopping board covered with slices of sausage and Patrick pops one straight into his mouth.

'You've got to try this,' Patrick says and I get a hit of garlic on his breath.

It's rare I'm this close to another human and I'm conscious of every exhalation and brush of our skin. I put a disc of sausage into my mouth and chew slowly, keeping my lips pressed together so no air can escape. Patrick tosses in three at once and continues speaking as he chews.

'You were telling me about on-the-job nudity. Don't let me stop you.'

I laugh. 'There's not much more to tell.'

Patrick rests his chin on his hands and switches to a serious expression.

'Honestly, why do you do it?'

'My job?' I ask to give myself time to think. I can't admit that the main reason was that Zippi didn't ask too many questions. 'It pays the bills.'

Patrick pours more wine in my glass. 'Please tell me to mind my own beeswax, but a woman of your obvious intellect can't have grown up wanting to deliver parcels.'

I've had enough wine in a short space of time to laugh at his audacity. It's not a typical job for women; I know I'm an anomaly. I see it in people's eyes when they answer the door. I wonder if this was the whole purpose of the date. Perhaps Patrick wants to report back to Bryce Cohen and the rest, but then I tell myself not to be so paranoid. I decide to throw him a little something – we are getting to know each other, after all.

'I made a career switch five years ago.'

Keeping his chin on his palms, Patrick clutches his face with his hands and leans even closer. 'And before?'

'I was a banker. Sales.'

He slaps the table and the wine glasses jump. 'There it is. I knew there was a story.'

I feel the smile fall from my face and work to revive it. 'There's no story.'

He sloshes more wine into my glass, though it wasn't empty.

As if sensing I'm not quite ready to open up, Patrick moves on. 'We'll get it out of you yet. Now, tell me about your siblings.'

The conversation reels and spools and I find Patrick's attention is like looking into the head of a flickering torch. One moment I'm blinking and answering a question and the next he's moved on to another topic. There isn't time for awkward silence. He tells me he's got three older sisters and they used to dress him up in girls' clothes. I don't mention that I know this already from the bio in his book.

Next, we spend a long time discussing whether there's a Spanish equivalent of *Francophile*. He calls Seb over for an opinion and a second bottle of Tempranillo. We settle on *Hispanophile* and Patrick proclaims himself to be one since he visits San Sebastian every summer. He tells me I must come if only to try the razor clams, and I feel a flicker of pleasure at the thought of us sitting outside in the warm sun, sharing seafood and more wine. I'm trying to weigh up whether it was a throwaway comment or a genuine intention but Patrick has moved on already.

'So you're an only child. What heaven. Tell me about your parents, then.'

We're well into the second bottle and my tongue is loose. My throat is feeling a little hoarse – it must be the most I've spoken in years.

'Not much to tell. They're in the old-fashioned mould. We're not huggers.'

He taps his fingers together. 'Go on.'

'My dad was a town planner, retired now. My mum was – well, is – a homemaker.'

Our family sounds very small compared to Patrick's large family.

'How often do you see them?'

'Once a year at Christmas.'

Patrick frowns. 'So infrequently?'

I hesitate. Perhaps it's the wine or the intimacy of the bar but I feel like I want to let him see something of the real me. 'We've had a bit of a falling-out. My dad refuses to accept my career change and so when we do meet he spends the whole time trying to convince me to return to banking.'

'Surely that's your decision.'

'I guess he just feels let down. They supported me through university and were so proud when I got the job at the bank. I think he hopes that a little persuasion will make me want to go back.'

'And does it?'

'God, no.'

'Well, I say good on you for getting out from behind a desk. I tried being a lawyer once. Three months as a paralegal was all I lasted before I was ready to stab myself in the eye with a pencil just to get out of work for the day. That's when I knew I had to try writing.'

He lapses into a monologue on his writing process and I'm happy to let his words wash over me. I've already said more than I should. It's the wine and the place, and Patrick is very inquisitive. I try to steer him back to women – I'd like to know whether he's dated since his ex-wife – but he is stuck on the joys of writing long-hand and I wonder again why he asked me out.

He breaks off mid-sentence. 'I hope I'm not boring you.'

I shake my head.

'You're too kind. When I get going on writing, you just need to give me a hard thump. Now, you will try a sherry, won't you?' He beckons over Seb and barrels on. 'Sherry is the most underrated drink. Most people think it's reserved for old ladies at Christmas but that's a crying shame. It can be the most marvellous thing.'

Seb appears at his shoulder and Patrick orders two sherries without waiting for an answer. I get the feeling that Patrick is plying me with booze and I vaguely wonder whether I should be worried by it. It might put another woman off but it's only making me feel more at ease. Perhaps we are better suited than it might first appear.

Seb places the amber liquid in front of us.

'*Gracias,*' Patrick says.

Patrick is right, it's delicious – bitter and viscous with a hint of orange.

'Back to your career change. Can I ask, was that a decision you made out of the blue?'

We're approaching dangerous ground, and even through my haze of tipsiness, I feel my senses sharpen.

'Not entirely.' I gulp my sherry.

'Shall we get the bottle?' Again, Patrick doesn't wait for an answer before waving over to Seb, who brings the bottle to our table and gives Patrick an indulgent smile. He is remarkably tolerant of Patrick's use of him as a personal waiter. 'There,' Patrick says, sloshing sherry into our glasses. 'Much better not to have any concerns about reaching the end of the glass.'

I keep quiet and hope the conversation has moved on but then Patrick fixes me with his hazel eyes and I can tell more questions are coming.

'Just tell me to mind my own business, but I'd love to know, what happened with your old job?'

My face feels hot and my thoughts are tumbling over one another. What's safe to tell him? The accident? Sophie? I don't want to lie but I'm not sure he'd look at me the same way if he knew the truth. I must tread carefully. 'I'm happy to tell you but can I ask that you keep it to yourself?'

Patrick looks offended. 'Of course. I would never repeat anything you tell me.'

I rest a placatory hand on his arm. 'I'm sure you wouldn't, I just needed to check since it's a bit sensitive with my work.'

'I understand completely. You have my word.' Patrick mimes locking his lips.

I take a deep breath. 'I think I told you that my husband died?'

'Yes, of course. You poor thing. I'm so sorry.'

'Thank you.' I pause. My words are coming out slowly but my mind is racing as I try to work out what to say. 'It's difficult to talk about. There was a car crash and . . .' I swallow more of the fiery liquid. 'He was . . . it was . . . well, my daughter was in the back in her car seat and she was . . . she was taken.'

His mouth hangs slightly open. 'What do you mean, "taken"?'

Licking my lips, I find my mouth is dry and when I try to speak, my voice cracks.

'Sorry.' I take a sip of water.

'Please, don't apologise. Are you trying to tell me your daughter was kidnapped?'

Searching Patrick's eyes, I see sorrow and what looks like genuine caring. No one has looked at me like that in years. I find myself nodding back.

Patrick puts his hand on my arm. 'Jesus, Laurel, I am so sorry. Did the police find her?'

'Not yet. There are leads all the time. I'm still looking.'

He takes off his glasses and rubs his eyes. I may as well tell him what happened next. I don't like to talk about Sophie but I learnt in sales, people will only buy what you're selling if they trust you. 'When that all happened, it was a lot to take. I wasn't able to keep working anymore, not in such a high-pressure environment.'

'Totally understandable. It's amazing you're still standing.'

I empty my glass.

'Well, I wasn't, not for a long time. I had a breakdown. It wasn't pretty but I got the help I needed and now I'm fine.'

Patrick covers my hand with his. The skin is warm, soft and a little damp. He must moisturise.

'Thank you for telling me. I think you're very brave.'

'You can see why I don't want people to know?'

'Yes, but you mustn't feel alone. Everyone has their demons. I mentioned my ex, well, at the end of our relationship she had a miscarriage.' Our eyes meet and his glimmer before he blinks a few times. I squeeze his fingers. 'I wanted to try again and she didn't. We couldn't go on after that.'

'Patrick, I'm so sorry.' I'm glad we're opening up but it's clear we both have issues.

The men on the next table suddenly fall quiet and we catch the end of the bald man saying, 'I did tell her it wasn't apple juice.' They roar with laughter. One of them slaps the table and a glass falls and shatters on the floor.

'Shall we get out of here?' Patrick says. 'I could do with some air.'

I nod and he goes over to the bar and deals with the bill. There are times when I like a man to take charge, and this is one of them. We've had a lot to drink and my head is swimming but I don't feel out of control.

The men are laughing again and I feel a sudden need for fresh air so I meander to the exit and wait for Patrick outside. It's dark and cold and I take grateful gulps of fresh air. As he opens the door, he pulls on his jumper, leaving his shirttails hanging like a rebellious schoolboy.

'Shall we stroll?' He offers me his arm, and with a flutter of pleasure I take it. Quickly we are both tense with the cold; we could each do with another layer. I feel the warmth of his body pressed up against my side. We walk in silence and I'm glad to leave our intense conversation behind.

He produces a tin from his pocket and gives me a grin. 'Smoke?' Inside is a neat row of pre-rolled cigarettes. 'I make my own tobaccos – have done since school. I've always enjoyed tinkering with my intoxicants. There's peppermint, liquorice and a salted caramel I've been working on. Can I tempt you?'

I accept a mint cigarette and we light them as we walk. After a few drags, I feel light-headed and I'm certain we're swaying. We're so close to Paradise Found that after a few turns we are upon it and we stop by the gate.

'Not very gallant of me – you've walked me home. My mother would be shocked.' Patrick laughs but then turns to me, suddenly serious. 'Will you come in for a coffee?'

I hesitate. 'No, I shouldn't.'

He takes my hand lightly. 'It's not like it's the first time we've met.' He intertwines his fingers with mine. I know I ought to refuse but the pleasure of being with Patrick for a whole evening, having him look at me like he is now, is too much to refuse, and the heady cigarette has left me feeling untethered.

'One more drink?' Patrick lifts my hand to his lips and brushes them against my knuckles. My stomach swoops and I find myself nodding as Patrick leads me through the gate.

Chapter Fifteen

It takes Patrick a few tries to get the key in the lock and when he opens the door, he lurches forward into the dark hall.

'Whoops!' He lets out another shout of laughter and I find myself giggling along with him.

Kicking off his deck shoes, he barges straight into the kitchen and turns on the light. By the time I get my shoes and jacket off and follow, he's already clattering about inside a high cupboard.

'I know we said coffee but shall we go straight to something stronger?' he says.

I'm already unsteady on my feet but Patrick produces a bottle of whisky and says, 'I make a mean old-fashioned. What do you say?'

It's a single malt and my mouth begins to water despite my brain saying I've had enough. 'Go on, then,' I say.

Patrick cheers and reaches for an orange from his fruit bowl. Before he slices it, he pretends to bowl, slinging his arm high in the air and muttering, 'Williams approaches the wickets.'

Shaking my head, I feel the sudden, urgent need to pee.

'Where's your loo?' I ask.

Patrick directs me out into the hallway to the guest loo under the stairs. The air is cooler outside the kitchen and I enjoy the break from Patrick's chaotic energy. I can still hear the clanks of the drinks being made, and figure I have a few minutes until he starts to wonder where I am. Turning on the spot, I study the framed pictures in the hall. From the book covers and posters he's chosen, it seems he's a horror fan: there are framed Stephen King covers and a large *Psycho* poster.

The stairs are divided into two short flights, the first leading up to a small landing and the second disappearing back over my head. I'm tempted to slip up and take a look around but a minute has already passed and I know I wouldn't have time. There's one more door from the hall. From the floor plans I found online, I know that most of the houses have a dining room set up at the back but the Addo-Smyths have knocked through so it's a single large living room. I wonder what set-up Patrick has gone for as I turn the handle as quietly as I can but it won't open. Frowning, I shove with my shoulder but it doesn't give. It's locked.

Patrick clears his throat and I spin around, heart pounding. He's in the doorway with a tea towel slung over his shoulder.

'Loo is right there,' he says mildly, pointing to the door under the stairs.

'Of course it is.' My face is on fire.

He doesn't go back into the kitchen until I'm inside the tiny bathroom. I lock the door and lean against it, wondering why have a locked room when you live alone? What was it Audrey said . . . '*and then he'll bury you under the patio'*. . . I consider it for a moment then laugh and shake my head. I'm being stupid; Patrick's a nice guy. I'm sure there's an explanation for it. I sit on the loo seat and breathe deeply to return my heart rate to normal before washing my hands slowly. On the wall is a photo of Patrick's schooldays. Rows of boys lined up in black uniforms with dated hairstyles. I look along the list of names until I find him at the front with the smaller ones, with floppy hair that can't hide a face full of acne.

When I return to the kitchen, Patrick has opened the folding doors and is smoking out into the black air. Two glasses filled with amber liquid sit on the table.

'Smoke?' he asks as I approach.

I accept a salted-caramel-flavoured cigarette and join him by the doors. A blast of wind hits me full in the face but I barely feel the chill as I take the first drag and wait for the nicotine to rush around my body. It hits me even harder than before and a wave of black flickers at the edge of my vision. I wonder exactly what it is he puts in them.

'I hope you weren't looking at the school photograph in the loo,' he says.

I feel a wave of relief that he isn't going to accuse me of snooping. 'It did catch my eye.'

'I'd like to think I was a case of the ugly duckling. I bet you were always attractive.'

Running my hand through my hair, I bask in the rare compliment, but I was never one of the good-looking girls. I wasn't ugly either. I was a wallflower. Even my unusual name was forgotten – Laura, they'd call me. It wasn't until university that I learned to play the game.

Make-up. Haircuts. Short skirts. And always laugh at their jokes.

'Are you flirting with me?' I ask with a coy smile.

He smoulders back. 'If you have to ask, I'm not doing a very good job.'

A silence settles between us and I glance at the house next door. I sense Patrick watching me and the silence stretches until it is nearly unbearable. I search for something witty to say. He moves closer and I blurt out, 'Do you know when the new neighbours are moving in?'

'Bryce Cohen said next week.'

I splutter and cough up a lungful of smoke. 'So soon?'

'Apparently they are going to rent the property from the Bateses so they can move in right away whilst the paperwork goes through. They must be champing at the bit since they've already been here with their interior designer, measuring up.' He raises his eyebrows. 'The street is really going up in the world.'

I'd hate to see what Patrick thinks of as down. He bumps his hip against mine and we both lose our balance and are forced to grab the doorframe to stay upright.

'Why are you so interested?' Patrick says teasingly.

I shrug. 'You get to know people on your route, that's all. I like this street.'

'It does have some rather charming residents.' He gives me a significant look and I can't help but laugh.

'Have you discovered anything unusual at Paradise Found?' he asks.

'What do you mean?'

'I'm sure you see things, coming here day after day. You probably know more about this street than I do.'

I think of my notebooks and a slow smile spreads across my face.

'So you have,' Patrick says excitedly, misreading my expression. 'Tell me.'

'It wouldn't be very professional . . .'

'Surely we're beyond professional?' Patrick slips his arm around my waist and pulls me close. His warm breath tickles my ear and my heart feels like it's trying to break free of my chest. I attempt to blow out a long stream of smoke with the sexy nonchalance of a French starlet.

'It would be against Zippi rules – they insist upon absolute discretion.'

'And I had you down as a rule breaker.' He squeezes me gently. 'How about I tell you a secret, then you tell me yours.'

I incline my head. 'I'm listening.'

'Let me see.' He takes a drag from his cigarette and blows smoke over my head. 'Got one. I didn't lose my virginity until I was twenty-three.'

I smile and raise an eyebrow. 'I'm not sure that's quite revealing enough for a trade.'

Patrick laughs. 'Ouch, I'm hurt. How about crushed dreams? You see, I always wanted to be a doctor but I failed chemistry. Twice.'

I suppress a snort. 'I'd feel sorry for you if you hadn't written a bestseller.'

There's another pause and I finish my cigarette so I edge out from Patrick's arm and put it out on the patio.

'Okay, here goes. The big one. You remember I said when I was younger my sisters used to dress me up? Well, the truth is, I enjoyed it.'

We both laugh.

'But is that really a secret?' I say archly and Patrick folds his arms, pretending to be offended.

'Okay, I'll tell you,' I say, 'but this is just between us.'

Patrick signs a cross on his chest.

I move back close, enjoying having our bodies touching, and whisper in his ear, 'Did you know that Harry Cohen sells antiques online?'

'Ye-es.' He bends down so my lips are against his ear as if he can't wait for me to spill the beans.

'I came across his website and realised that I'd delivered some of the items for sale to his house.'

'No harm, no foul in that is there?'

I leave a dramatic pause. 'The items were from department stores.'

It takes Patrick a moment, but then he gets it and gasps. He removes his glasses and rubs his eyes, then he shoves them back on and blinks at me. 'That old dog! He tried to flog me a bed once for three grand. Said it was Victorian.'

'Shh!' My finger goes to my lips. 'Come on, let's go back inside.'

We return to the kitchen table and take a seat side by side. Patrick sits back in his chair, crossing one leg over his knee and cradling his drink against his chest. I sip mine. 'This is good.'

He nods. At the far end of the table is his laptop and a pile of papers.

'How's the novel going?' I ask.

'Dreadful. I can't bear to talk about it. There's so much pressure after the last one. That's why it's taken me years and several discarded drafts.'

'It was fantastic. Gruesome but a page-turner.'

Patrick's expression lifts. 'You've read it?'

'Of course. When it came out. You could hardly miss it.' I don't mention that I've been re-reading it late at night, sitting in my chair and jumping at every creak from the estate or whistle of the wind. It's been keeping me awake but it doesn't matter, I don't sleep much anyway.

'I suppose it was everywhere. That was a hectic summer. I was doing interviews with the Sunday papers one week and jetting off to Hollywood the next . . .'

I think back a decade to when his book was released. Pre-Sophie. I was working at the bank and things with Dominic were still in the honeymoon phase, but it was around that time I met Simon. We were colleagues first, then friends for a long time before anything happened and it was only after Sophie was born that things really took off.

'Listen to me, humblebragging. I'm only trying to impress you.'

I smile and take another sip of wine. 'It must have been exciting.'

'Yes, Maria certainly thought so.'

There she is again. The ex-wife. There are no photos of her that I can see, and the house feels and smells like Patrick, but there are distinct traces of a woman's presence. In the line of recipe books on the shelf next to the cooker is one for Argentine beef dishes. On the corkboard behind the door, pinned above eyeline, are faded wedding invitations addressed to 'Pat and Maria'. I bet somewhere there's a wardrobe filled with her clothes.

'Have there been many other girlfriends?'

He glances back at me with a half-smile. 'A few, I admit it. These dating apps mean it's almost impossible not to meet someone if you really want to. I just haven't met anyone special. And you?' he asks.

'Not really. I've been taking it slow after what happened.'

'Of course.' Patrick rubs his chin again. 'Such an awful thing.'

I smile brightly, determined not to bring down the mood. 'Loo again.' I stumble back into the hallway and realise just how drunk I am. I make it into the toilet and find I'm suddenly desperate. I only manage to get my knickers down just in time and as I lean back my head lolls. Feeling myself drifting off, I sit up sharply, rubbing my face with my hands. My body feels strangely floppy and I use the towel rail to haul myself upright so I can stare in the mirror above the sink. My cheeks are flushed and my pupils are pinpricks. I vow not to have another of Patrick's home-made cigarettes; they're lethal.

Trying to pull myself together, I splash cold water on my face and look again at the row of schoolboys. Simon went to a boarding school like that. Brutal is how he described it, and it damaged him for life. I slap my cheek once. I don't want to think of Simon, not now. Sucking in some air, I head back into the kitchen and find Patrick standing on a chair, reaching for something at the back of the cupboard.

'Where is that . . . ?' He pulls out a bottle. 'Here it is. Ouzo I got on my travels.'

'I'm fine. Honestly—'

But Patrick brushes the dust off the bottle as he gets down and produces two shot glasses that he sloshes liquid into. 'A toast. To us.'

I hesitate, then pick up mine. The glass is sticky. It doesn't feel like a good idea, but it would be awkward not to now.

'To us,' I say, and we knock them back.

'Shall we dance?'

Patrick goes over to the corner of the room where there's a record player on a bookshelf. He puts on Fleetwood Mac and dances towards me, reaching for my hands. The ouzo hits my stomach and I let him pull me forward. His skin feels clammy. We dance around the kitchen, acting silly, until a slower song comes on and he pulls me close. All I can think is that I hope we're not disturbing Evelyn next door until he looms and kisses me and all thoughts other than the feel of Patrick's mouth on mine evaporate.

Chapter Sixteen

I jolt awake and my eyes snap open. I drag in my first waking breath as if I've emerged from the bottom of a swimming pool. My heart pounds. It takes me a moment to realise that I'm in Patrick's bedroom and his arm is draped across my body, pinning me down.

Pushing it off, I sit up, grimacing. I'm in Patrick's bed but I can't remember how I got here. I remember the wine bar of course, then the kitchen, but after that, there's nothing. My stomach lurches and I collapse back onto the pillow. Patrick is dead to the world beside me but I can see his chest is bare and surprisingly hairy as if he's wearing a mohair sweater. There's a long, red scratch down his back onto his buttock. Did I do that? I close my eyes and try to remember but it's a blank nothingness.

I lift up the duvet and see that we're both naked. Our bodies are giving off an earthy, stale scent and there's a dampness between my legs that tells me we had sex. It's been five years since I slept with anyone. I'd like to say it was with Dominic – that's what a good wife would say – but sex with Dominic dried up way before. After Sophie was born, we tried a few times but something had changed. Dominic was so focused on being the perfect dad, and I had my work. And Simon.

As I peer blearily around, through the fog of my hangover I'm struck by the neatness of the room compared to the clutter downstairs. The bed linen is a smooth navy cotton that smells fresh. The curtains are drawn but pale light seeps in at the edges, and I can tell it's early. I try to stand but have to sit back down immediately. My head is killing me. I dig my fingers into my scalp and massage my skull but it's no use – the pain doesn't budge. Next to me, Patrick is sleeping heavily, a light snore catching at the end of each inhalation and I take the chance to study him. The drinking session hasn't done much for his skin – it's pale and there's a sheen of grease across his forehead and around his nose. His usual lustrous hair is pasted to one side. But there's something beautiful about a man so open and unencumbered. It makes me feel special to be allowed to see him this way.

A gentle snore is followed by a huge one and Patrick almost wakes himself up, rolling over and muttering. I know it's childish but I'm not ready to face him so I push myself out of bed and this time I manage to stay on my feet. Creeping to the door, I notice that the snoring has stopped.

'Laurel?' Patrick's voice is croaky.

'Just going to the loo,' I say lightly.

He grunts and rolls over. I brace my arm against the doorframe as the room comes in and out of focus and it takes a minute to feel strong enough to move. Using the wall for support, I gather my clothes in the half-light, retracing what must have been our route from the night before. My jeans are at the foot of the bed but my bra is draped over the bannister in the hallway and my blouse is in a puddle on the floor at the top of the stairs.

I make it to the bathroom and drop the bundle of clothes. It's more modern than I expected from Patrick's traditional style, with a round mirror over the sink that's like a ship's porthole and doesn't help with my hangover. I try to look at myself but there seems to be something wrong with my eyes – they won't stay in one place. I turn the shower as hot as it will go and stand under the steaming water with my teeth chattering, wondering what the hell we did to ourselves.

I don't want to make the journey home but I need to get out of there. I'll message Patrick and explain; I'm sure he'll understand. Dressing takes longer than usual but I finally manage to get my clothes on and peep around the door of Patrick's room. He lets out a low moan from inside the mound of duvet.

'We may have overdone it,' he says.

A weak giggle comes out of my mouth.

'Don't go,' he says.

'I have to. I need to pop home and get ready before my shift starts.'

He emerges, blinking like a mole from a hill, and fumbles for his glasses on the bedside table.

'I'm sure I have things you can borrow. A toothbrush, shampoo . . .'

A toothbrush isn't going to cut it. I need a darkened room and a bucket.

'I need to pick up my uniform, but thank you for last night.'

'Laurel?' He holds out his hand and I go over to take it. He pulls me down onto the side of the bed. 'Last night was really fun.' He drags me further so I'm next to him, our heads on the same pillow. 'I'd like to do it again.'

My stomach gives a small flip. 'Me too.'

'I'll call you.'

I push myself up, give his hand one last squeeze, then leave the room and pinball down the stairs, bouncing between the wall and the bannister. My shoes are on the floor in the hallway next to Patrick's and my new leather jacket is slung on top of the tub of Halloween sweets. Before I put them on, I freeze and listen. It's quiet upstairs. I tiptoe in my bare feet and try the handle of the closed door. It's still locked and I frown but then I shake my head. It's really none of my business.

From upstairs I hear the bed creak and I scurry back to the front door, jam my feet into my shoes and grab my jacket. I hurry outside, stumbling over the threshold. It's been raining, the pavement is wet and I can make out tiny drops of dew on the grass, shimmering like pearls. The sky has a pale underbelly that tells me morning is on the horizon, but it's dark enough that there are lights on at number three, where Mr Addo-Smyth must be getting ready for work, and at number five. I stop and stare for a moment, confused. Could it be the new neighbours already? One room upstairs and the hallway are lit up but I swear Patrick said they weren't moving in until next week.

Though my head is pounding and my stomach roiling, I can't help myself. I walk along the row and up the short path to their front door. It's what any good Samaritan would do, I reason. They could be being burgled. The Bateses' curtains have been removed and there's nothing to obscure the view. The walls in the hall have been stripped; I can see the salmon-pink plaster. A figure crosses the window and my heart quickens. Before I can move away, the door opens.

It's a man. Blonde, with one of those too-perfect side partings. Dressed in a well-fitted navy suit with a black trench coat thrown over his arm.

'What do you want?' he says.

I'm suddenly aware that my palms are drenched in sweat and go to wipe them on my trousers before I realise how this will look and let them hang stiffly by my sides. 'I just delivered a package next door,' I snatch at my usual explanation but his eyes narrow and I remember too late that I'm not in my fleece and it's early.

'I work for Zippi.' Even to me this sounds desperate. I mentally kick myself for not just saying I was at Patrick's.

He steps closer, forcing me to move back. From the curl of his lip it doesn't look like he believes a word I'm saying. 'And what are you doing at my house?'

'I saw the light. I was just checking there was nothing untoward going on.'

'Untoward?' He sounds angry now. 'Like a service provider peeping in the windows?'

I feel my face burn. 'That's not what—'

'I have a child in the house. You shouldn't be creeping around here.'

'I'm sorry. One of the neighbours told me you weren't moving in until next week, and I thought—'

'And that's your business how?'

I take a deep breath and force myself to think. I know the type from my banking days. This man doesn't want an explanation, he wants to make me feel small. I lower my eyes to the floor and rearrange my features into what I hope is a contrite expression. 'I'm sorry, sir.'

His eyes remain narrowed. 'Zippi did you say?'

I nod.

'What's your name?'

It wouldn't take him long to find out now he knows the company name, and I'm around here often enough, so I decide to tell him the truth in the hope of placating him. 'Laurel.'

'And is it part of your job, Laurel, to sneak around outside people's homes?'

I drop my gaze again to his overshined shoes. 'Sorry, sir.'

'I think I ought to send an email to your superior.'

There's a pain in my stomach like I've been punched. My hangover threatens to overpower me so it's all I can do to let my head hang and nod.

'Run along, then.'

My body doesn't feel like my own as I walk back to the main gate with him watching every step. I can tell that he's the type who will send a complaint to the company and follow up to make sure it's been received. Worry tightens my chest but I can't think about it now – I need to focus on getting home without being sick.

As I get into the van and turn on the heaters, I try to tell myself that Zippi will understand. Only there've been a number of complaints to previous employers before, from busybodies and pedants, and I've been forced to move on. It's been easy enough to rent a new flat or change delivery companies. But Paradise Found means more to me than any of the streets before. Biting back tears, I promise myself I won't let it, or Patrick, go without a fight.

The van's heaters are slow to warm up and I shiver most of the drive home. I can't seem to get my body under control – my muscles twitch and jerk waywardly. Patrick and I must have put away enough between us to tranquillise a horse, and I am definitely still over the limit. I'm finally warm when I pull up in the alleyway where I park.

The estate is silent as I make my way up to my flat and when I reach my floor, I'm pleased that it's too early for Ramzan to be outside, I wouldn't want him to see me in this state. As I approach my door, I'm going over the conversation with the new neighbour in my head but when I reach the doorstep, I stop suddenly. All my muscles tense. Jammed below the door is a folded piece of paper. I bend down slowly and pick it up, my hangover making it hard to think clearly.

Unlocking the door, I take the note to my desk, already coated in cold sweat before I've read it. My heart beats hard, and I half expect someone to jump out at me but I know my demons are on the paper. On my desk is the half-drunk bottle of whisky. I'd love a slug but I force myself to take ten deep breaths instead. Sophie's photos watch over me. Moving quickly like ripping off a plaster, I open the note and see Simon's handwriting. My heart plummets though it could only be him.

'*I need to see you, Laurel, please. I'll be back soon.*'

Chapter Seventeen

A while later – it could be a minute, it could be an hour – I push myself up and stagger back out into the morning air. There's a fresh breeze but I'm already shivering and I wrap my arms around myself as my teeth chatter even though I'm drenched in sweat. My body feels like a wet rag, and again I curse Patrick for getting me so drunk. It feels more like an out-of-body experience than a hangover, like my mind is a helium balloon that's floating somewhere above my head. I wonder again whether there was something in the cigarettes. Hangovers I'm used to, this feels like something else. I'll have to be more careful when Patrick's around. I don't want to embarrass myself in front of him.

I use the balcony railing to hold myself upright and look out at the soft, grey haze on the horizon, feeling the wind on my face, and in that moment a steely resolve comes over me. I resisted Simon once, I can do it again. The whisky bottle is still in my hand and I sit down heavily in Ramzan's deckchair, suddenly feeling defeated. I unscrew the cap and take a sip. It's been five years, but the memory of Simon is still so fresh – the shape of him, the feel of him. I screw my eyes shut to try to block it out. I thought I'd managed to cut him out of my life forever. But he's been here and I know he'll keep coming back until he gets what he wants. He always was persistent. I yearn to take another sip and keep drinking but that would be giving up. I'm building a new life – a real one – away from here, at Paradise Found, with Patrick.

I'd like to spend the day sitting here, drinking, but I need to shower and get ready for work. Lifting the neck of my shirt, I sniff my skin – there's a sweaty, sickly smell and when I shift in my seat I ache in places that make me certain that Patrick and I had sex. The alcohol has forced every memory from my head after the ouzo, and just remembering the shot makes me gag. It's not the first time I've had sex blackout drunk but I'm furious with myself. I wanted it to be special with Patrick and I thought I'd got those impulses under control.

I'm close to breaking down but I force myself into action. Taking one last sniff of the whisky, I screw the cap back on and put the bottle under Ramzan's deckchair so I'm not tempted to keep drinking, and go back inside. I go straight into the bathroom, take off my clothes, and stand under the shower with the water as hot as it will go. Quickly, my hands and feet turn bright red and tingle as they warm up from the cold. My body is tender but I scrub hard with handfuls of shower gel.

Once I'm dressed in my uniform, I hurry down to the van and try to find some music but I flick between albums until I just turn it off. I don't feel like myself this morning. Popping in a couple of sticks of gum, I chew so quickly my jaw aches as I drive to the depot. There are no packages for Paradise Found but while I feel its usual pull, the blank in my mind where the end of last night should be makes me uncomfortable. Patrick seemed happy enough this morning but I can't be certain of what I did or what I said.

The sky never lightens, remaining heavy and brooding for the whole of the morning and well into the afternoon. I keep expecting rain but it never comes. By the time I'm approaching the end of my route, I can barely sit still from the tension. While my right leg works the pedals, my left leg jiggles uncontrollably. The palms of my hands are leaking sweat and every few minutes I have to wipe my hands on my trousers. I'm dreading delivering the final parcel since I don't want to go home.

Once I've completed the final delivery, I run over other possibilities in my head. The pub is an obvious answer but I really don't want to drink. It's not Tuesday so there's no group – and I'm not sure I could cope with Denise at the moment, anyway. I can't go to Paradise Found, not without an invitation. I need to tread carefully with Patrick. But I can't go home. Simon could be there. I grip the steering wheel and feel panic rising in my chest. It feels harder to breathe and I start gasping for air. Tears leak from the corners of my eyes and I realise I'm close to the edge.

Indicating, I take a sharp left and head in the direction of Paradise Found. I won't go inside the gate, I promise myself. I'll just park up nearby and sit in the van. It's the one place that makes me feel better. As soon as I've made the decision, I feel lighter. The tightness in my chest eases. It's a pleasant evening now the colour is draining from the day and the grey overhead has been traded for inky blue. Perhaps I'll go for a walk around the block.

There's a free space within sight of the gate so I pull in and once again give silent thanks that Zippi don't have branded vans. My body still aches from the hangover but I roll my neck from side to side and feel some of my tension lift. It doesn't take long for the gates to open and Stephanie to appear in her running clothes. She turns my way but I slump down, following her with my eyes. Surely it's not healthy to run so much in this pollution? I watch her in my mirrors until she turns along the footpath and disappears.

After another few minutes, I feel well enough to turn on the music and select Take That's *Greatest Hits*. It reminds me of my teenage years when things were a lot simpler. I go through the album once and find I'm singing along so I start again at the top. The gate opens and Harry Cohen comes out with his collar turned up and his dog on a lead. I sit up straighter in my seat. I haven't seen Harry since our conversation. Our eyes meet as he passes and I give him a little wave. He ducks his head but I convince myself that the way he pursed his lips was almost a smile.

'Never Forget' comes on and I join in the chorus at full volume. It feels good to clear the cobwebs until I turn back to the front windscreen and my heart almost stops.

There's a figure standing in front of the van, looking directly at me. My hands brace against the steering wheel, then to my face to cover my mouth. It can't be, I tell myself, not here, at Paradise Found, but the outline looks like Simon. I slam my hand down on the door lock just as he lifts his hand and gestures to me to open the window. I long to start the engine and speed away but he's blocking my path. My breathing is unsteady and my hangover is rising again, making me too hot and too cold at the same time.

With a shaky hand, I wind down the window two inches, not enough to get an arm through. Simon walks around to the driver's side and stands close enough that I can see each of the five years that have gone by in his face. The wrinkles at the corners of his eyes are deeper and the whites are a little bloodshot. The twin peaks of his forehead are higher. But he's still got it and he knows it. The year-round tan covers most of his sins and there's that glint in his eye that always was my weakness.

'You've been hard to track down,' he says lightly.

So many questions bombard me in my head but my jaw clamps together and I know I couldn't speak if I tried.

'Laurel, please, look at me.'

I stare straight ahead out of the front window.

'I know you blame me but what happened wasn't my fault. How could it be? I wasn't even there.'

I feel my face screw up and tears begin to slide down my cheeks. I wipe them away on my sleeve, not wanting him to see but it's too late. His voice softens. 'Laurel, I want you to know that I've thought about you, and Sophie, every day since. I've tried to get in touch so many times. I loved you.'

I still refuse to turn to face him but I hear his voice crack. I won't feel bad for Simon. He never thought about anyone other than himself. Not his wife or four kids or me or my marriage – Simon just sucked me in and when things fell apart, he let the pieces fall where they may.

'Just go,' I say, through gritted teeth.

'Not until you look at me.'

'No.' I refuse to give him anything he wants, not any-more.

'Look at me!' he shouts and slams the glass with the flat of his hand. I flinch with each slap until he stops sud-denly and I hear muffled voices outside. Simon's talking to someone.

Finally, I turn his way and feel like crying harder when I see Stephanie talking to Simon, speaking low and intently. He lifts his hands into the air and backs away.

'Laurel, tell this woman that you know me.'

I rub at my eyes with my fleece but keep the door closed.

'You need to go or I'm going to call the police,' Steph-anie says.

'Tell her, for fuck's sake!' Simon smacks the side of the van this time with a loud bang, but I keep my teeth gritted until he turns and jogs away. I wait until he rounds the next corner before shakily unlocking the door and opening it a crack. Stephanie's forehead is creased in concern and she reaches in and takes my hand.

'Are you okay?'

I nod but can't seem to stop the tears rolling down my cheeks.

'Come on,' she says, helping me out of the van, but halfway out I realise what's happening and try to get back in.

'I'm fine, honestly. It was just a surprise that's all. A blast from the past.'

'You don't look fine.'

I pull my hand free. 'I just need to get home.'

'You can't drive, not in this state.'

Glancing behind her to the gate, I shake my head. Patrick doesn't need to see me like this. He'll only ask more questions and I don't need to give the new neighbour any more material for his complaint. Stephanie follows my gaze and a look of realisation dawns on her face. 'Would you like to go somewhere away from here and get a drink? You can tell me all about it.'

I search her face for any indication that she's joking but she seems to mean it. Fresh tears leak from my eyes but I soon gather myself and nod. 'Only if you're sure you have time.'

Stephanie fiddles with her ponytail and grins. 'I'd like to. Oliver is with the kids and I so rarely get the chance these days. There's an old-man pub a few doors along. Does that work?'

'Perfect.'

She leads the way to a dingy pub with a low ceiling and dirty carpet, but at least it has character. We take one of the booths that run along the side with stiff, dark green leather seats that are slightly tacky.

'What can I get for you?' she asks.

'I should get these.' I start to get up but Stephanie beats me to it.

'No, let me.' She says it self-consciously, as though she knows how much I get paid. 'Please.'

'White wine, then. Thanks.'

She goes to the bar and returns with two large glasses of white.

'It feels a bit naughty on a school night,' she says with a smile.

'Cheers to that.' I raise mine and we chink them together, then I take several large gulps. The wine circulates and it doesn't take long before I'm feeling more steady.

'So, who was that guy?'

Cradling the glass in both hands, I stare at the wine. I can't bring myself to look at Stephanie.

'The man I had an affair with.'

Her eyes open wide and she covers her surprise by sipping her wine. Her glass is still full while mine is already half empty. I put mine on the table and force myself to sit back, putting distance between me and it.

'What happened?'

I hesitate, trying to work out how to say it, and when I do, my voice is a whisper. 'He broke me.'

'I'm sorry. We don't have to talk about it, if you don't want to?'

'No, I'd like to. I just hope you won't judge me too much.'

'Of course not.'

I meet her gaze. It's hard to tell whether what I'm about to say will send her running or bring us closer. But I can't lie to her – I like Stephanie and I've been suppressing the truth for too long, a little bit of it needs to come out.

Chapter Eighteen

It was one of those mornings where you're fighting a losing battle. Dominic had told me he had an early client, so I should have been prepared but when I felt him slide from bed before six and heard the clank of the dumbbells knocking together inside his bag as he left the flat, I'd allowed myself five more minutes. That was my first mistake.

It had been a late one the night before. A client dinner that began with air kisses and apple martinis and ended with the investment manager I was meeting vomiting down the side of a black cab, his head hanging out of the window like a dog's. I'd felt a little swirly myself but had dropped him off at home, given the driver a large tip, and made it to bed.

Perhaps that's why when I next opened my eyes it was seven thirty and Sophie was wailing. She'd just turned two, was still in her cot, and didn't like to be forgotten. Not ready to face her yet, I lurched from bed and into our en suite. Her fire-engine siren broke into softer whimpers and I wondered how long she'd been crying, but I turned on the cold tap and splashed my face. There were black smears beneath my eyes, the whites were pink and my skin was puffy – a clear tell.

'Daddy!' Her voice rang through the flat in one unbroken, furious wail.

I should have gone to her then, but I just needed a few minutes to gear up to it so I turned on the shower and let the hot jets massage my shoulders, taking the time to lather my hair and deep condition. When I came out, Sophie was quiet. I thought she must have dropped back off to sleep. That gave me enough time to pat myself dry with a fresh towel, rub lotion onto my skin, and do my face. What takes twenty seconds now took twenty minutes back then.

I had a breakfast meeting with Simon so I dressed carefully in matching underwear, a crisp white blouse and a leather pencil skirt. I finished the outfit with a pair of killer heels. Dress up for a hangover, that was my rule. There was still no noise from her bedroom so I checked my emails as I filled a beaker with apple juice from the fridge. Dominic only allowed her to drink juice in the evenings but I needed something to get her onside. There was an apology from the client, which I replied to with a cheery brush-off and I pinged a message to Simon.

One of these days these shoes are going to walk all over you, accompanying a photo of my stilettos and a smiley.

I twisted the spout lid onto the beaker and walked along the hallway to Sophie's room. My heels click-clacked on the wood like a clock, counting down. The door to her room was partly open. The air was warmer than the rest of the flat, and heavy with Sophie's sweet, milky smell and an edge of ammonia from her soaked nappy. Wrinkling my nose, I felt a pang of guilt for not changing her yet. Her little body was tangled in her comfort blanket in the cot and the llama head stitched to it was pressed to her nose.

She looked peaceful. Her pale eyelids were closed and I could see the tiny blue veins behind them. I watched for a moment even though there wasn't much time, feeling a rush of love for my daughter and wishing I could watch her sleep for longer. Loving her was never the hard part but sometimes taking care of her was a struggle. I put my hand gently on her shoulder.

'Sophie?'

Her eyelids snapped open and her dark brown eyes took me in and I saw I wasn't fooling her. I never had.

'Want Daddy not you.'

Children have a sixth sense for weakness. I lifted her to sitting position and tried to hide my hurt. 'Tough luck, bubba.'

She let out a yell of frustration but I jammed the beaker into her mouth before she could really get going. She resisted for a moment until the sweet juice touched her tongue, then her eyes widened and she relaxed. The battle had begun and I'd won that round. *It's a phase*, Dominic said. *Girls always fight with their mothers. Just have patience*. But did it usually begin at two? I must admit that I worried there was something wrong with me; I loved her fiercely but my maternal instinct always seemed to fade just when I needed it the most.

The juice served as a distraction while I changed her nappy and wrestled her into the clothes Dominic had left out. The flat had an underground car park so we sailed down to the basement in the lift and out to the car. It was eight thirty and I was meeting Simon at nine – I needed to hurry to get there on time.

As soon as I opened the rear door, Sophie began kicking and screaming and thrashing her head from side to side. There was rarely a specific reason, perhaps it had sunk in that there really was no Daddy this morning or that she was going to have to wait until we got to nursery for breakfast but I didn't have time to reason with her. I shoved her into the seat with one hand and forced the straps over her shoulders with the other.

When Dominic put her in he always sang a silly song he'd made up. I don't remember all the words but it ended with: *'And then Mr Strap Man tickles you under there,'* and she'd squeal with delight. I could never get her to make that noise even when I tried and if I sang the song she'd pull a face and shout 'wrong!' in my face.

When she was safe in her seat, I slammed her door and took a moment to myself even though she continued to cry. That's all you get with children – snippets of time that you wish were longer. I rubbed the back of my neck and tried to stretch out the muscles, before I took a deep breath and slid into the driver's seat.

'Enough already,' I pleaded. 'We'll be there in five minutes.'

A little white lie since it was a ten-minute drive, but it did nothing to placate Sophie – if anything her howls edged up a notch. Glancing in the mirror, I saw real tears and she began kicking the back of the passenger seat – *Bang! Bang! Bang!* Snot glistened around her mouth and nose and her cheeks were an angry red.

Out of desperation, I turned on the music and her nursery rhymes playlist started in the middle of 'Incy

Wincy Spider'. She only cried louder. I would do anything to go back in time and have stopped, taken her
from the seat and soothed her, then turned around and
taken her home, where she'd have been safe, but we were
already late. I had ten minutes to drop her off and get to
the Ace Hotel where I was meeting Simon.

Backing the car out of the space, I left the car park
and joined the early morning traffic. I wasn't a confident
driver and it was the cyclists I really feared. The way they
hugged the pavement but not far enough over for you
to edge by – one wrong wobble and they'd be flat on the
ground. I was desperate to avoid hurting anyone.

The next track came on – a 'Wheels on the Bus' remix
in double-time – and Sophie screamed over it. My head
pounded. The traffic light changed from green to amber and I hesitated. There wasn't really time to squeeze
across so I lifted my foot and eased off but then I remembered Simon. I didn't want to be late so I slammed
my foot on the accelerator, flooring it. We sped across
the junction, a moment too late, but fast enough. In my
rear-view mirror I saw the car brake to avoid us, and a
white van slam into the back of it shunting it onto the
junction. The blonde on the bike had been waiting at the
lights. She'd just stood up to get the pedals turning and
she must have been distracted by the commotion and
slipped.

Her platinum hair caught the sun as she fell, coming
down hard against the kerb. Her bland expression went
from surprise to terror in a moment. She was young –
twenty-five I found out later – and though her face was
too wide for true beauty, she had the allure of youth.

Dewy skin, and a baby pink T-shirt that bagged in the wind.

I heard nothing beyond the music and Sophie and the roar of blood in my ears. There must have been a loud smack when the van hit the car and a quieter crunch when the woman's bike went down. My heart was pounding and the back of my blouse was drenched. In front, the cars were moving so we quickly left the scene. A wisp of cloud floated on the horizon.

The final minutes of the journey I drove like it was a driving test. Straight back, hands at ten and two, eyes darting frantically between the mirrors. I'd gone through a red light and I knew if I was pulled over there would be repercussions. Shame certainly, but in that short window even prison crossed my mind. Who knew what the alcohol levels were in my bloodstream?

When the arched entrance of the multi-storey car park between nursery and work came into view I let out a breath I hadn't known I'd been holding and eased the car onto the upward slope and out at the first floor. The spot I usually parked in was taken – I was later than normal – so I went up and up, searching for somewhere I could drive straight into. My body was shaking and I knew I couldn't handle a manoeuvre.

I drove up and out onto the top floor where all that was above my head was the wide expanse of clear blue sky. There was only one other car and the sun dazzled off its windows. I glided into a space and turned off the engine, letting out a sigh of relief as the music stopped. The silence hummed in my ears. It took effort to let go of the wheel and peel my shirt from the seat. I stepped into the wind, my hair whipping out behind me, and I filled my lungs, breathing deeply for ten seconds. It was still cool but the small cloud must have blown away and I could tell it was going to be a scorcher.

I took out my phone and texted Simon. *There in 5.*

It was only later when I discovered that the cyclist didn't make it. An 'unfortunate accident' was how it was described in the tiny paragraph in one of the free papers. She hit her head on the raised corner of the pavement and never regained consciousness. Her parents donated her organs and gave the interview to raise awareness of what can happen if you don't wear a helmet.

Chapter Nineteen

It feels good to tell Stephanie part of my story, even though it's only a fraction of what happened. What I didn't know then was that the cyclist would be consigned to a footnote in the worst day of my life. In that moment, the poor girl having a nasty fall weighed on my mind. Was it my stamp of the accelerator that caused her to hit her head? It's easier to blame myself for that than for what happened after.

When I finish, wiping the tears from my face, Stephanie leans over the table and gives me a hug. Her skin smells of almonds even though she'd been out jogging and her large diamond earrings knock against my cheek. I smooth my hair over my cheap moon pendants and indulge in the fantasy that we're equals.

'It wasn't your fault,' she says in my ear, and I allow myself a moment where I believe her.

That night, I'm able to sleep. Simon may have tracked me down but I feel stronger this time, more resilient. I'm building a new life at Paradise Found and my past is behind me. Sometimes I think that driving a van is my daily penance and after five years, I'm an experienced driver. I try not to let myself think of the girl in the pink T-shirt too often because I need to be able to get out of bed each day. We all take our chances – that's what I tell myself. It can't be solely my fault that her time was up. It just can't.

Before I leave for work, I check my emails. There's one from Zippi that makes me sit heavily in my chair and click the mouse desperately, as if opening the email faster will change anything. The subject says 'Customer feedback' and as I scan the text, one sentence jumps out: *As a result of negative customer feedback, your route is being reallocated.* My mouth goes dry. I read on to the end. *It's never too late for a fresh start. You should receive details of your new route soon and until then, we remind you of your status as an inactive driver – your app will not work on the entry scanner at the depot and you are not able to sign up for shifts.*

So that's it. Paradise Found is lost. I feel numb. I wait for the feelings to flood in and tear me down but they don't come. One advantage of having your child ripped from you is that it gives you perspective. The email ends with '*a little reminder*'. Any further customer complaints and I'll be out of a job. This thought fills me with panic since I've already worked for Amazon, DHL, Swift, Hermes and UPS, and Zippi was the last delivery company I could find. With my track record, I fear I'd struggle to find employment in finance again and I don't want to have to stack shelves in a warehouse.

Without a route, I have no reason to leave the flat so I find myself pacing listlessly, torn between wanting to crack open a bottle of whisky and looking up at the photos of Sophie and knowing that once I begin, it will be impossible to stop. The morning is a battle and I feel my resolve slipping when around lunchtime, a text beeps in.

It's from Patrick. *Chicken pie tonight?*

I feel a rush of relief and I'm embarrassed to admit that tears spring to my eyes. I may not be delivering parcels to Paradise Found anymore but Zippi can't stop me meeting Patrick. I'm thrilled to hear from him but there's also a wriggle of discomfort in my stomach at the way we left things. I still don't remember sleeping with him, but he doesn't seem bothered, so I try not to be.

I reply right away: *What time?*

We make our plans and as the light fades, I shower and dress in jeans and a frilly, whimsical blouse that I think Patrick will like and select a nice bottle of red from my collection. The last thing I do before I leave is brush my teeth and shove a clean pair of knickers into my handbag, just in case.

Ramzan whistles as I step outside. 'Where are you sneaking off to?'

I haven't seen him in days and have to fight the urge to give him a hug.

'Just meeting a friend.' Somehow this sounds ridiculous.

'Don't tell me you're meeting that guy?' He gives me a teasing grin, flashing his perfect, white teeth.

I duck my head. He cheers and breaks out into a chesty cough.

'You okay?'

He taps the packet balanced on the armrest. 'Been smoking too much.' He takes one out and lights it. 'You want one?'

'No, I'd better get going.'

'Don't want to keep him waiting.' He winks.

I stick out my tongue playfully and skip down the stairs and take an Uber to Paradise Found. It feels good to step out of the car and through the green gate. I don't need to buzz Patrick since they haven't changed the code. Inside it's peaceful as usual. A quick glance to the end of the row and I see number five is in darkness. I relax a little more and turn towards number one.

I push Patrick's bell and after a moment, he answers, letting out a warm, rich smell of home cooking. He's dressed in the chunky-knit maroon jumper he's often wearing and one of his big toes is poking through a hole in his sock. The knot in my neck eases slightly at the sight of him.

'You came!' He sounds pleased. 'You look fantastic, as usual. I hope you're hungry.'

He takes my arm and leads me through into the kitchen, the beating heart of his home. The lights are blazing and there's a tray of freshly baked muffins cooling on the counter. The day's papers are spread on the kitchen table next to a half-drunk cafetière My eyes travel to the back of one of the chairs where a peach-coloured scarf with white embroidery is slung over the back.

'Sorry about the mess,' he says, taking the cafetière over to the sink and swilling it under the tap. 'Have a seat.'

I remain standing in the doorway, feeling as if my blood has slowed. Patrick may dress sartorially but surely that's a woman's scarf. My mind goes back to the used condom I saw in the bin and the internet dating he admitted to; can I trust him?

'Patrick, what's going on?' My bottle of wine is still clutched under my arm. He follows my gaze across to the chair, and lets out a strained laugh. 'Oh that. It's not what you think. Come, sit.'

After drying his hands, he gets glasses from the cupboard and takes them over to the table. I hesitate but join him and put the bottle of wine down with a clunk. I may be overstepping the mark but if Patrick has had another woman in his house today, I deserve to know.

'So?' I say.

'I had a visit this afternoon from my sister-in-law, Clara.'

'Oh.' Heat rises to my cheeks. 'Sorry, I thought . . .'

'I understand.' He unscrews the cap of the wine and pours us each a glass. 'It's all a bit of a mess, really. Her sister has run off with some undesirable and Clara wants me to help find her. Well, actually she wants my money. She seems to think that because Maria is my ex-wife I should pay to help the family track her down in Peru or Thailand or wherever she's wound up this time.'

'This time?'

'Maria likes to think of herself as a free spirit. She goes wherever the wind takes her. That worked in my favour when I married her because it brought her to London. But for her family, it's a constant nightmare. She just ups and disappears without so much as a postcard. I've given Clara money before but this time I just don't have it to spare.'

He goes over to the oven and opens the door. A blast of heat comes out and his glasses steam up. I never knew he was having money trouble; I wonder if his house is at risk. The sudden terror I feel is irrational, I know, but I can't lose Paradise Found.

'Let's not let Clara ruin our evening.' He touches my shoulder. 'Pie is almost ready, if you're staying?'

I take a big gulp of wine. 'I'm staying.'

I spend the night at Patrick's and when I wake up in his arms, I feel like I need to pinch myself. It's safe and warm and this time my head is clear enough to remember the sex. It was loving and gentle. I can't help but compare him with memories of sleeping with Simon and though sex with Patrick wasn't as exciting, I remind myself that that was what got me into trouble in the first place, so perhaps it's not a bad thing it was more emotional than explosive. I try not to disturb Patrick as I reach out of bed and check my phone. Reading my emails, I groan softly when I see that my new route has come through. It's five miles east and a longer loop that leaves me no opportunity to swing by Paradise Found.

'You okay?' Patrick says.

I put my phone face down on the bedside table and roll over so my head is next to his on the pillow.

'Better now.' Twirling my fingers through his hair, I marvel at the thickness. It's like a lion's mane of grey and brown. I kiss the curve of his cheek and wait for him to turn towards me but he sits up quickly and cold air whooshes inside the duvet.

'Breakfast,' Patrick says with gusto.

I feel a rush of disappointment but I start to get out of bed when he says, 'No, you relax. I'll bring it up.'

Settling back against the pillows, I listen to his footsteps going downstairs and into the kitchen. He starts singing a David Bowie song as he clanks the pots and pans. I try to enjoy the moment but my mind keeps going back to the email. After a few minutes, I can't lie still any longer and I jump out of bed and throw on Patrick's crumpled shirt from yesterday, hoping it looks sexy rather than grubby. Buttoning the middle only, I follow Patrick to the kitchen.

When I open the door, he's making porridge on the hob and he turns with a look of surprise.

'Didn't fancy breakfast in bed?'

'No, I just . . .' I sigh and sit heavily at the table.

'Coffee?' he asks.

'Please.'

The sounds of Patrick boiling the kettle and filling a cafetière come from behind me while I look out at the overgrown grass in the garden. It's thick and coarse and really does need cutting. I don't hear him approach and his hand on my shoulder makes me jump.

'Your coffee.' He puts it beside me but remains standing, placing his hands gently on my neck.

'What's wrong?' he asks.

'Nothing.'

'You're not still worried about Clara are you?' His thumbs slide up my neck and he begins rubbing small circles at the base of my skull. I close my eyes and shake my head. To be honest, I'd forgotten her with everything else that's going on in my head.

'What is it then?' His hands slide down to my shoulders. 'Tell me, maybe I can help.'

I hesitate, and then say, 'I had a run-in with your new neighbour at number five.'

His hands stop massaging. 'Stanley Winters?' His voice is clipped. 'Why?'

It's the first time I've heard his name, and I mentally log it. 'When I left here the other morning, I saw a light on and I walked over to check nothing was amiss since you'd said they weren't moving in until next week, and Mr Winters was there.'

His fingers restart, kneading gently. 'Well, that doesn't sound serious.'

'He reported me to my company. I've been given a new route.'

Patrick drops his hands and goes back over to the porridge.

'Is that so bad?' My frown returns and I feel a fizzle of anger as he says, 'A change is as good as a rest, as they say.'

I open my mouth to protest, but what can I say? Instead, I say as lightly as I can, 'It's just inconvenient chopping and changing at such short notice over nothing.'

Patrick begins whistling softly.

'Have you met Mr Winters?'

'Once. He and his wife dropped by to say hello.'

'And did you get on well with him?'

'It was just hello and goodbye and see you soon, but he and I look like we come from different planets. There was him in a designer suit and me in my apron.' Patrick snorts.

'So you don't think you have anything in common with him?' I'm surprised he can't see where I'm going with this.

'Not a dicky bird. Honey?'

It takes me a moment to realise he means on the porridge. 'Yes, please.' I clear my throat. 'But he's a neighbour – you have that in common. Maybe you could explain what happened and ask him to retract his complaint? He might listen to you.'

There's a strained silence and since I'm facing the window I can't see his face but after a moment, Patrick bangs the cupboards and I hear him taking out bowls and spoons and jars and packets.

'I'm sorry but I just don't think that's a good idea.' I turn around in my seat to look at him but he avoids my gaze by busying himself with the porridge, adding random toppings without asking what I like. 'Listen, Laurel, I'm really enjoying getting to know you but I think it's best if we keep it between us. We don't want the whole street knowing our business.'

He puts the bowl on the table in front of me with a thud and kisses the top of my head. I open my mouth to say something but I don't quite know what he's saying other than he won't help me.

'Eat it while it's hot.'

Patrick sits opposite me and eats hungrily, flicking through the paper that got delivered earlier. A dollop of porridge falls from his spoon and lands on his T-shirt.

'White rabbits,' he says.

I'm sitting in a daze and I still haven't picked up my spoon. 'What?'

He turns the paper so I can see the front page. There's another headline about the virus.

'It's the first of March.'

The porridge is too hot. I eat a few mouthfuls, blowing on each one, before I put down my spoon again. I don't like nutmeg.

'I'd better get on. I've got work.'

'So soon?'

'Afraid so.'

I go upstairs to get ready. I half expect him to come up and apologise but when I'm showered and dressed, he's still downstairs. I hover in the hallway but he still doesn't come and I'm unsure whether to go into the kitchen or just leave. It feels like a stand-off even though he's the one who's let me down.

'Bye then,' I call out.

This brings Patrick into the hallway, still chewing. I turn my face as he goes to kiss me goodbye. He frowns.

'I hope you're not upset. I just think it's better for both of us if we keep this to ourselves until we know what it is.'

'Of course.' What else can I say?

He bends to kiss me again and this time I let his soft lips touch mine before I slip out into the fresh morning air. It's cold but dry and I stand for a moment, taking in the houses around me, before I stride out of the gate.

Chapter Twenty

I pick up my van and drive to the depot to collect the packages for the new route. It's a day for angry guitars. I turn the volume up high and set off east against the worst of the traffic.

The area I arrive at is mostly newly built cul-de-sacs that hold no interest for me. I prefer a bit of history. There's no elegance in a red-brick two-up two-down. I work through the deliveries as fast as possible, not bothering to complete all the details when I leave a parcel in a safe space and certainly no small talk. It's too suburban here and I'm out of my comfort zone; I need the hustle and bustle of zone one. I even miss the taste of diesel at the back of my throat.

When I'm finished, I check my phone outside the final stop, a block of affordable modern flats where I have eight items for four different floors. There are no messages. Not even a 'hello' from Patrick, let alone an apology. It's only mid-afternoon and the sun is bringing people out and about, but I have nowhere to go.

There's an off-licence next door to the flats and I think about picking up a couple of bottles of wine. White followed by red. Perhaps Italian. Or I could go for one of these new gins that have become ubiquitous. I enjoy a juniper flavour – it takes the edge off drinking it neat. I make for the door but a mum comes out with a double pram. I glance inside and see two sleeping faces. The woman raises her eyebrows and says, 'I feel like I've earned a glass.'

I smile but veer away from the entrance and head back to my van, giving myself a mental shake. I've promised myself I'll cut back and not drink my life away. It's Tuesday. My group is on Tuesdays. I've been avoiding Denise since she tried to drag up details of what happened to Sophie without my consent but I shouldn't allow her to take away my support network. I need all the help I can get.

I sit in traffic on my way back to central London. It's the usual carnage. Zippi doesn't provide branded vans because they don't want complaints about bad driving. Instead, we delivery drivers must use our own vehicles and pay for our own fuel and insurance out of the meagre hourly rate. Despite the cost, I prefer it this way. White vans are anonymous and I can take my frustration out on the road without fear of retribution. It wasn't the same when I worked for DHL.

The light fades as I drive and it's dark when I reach Upper Street. The shops are closing but the restaurants and bars are filling up. I find a parking spot outside a pub where people are spilling out onto the pavement. I walk through the cloud of smoke and the fug of booze and fags makes my mouth water, and I consider stopping. It would be easier than returning to group but that's what the old me would do so I force myself to go on.

The door to the church hall is propped open. I'm a few minutes early but I go in and head straight for the tea urn. Someone – Elaine, surely – has put a plastic bottle of hand sanitiser next to the plate of bourbons. There's a short queue.

Audrey is at the front and what looks to be Sharon is behind her. I stare at the yellow-blonde bob with its black roots.

'Sharon?'

She turns around. Her eyes are ringed with black eyeliner and her foundation is several shades darker than her face.

'Laurel, isn't it?'

'I thought you'd found your daughter?' I wouldn't usually ask so directly but her being here has caught me off guard.

Audrey finishes stirring sugar in her tea and turns around. She puts a meaty hand on Sharon's shoulder, and Sharon gulps. 'I did but she's done a runner again.'

'Awful,' Audrey says. 'They really play with your emotions.'

Sharon sniffles and reaches for a styrofoam cup.

Anger builds inside me until I can't hold it in any longer. 'It's not really awful though, is it?' I say sharply.

The sound of people chatting and shuffling to their seats stops.

'What do you mean?' Sharon says.

Audrey puts a biscuit in her mouth whole.

'This group is for mums who can't see their children. You have seen your daughter.'

Sharon opens her mouth to speak but nothing comes out, and she closes it again like a goldfish. She pulls a tissue from her pocket and presses it to her lips.

'Laurel, that's not fair.' Elaine appears from behind me with a clipboard in her hand.

'Someone must agree with me?' I turn on my heel and scan the room. My eyes stop at Denise, who is standing in the doorway in a yellow overcoat and a printed headscarf. 'Denise? After what you've been through you can't think Sharon's situation is comparable? Her daughter's only moved away, she's not exactly gone.'

Denise's boot heels clack on the floor, and as her gaze meets mine, I know I've gone too far. Sharon stops sniffing. We're all waiting for Denise to react but she touches my shoulder and says gently, 'Let's get some air.'

Audrey looks disappointed, as if she was hoping for a blow-up. I follow Denise back outside and zip up my fleece.

'I'm worried about you,' Denise says.

Across the road is the pub. Workers in suits and skirts drink and chat in groups. That was me five years ago. Look at me now.

'Are you taking care of yourself?'

I wish she was angry. Her pity is harder to take.

I fold my arms tightly and turn slightly away from her. 'I'm fine.'

'You seem . . . chaotic.' She must see my frown and quickly says, 'Distressed. Has something happened recently?'

She wouldn't understand about Paradise Found. To her, I'm sure one street would be the same as any other. People think I'm only there to deliver parcels; they don't realise the effort I put in, the amount of myself I give in those little exchanges. Is it too much to want something back?

'You said you'd met someone?'

'Patrick. He's great. We're fine.'

'Does he know what happened to your daughter?'

I nod, but then Denise reaches out to touch my arm and I finally meet her eyes once more. 'Does he know the truth?'

A dad and his brood walk along the pavement past the pub. The smallest child is a girl with long brown hair. She's wearing a ballet outfit beneath her coat. I always wanted Sophie to do ballet but she was too young. She loved her Little Splashers swimming class that Dominic took her to, though. He said she was the bravest in her class and never cried when the water splashed her face. I always hated public pools, with their slimy floors and draughty changing rooms, so I never went.

'Laurel?' Denise says gently.

'I've told him she's gone.'

'Have you told him she's not coming back?'

I flinch.

'She is.' My voice sounds small and defeated, and I feel a surge of fury at myself. I have not given up.

Denise puts her arm around my shoulder but I shrug her off. 'I'm sorry, Laurel, but I've spoken to Elaine and we don't think Missing Mums can help you. Not until you admit the truth.'

I turn to face her, tears welling in my eyes. It's clean-cut for her. The police have ruled that Dion was murdered. Denise isn't looking for her son everywhere she goes. 'What would you do if there was a chance Dion was still out there?'

She frowns and says, with a hint of steel, 'That's not the point.'

'What would you do?'

Her eyes go to the sky. Eventually she says, 'I'd never give up, but—'

'Then you know my answer. I guess this is goodbye.'

I jog across the road, away from Denise. A burst of laughter spills out from the pub. I glance back and see with relief that Denise has gone. I've been resisting but I feel my internal defences crashing down and I veer into the pub. I should be disappointed in myself but all I feel is building excitement as I make my way to the bar and when I take my first sip, a sweet release.

'Miss? Miss?' I rub my eyes and realise I'm slumped in the van's front seat. My mouth is dry and tastes rancid. I must have been asleep with my forehead against the window and my head is throbbing. There's a tapping on the window close to my head and the voice comes again: 'Miss?'

I turn my head slowly and see a policeman in full uniform rapping on the glass. It's light but the road is still quiet so I guess it's early morning. There are uncollected bin bags piled by the lampposts. I'm painfully aware of how I must look – and smell as I roll down the window a few inches.

'Hello, officer,' I slur and cough quickly to try to cover it.

He's a young Asian man, not much older than Ramzan, with neat, gelled hair and a strong underbite. The words COMMUNITY SUPPORT are emblazoned across his yellow bib and he has a small blue badge that says TRAINEE.

'Step out of the vehicle, please, madam.' The switch to madam doesn't escape me, and I feel the familiar, dull weight of dread in my stomach. I swallow a few times but I don't open the door. I wish I had a mint.

'I need to get my returns back to the depot,' I say, trying for a bright smile. 'I'm a delivery driver. I don't want to keep customers waiting for their refunds.'

His thick eyebrows knit together. 'I'm sure you're aware it's a criminal offence to be intoxicated behind the wheel of a parked vehicle. Have you been drinking?'

'No, sir,' I say, trying to expel as little breath as possible.

He glances back and I see his colleague, a woman closer to my age, walking along the road towards him. The darting movement of his eyes gives away his nerves. I wonder how long he's been on the job. By rights he should breathalyse me, and that would be it – fired by Zippi, Paradise Found never returned, and the embers of my relationship with Patrick would surely be stamped out.

'I feel so embarrassed.' I attempt another smile. I run my fingers through my hair and try to wind a strand around my finger but it's too knotted.

He doesn't smile back. Behind him, his colleague stops outside the Sainsbury's Local to speak to a man with a dog. She's only twenty yards away. I have a feeling that she will be much more forceful in her treatment of me.

'I know how it looks, but honestly, I just stopped for a break because I was so tired. I work two jobs to feed my daughter, deliveries and cleaning offices – hard, physical work. My eyes were heavy and I know tiredness kills, so I pulled over.'

His cheeks pull in as if he's sucking from the inside.

I open my eyes wide. 'I'm sorry.'

The female officer is pointing in the opposite direction, directing the homeless man somewhere. I lick my dry lips.

'I need to get back to the depot. I can't afford to lose this job.'

He drags his gaze to my face, and I lift my chin and meet his eyes. I can practically see his brain whirring as he weighs it up, and I don't dare look away. In my periphery, I see the woman walking towards us. He shifts from foot to foot.

'Please.' My voice cracks slightly.

He nods once. 'Off you go, but I don't want to find you here again.'

I start the engine without another word. The female officer reaches us just as I jam the van into reverse and execute a U-turn towards the city. I'm shaking, but whether from the encounter or the booze I'm not sure. I think back over last night, trying to piece it all together. My memory of the evening is patchy. I know I ordered a couple of rounds in the pub and got talking to some graduate accountants. The last I recall is a toast I made to 'no regrets'.

That's rich, I think. Children never were a priority for me. It was Dominic who wanted them, Dominic who cooed over babies and asked toddlers how old they were and what their names were. I always forgot you are meant to feign the expected interest in other people's kids. I gave in to his pleading, in the end, and found he was right: it is different when it's your own. They don't change who you are, but you can't help but love them with all of your being.

I make it home and have to stop a couple of times as I walk up to my flat. By the time I get through the door, I'm shaking like a leaf and the thought of another tour of suburbia fills me with dread. Without the threat of losing

Paradise Found hanging over me, I find it much easier to tap the keys and call in sick via the app. The late nights are catching up with me. I always used to have excellent stamina.

At the top of the stairs I see several suitcases outside Ramzan's flat. Panic makes me stumble. I grab the metal railing and take deep breaths. I can't lose him too. There are footsteps on the stairs, and I turn to see someone jogging up towards me. The man looks like a younger, flashier Ramzan with sculpted facial hair and a diamond stud in each ear that are larger than Stephanie's. He reaches for the cases and heaves one in each hand.

'Where are they going?' I ask.

'You the neighbour?'

'Yes.' I point to my door. 'That's me.'

'Ram's got corona, man.'

'What?'

'He went to hospital but they've sent him home already. He's in bed but Rashida and the kids need to stay away. She's pregnant again.'

It's a lot to take in. Three kids and the virus. My mind is spinning but mostly I feel a churn of worry for Ramzan.

'Is he okay?'

He shrugs. 'They said to stay at home unless he can't breathe.'

Our eyes meet and I see a flicker of fear in his warm, brown eyes but he looks away quickly. 'Take it easy.'

I don't move until his heavy tread reaches the bottom and the back gate clangs behind him. I unlock my flat and go straight to the desk. I have notebooks and Post-its but no writing paper or envelopes. I select one of my spare notebooks and carefully tear a page from the back to write Ramzan a note. *I'm next door if you need anything. Just put a note through or call me. Got you a few things to tide you over.*

I add my number and put the note in my pocket. I'm moving slower than usual and it takes me an hour to get to Tesco and back. I buy a bag of basic food for Ramzan – bread, milk, rice, hummus – and chuck in a copy of *Wired* and a bottle of scotch. I get one for me with just the scotch. Leaving the bag by his front door, I put the note through the letterbox.

Back inside my flat, I sit at my desk and pour myself a couple of fingers of the scotch, pondering the injustices of life. Things don't work out how they should. Ramzan doesn't deserve to be sick and I shouldn't have been kicked off my route. Paradise Found is the one thing that still makes sense to me; the street has burrowed into the fabric of my being. It reminds me that normal life goes on. In a parallel world, Dominic, Sophie and I live there or somewhere like it. We watch movies on Friday nights and Sophie has a bath every Sunday before school. Dominic and I are happy. If Patrick won't help me get it back, I'll find another way.

I go on Google Street View and put the little yellow man in the middle of the street. I can tell that the images were taken before the Bateses left, because their window box is bare. If I zoom in, I can just make out the tub of sweets at Patrick's house. I'd immediately replace that with a nice pot plant and the window could do with a new blind. Thinking about my imaginary future cheers me up, and I go through his rooms in my mind, happily moving this, replacing that, lost in what could be.

I pour myself a second glass and a third. I know I should slow down but what's the point? Through the wall I hear Ramzan having a coughing fit and flinching at the awful sound, I add another couple of fingers to the glass. On and off all day, his coughing reverberates through the thin wall between our flats, driving me slowly mad. When I can't take it anymore. I put on my cap and set off for a walk.

Outside, the sun fades and the sky clouds over. It's the turning point between afternoon and evening. The streets are busy and there's the happy energy people have when they're between work and home. I love this time because it's when people are most likely to be free from responsibility and heading to the gym or popping to the pub for one with friends. I may not do those things anymore but it's still nice to see others walking along with a smile.

It's dark by the time I reach Paradise Found. I walk along the back passage and run my hand along the fence as I go. When I get to the section that's behind Patrick's house, I look through the eyehole and see that the room is still in darkness. It can't be the kitchen it looks onto since that's always lit up and homely. It must be on the other side – behind the locked door. That room is a mystery and I promise myself that I will find out what's inside, though I'm sure there's a straightforward explanation.

There's nothing to see here so I walk around to the gate. Peering through the bars, I can see that the street is deserted. I move to the entry buzzer and my hand hovers over the keypad. It's a six-digit code and if I use it I can wander freely, anonymously inside, but the little voice in my head tells me the code is not for personal use. I press the first number but stop. Instead, I take out my phone and call Patrick.

'Hello, you.' He sounds happy to hear from me.

'Hi. I'm just finishing up my round and I'll be driving by. I wondered if you fancy a coffee?'

I hear him hesitate. 'That would be nice but I'm on a roll with my writing so I better not. Can I call you later?'

I feel a hit of disappointment but I say brightly, 'Of course. Another time.'

We hang up and I stare at his house through the gate. The front kitchen window is lit up and I'm sure inside will be warm and filled with delicious smells. It's now hard to believe that it was only yesterday morning when I left Patrick's and he kissed me goodbye. I know I should leave before anyone sees me, but I can't seem to make my feet move.

Glancing at my phone, I see it's just after seven and the sky is clear and cold. The street is well lit by streetlights that are designed to look like old-fashioned gas lamps and I know that anyone could see me at any moment, so I shouldn't linger. But something draws me in and before I know it I find myself punching in the key code. The gate whirs open.

I walk along the short street, studying each house in turn. I'm drawn to the glow at Patrick's like a moth to a flame. As I pass the window, I slow my pace and peer inside, hoping to glimpse him hard at work. The table where he writes is at the other end of the room so I'm not expecting to see much but a flicker of movement makes me jump. Inside, Patrick is standing with his back to me, wearing a baggy T-shirt and a pair of shorts. I watch as he bends over to one side, then the other. It takes me a moment to realise he is stretching. Why didn't he tell me he was working out?

He begins a set of lunges and I force myself to move, frowning as I try to work out why Patrick lied. Perhaps he's trying to get in shape for me. This thought makes me smile as I continue along the row. There's no sign of life at Evelyn's but the next two houses are lit up like Christmas trees. The Addo-Smyths' electricity bill must cost a fortune. The final house, the Winters' place, is in darkness but as I approach, still thinking about Patrick, a floodlight comes on.

I freeze in the glare, my heart thudding against my ribs. The light is new, as is the fancy doorbell that records passers-by through a tiny camera. They've been getting more popular on my route, especially at the more expensive houses. But Paradise Found is a gated community, so there's already ample security. It makes me wonder about the Winters. What are they hiding?

At that moment, the door opens. It's too late to hide, and all I can do is stare as Stanley Winters appears in the doorway, framed by the light spilling out from behind him. I can't see his features but his arms are folded across his chest and his shoulders are set.

'I thought I saw someone,' he calls out.

I remove my cap and walk towards him. This is the last thing I wanted to happen, but now I'm here, perhaps I can get him to listen to reason and withdraw his complaint. I take a deep, shaky breath and try to speak clearly and calmly. 'Mr Winters, I wanted to come here in person and apologise again for my actions. I have been reprimanded and I fully accept the consequences.'

There's a strange glint in his eye, as if he's amused, and I feel a sudden burn of loathing for the man.

'So you're apologising for disturbing me by disturbing me again?'

I lower my head. 'I'll go now. But I hope you accept my apology and consider retracting your complaint. Sorry once again.' I turn to leave.

'Laurel?' I spin back around to face him, and to my surprise he is smiling. I never noticed his dimples before. 'Let's put this behind us.'

I feel a flicker of hope. He unfolds his arms and holds out his hand.

'Stan?' a woman's voice calls from behind. 'Dinner.'

He reaches behind him and pulls the door so we're alone. Despite his newly friendly demeanour, I hesitate at his outstretched hand.

'Come on.' His hand is still hanging in the air. 'I don't bite.'

I have no choice but to grasp it, and his fingers close tightly around mine. Too tightly. I try to pull away, but he doesn't let go.

I gasp. 'You're hurting me.'

'Stan?' His wife's voice is behind the door but he keeps his other hand on the handle so she can't open it.

'One minute,' he calls and then drops his voice to a hiss and pulls me close to him. 'I know your type, so I'm going to say this once and once only. Stay away from me and stay away from my family.'

Still grinning, he drops my hand and goes inside.

'Smells delicious,' I hear him call as tears roll down my cheeks and I turn and hurry back through the gates, rubbing my fingers. When I reach the street I take a few deep, steadying breaths, and after a few minutes my fear and shock are replaced with a rising, steely anger.

Chapter Twenty-One

I sit up most of the night with a bag of frozen peas wrapped around my hand, trying to work out my next move. There's only one person I can think of left to ask for help – Simon – but I feel like I'm one step behind him. I can't figure out how he got my address or how he found me at Paradise Found but I keep coming back to Priya. They knew each other at the bank and Simon returned just after I saw her – that can't be a coincidence.

Opening my emails, I find the one from Priya and send a reply asking her to meet. Perhaps she can help me find out a way to put pressure on Simon. It's not a great plan but it's a start.

I can't afford to lose another job, so when morning comes, I get dressed and force myself to complete my deliveries. As I drive, I listen to the *Pulp Fiction* soundtrack and pretend I'm an actress in a role. Let none of this be real – Ramzan being ill, Simon being back and Paradise Found being on a knife-edge.

I'm halfway through my route when I see that Priya has emailed and can meet this afternoon. I reply: *Name your time and place*.

The café she chooses is a small independent in Clerkenwell and I haven't quite finished my route by the time we're due to meet. A handful of parcels remain in the back of the van but I make a turn in the road and drive back to the city. If anyone at Zippi notices, I'll just have to say that I had engine trouble.

It's late afternoon and almost feels like summer. Men are out in shirtsleeves and a few people are even wearing sunglasses. It's stuffy inside the van and I crack the window. Someone leans on the horn and I realise the traffic light is green. I push down the accelerator and the van jerks forward into a stall. I swear under my breath and restart the van as the person behind me honks again. I speed up and take the corner far too quickly. A cyclist swerves and slaps the side of the van as I drift too close. My palms are damp and I can't get a grip on the steering wheel. My feet are clumsy on the pedals.

I pull into a space near the café and tumble out. It's gusty as well as bright and I take deep breaths of fresh air to calm down. I try not to think of the girl in the pink T-shirt. The look on her face as she realised what was about to happen. I feel suddenly nauseous. I stagger to a bench and sit down, gulping in air. As my heart rate returns to normal and I start feeling less dizzy, I stare up at the buildings. One problem at a time. I'm here to meet Priya so she can help me track down Simon.

Five minutes before our meeting time, I get up and make my way to the narrow alley off the main road where the café is. As I turn the corner, I see that overhead is strung with bunting and I tip my head back to watch the pink and blue flags fluttering in the breeze. At the end is a chalkboard advertising their happy hour. So it's a wine bar as well – a turn-up for the books, I think brightly. Priya may not be drinking with a new baby but it's after midday and a glass of white would really grease the wheels.

This plan carries me the last few strides into a small courtyard filled with outdoor tables with more bunting overhead and enough potted plants to give it a woodland feel. Through the window I see that Priya is already seated. She's dressed up today in a black rollneck and full make-up – black eyeliner always was her trademark.

She waves but I'm scanning the space around her. There's no pram, no carrier – the baby isn't here. I feel a crushing disappointment I didn't expect, and smile brightly to conceal it.

'Hi there,' she says as I approach.

It's toasty inside and I take off my fleece. 'Hi.'

'Please, have a seat.' She gestures opposite her. 'What can I get you?'

I pretend to consider it. 'You know, I think I'll have a white wine, since we're catching up.'

She beams. 'I'll join you. Anything in particular?'

'You choose.'

She beckons the waitress and orders our drinks and some nibbles. I'm pleased that she goes for a full-bodied Chardonnay – underrated in my opinion.

'No Hugo today?' I say casually.

Priya puts her hands together. 'No, thankfully. He's with my mother-in-law. She was convinced we weren't going to have kids so this late bonus has really sent her doolally. I have to prise him from her hands when I pick him up.'

'That must be a big help.'

Dominic's mum died when he was a kid and his dad lives in Bristol. My parents preferred us to visit them so we didn't have much help day-to-day.

'Yes. I complain but really it's a godsend.'

The waitress brings our drinks and places a bowl of glossy olives between us. I go straight for the wine and take a long sip.

Priya fixes me with a direct look that makes me feel immediately nervous. 'Look, let's not beat around the bush. We've both got a lot going on personally. I want to talk to you about work.'

I pop an olive in my mouth to slow my drinking.

'You were one of the best salespeople I worked with. You knew your stuff and didn't step on the traders' toes. It's a difficult balance. After my maternity leave, I'm not planning to go back to the bank. I've decided to start my own fund and I need someone who can talk to investors. Someone like you.'

I take another gulp of wine, then catch myself and hold the liquid in my mouth, savouring it. I can't empty my glass before Priya has even taken a sip.

'I know you've left finance, but hear me out.'

I nod as the wine stings my tongue. There's no harm in listening.

'It will be flexible working, as much from home as you like. You don't need to be chained to a desk. And I'll make it worth your while financially, of course.'

Finally, I swallow, feeling a little buzz of excitement that's not just from the wine. I must admit, I always enjoyed money. These past five years have been tough. But I could never be as free as I am now.

'You'd work alongside me after everything that happened?' It's hard to say but she meets my eye and smiles gently.

'We all make mistakes. Who am I to judge? This is business only and I know you're reliable in that arena.'

There's a caginess to her answer that makes me think that she wouldn't trust me with her son. I suppose I can't blame her.

'Look, Laurel, you were the top salesperson at the bank, and I want the best. What would it take to convince you? I can send you the package by email, but I think you'll be happy. It's a big number.'

'Thank you. That's really kind. Do you mind if I think about it?'

I empty my glass and stand up. Her perfectly made-up eyes widen and she nods, and for a moment I feel bad that she's wasted her eyeliner.

'You don't have to go yet. You've only just sat down.'

'I'll leave you to enjoy a moment of calm. I remember what those early days with kids are like.'

'You will think about it though, won't you?'

'I will. Thank you.'

And I do appreciate it. But of course I won't accept. I can't. It would be impossible for me to walk back into my old career as if nothing ever happened. I'm a different person now. I take a couple of steps, then turn back as if I've suddenly remembered something rather than this being the entire purpose of the meeting.

'Priya, just out of interest, how did you get my email?'

'Oh, I asked Simon Morrison.'

It had to be.

'I know you and he were . . .' she twists her rings '. . . close. I asked for your personal email and he sent it over. I hope that's okay?'

I blocked Simon's email address the day after it happened. He used to set up new ones every once in a while and try to get in touch but it only took a couple of clicks to stop them. He hasn't sent one in years.

'That's fine.' I keep my tone light. 'Did you mention anything else to him?'

'No, nothing.' Her face is blank and then she frowns as if her mind has snagged on a memory. So there was something.

'Nothing at all?'

'Only I may have said you are working at Zippi.'

There had to be some connection with Zippi – how else would he have tracked me down? I paste on a smile. 'Great. You know, he and I have rather lost touch. I don't suppose you have his mobile number that you can pass on? I'd love to join up with him.'

'I have his work number.'

'That's fine. Simon's always been a workaholic so I'm sure I can reach him.'

She pulls out her phone and taps at the screen.

'I've emailed it to you.'

'Thanks again, Priya. I'll be in touch.'

When I'm back in my van, I text Simon and feel a hit of nerves when my phone beeps almost immediately. He always had that effect on me. Telling myself not to be silly, I read the message and ignore the slight tremor in my hand.

Lovejoy! I knew you'd crack. Would be a pleasure to see you. Tonight?

He gives me an address in the city and we agree to meet. There are butterflies in my stomach and I reach into the glove compartment for my flask. The hit of vodka kills all other feelings and I'm glad.

I don't go home and change or even look in the mirror of the van. It's not a date, I tell myself. Instead, I drive around, and as the clock ticks closer to our meeting time, I turn towards the city. My route passes close to where I used to work but so far I've avoided driving past my old office. As I approach the soaring glass building, I feel cold creep over me. It's mostly in darkness but there are signs of the 24/7 work going on inside – the light-flooded lobby, a couple of black cabs idling outside, a Deliveroo driver leaving by the side exit next to the revolving door in tell-tale turquoise.

When Sophie was born, I was happy to be the breadwinner. We needed to pay our mortgage and nursery fees and Dominic's handful of personal training clients didn't scratch the surface. I couldn't spend the day making macaroni artwork with Sophie or drawing a treasure map, however much I'd have liked to, and over time, our roles shaped us. Dominic became the one who knew what paint didn't aggravate Sophie's eczema and how she liked her sandwiches cutting, and I did my best not to resent it. I must admit it hurt that they had their club of two, perhaps that's why I sought out Simon.

The rest of my tour doesn't take long. I pass the hotel where Simon used to book a room every Thursday while I told Dominic I stayed in one of the office sleeping pods. I don't turn onto the back street where the hotel we used to pay by the hour is. I keep going along the main road until I've passed the last pub – I was a regular at most of them along that stretch – and I reach the address Simon gave me, where I park up and leap out into the cold night air. My body is tingling and shaking and doesn't feel like my own as I walk to the door and push the buzzer before I can back down.

'Hello?' Simon's voice crackles over the intercom.

'It's Laurel.' The door buzzes open and I enter a brightly lit lobby. My eyes are dazzled and I don't take much in as I wait for the lift and head up to the fourth floor. There's a thick, blue carpet underfoot and I walk slowly to the right door. My heart thrums in my chest. It opens before I get there and Simon appears in the doorway looking fit and healthy, a smile playing on his lips.

'So now you want to see me?'

He holds the door for me and I follow him inside. It's a serviced apartment, probably provided by the bank, and inside is decorated with anonymous yet expensive taste. Lights from the office blocks sparkle through the floor-to-ceiling windows and I take a seat on the small sofa, wiping my damp hands on my trousers.

'Drink?' Simon asks.

I nod and he pours me a glass of white wine that I notice is one of my favourites. It's like we're dancing to the same old songs again, the choreography hasn't changed. He brings the glass over and sits next to me. The sofa is for two but I'm painfully aware of how close he is, his familiar woody cologne and the heat of his thigh against mine. I drain half of my glass in one gulp.

'I've missed you,' he says.

'Simon, please.'

He turns to me, our faces now only a couple of feet apart due to the confined space, and I see his soft brown eyes between thick rows of eyelashes. I have to stop myself from lifting my hand and touching the mole on his cheek.

'Don't you think I deserve an explanation?' he asks.

I frown and shake my head.

'I thought we were in love. You were the one who pursued me, and then when everything happened, it was like a switch was flicked. You just turned off your feelings.' I'm surprised to see tears shining in his eyes. 'I would have left my wife for you, you know that?'

Sipping my wine, I close my eyes for a moment. I told myself I never wanted to see Simon again because I blamed him for everything that happened to me and Sophie, but now I have to admit to myself the real reason is that he reminds me too much of my own weakness. I loved Dominic but it wasn't enough. I had embarked on the affair that lit the fuse that blew up my life. It's easier to blame Simon than to face up to what I did.

He puts his glass down and his hot hand slides onto my thigh. I jerk back from his touch even though I've been expecting it.

'Don't tell me you haven't missed this.' His hand inches higher and he leans in to kiss me but I turn my head. I want to go back to how things were between us – I want to more than I can admit to myself – but I'm trying to be a better person. Simon is married and I've moved on with my life. There's Patrick to think of and I can't get entangled in another affair, not after what happened.

'Just tell me to stop.' His lips slide across my cheek to my neck and his fingers twist into my hair. I close my eyes and allow myself to enjoy the closeness and the memory of Simon for a moment before I say, 'Stop, please.'

He pulls back and there's hurt in his eyes. 'I thought this was why you wanted to meet?'

I shake my head. 'I need your help.'

He picks up his wine glass and drains it. 'Why should I help you? All you've done is use me.'

Wincing at his words, I try to think of how to persuade him. The old me might have given in and followed him to the bedroom but I'm not that person anymore.

'I loved you,' I say softly.

He drops his head into his hands and sighs. I feel the urge to run my hands through his hair and hold him close but I resist. I force myself to put my glass on the coffee table and go to stand but he catches my hand.

'I should go.'

Simon lifts his head and looks at me between his fingers. There's a mix of sadness and regret etched on his face but then he smiles. 'Things are never simple with you, are they? What is it that you think I can help with?'

'When you came to my van, how did you find me?'

He turns away and rubs his chin, refusing to meet my eyes.

'Luck.'

'Come on.' We're both far too cynical to believe that.

'You're not going to like it.' He massages my fingers. 'You have to promise not to get mad.'

I nod.

'And remember, you're the one who's been avoiding me. You forced me to do it.'

'Okay.'

'I was at school with the CEO of Zippi.'

Disbelief washes over me. 'They gave you information on me?'

He holds up his hands. 'He owed me a favour. I'm sorry. I had to see you.'

'What about data protection?' My voice is tight with fury.

He bows his head, at least pretending to feel ashamed. 'I told him what happened with your daughter and that convinced him you wouldn't be a problem . . . Sorry, Laurel, but you're hardly likely to bring a legal claim after what happened.'

My cheeks grow hot and there's a tight ball of anger in my stomach but I tell myself I got what I needed. I suspected it had to be something like that. I rub my jaw and try to unclench my teeth.

'I understand.'

'You do?' He sounds surprised.

'Yes but now I need you to do something for me. Can you speak to your friend and have me reassigned to my old route?'

'Laurel, I'm not sure . . .'

'Just do this one thing for me, please.'

Our eyes meet and I kiss him, on the lips this time, but it's less a promise of something than a goodbye. Simon doesn't resist as I pull back and stand. He follows me to the door.

'Will you do it?' I ask, my hand on the door handle.

Simon nods. 'You're a hard woman to refuse.'

He takes the moment to kiss me again, catching his fingers in my hair and pulling me close. I close my eyes, allowing myself to go back to all those stolen moments we shared before I break off. If only I'd had more control five years ago, none of this would have happened.

'Goodbye, Simon.'

I hurry back outside and return to the van. As soon as I'm inside, I lean across and get the flask from the glove compartment, fumbling the cap as I try to unscrew it. There's not much vodka left but I drain the flask and walk as quickly as possible to the nearest off-licence. One of my old haunts.

It's too bright inside and I wince. I go straight to the shelf and pick up a bottle of Smirnoff. The son is behind the till. He was finishing college when I was a regular. He wanted to study medicine. I wonder if he got the grades.

I put the bottle on the counter and he looks up and grins. 'Hello again. Long time no see.'

I'm not in the mood. I nod curtly and he drops his gaze. He always was a smart boy. Back outside, I crack open the lid. I don't bother pouring it into the flask but I drink from the bottle until the memories of Simon that have been trying to force their way back into my head are silenced.

The next morning, I wake in my chair when it's still dark. I check my phone, but there are no emails from Zippi. I try not to feel disappointed, reasoning that it's only been a few hours since I extracted the promise from Simon and he hasn't let me down before.

His accusations weigh on my mind. Did I use him? It's hard to see it that way when I suffered so much and he simply slunk back to his comfortable life, to his wife and kids and respectable job. But he was there when I needed him and if I'm honest, I enjoyed it. Being with Simon was easy, it was the rest of my life that was hard, but all that is behind me. I feel a flush of pride that I resisted him last night. I may not be perfect but I'm trying to move on.

The estate judders into life again as I shower and dress, and I return to the van as the sky is smudging into grey. I arrive at the depot nice and early and scan the app to enter. Pulling into the delivery bay indicated, I wait for the delivery log. It pops up and I see Paradise Found on the list. I smack the steering wheel and hit the horn in triumph and pure, unadulterated joy. Another driver glances over but I just raise my hand and smile.

It's not what you know but who, my dad always said. Even with my degree, I struggled to open doors. Interviewers probably spotted my awkwardness or saw lack of polish and didn't want to take a chance. It was an open day where I got my first break. The bank put on a tab in an underground cocktail bar with applicants for the graduate scheme there to mingle. One of the managing directors stayed late, topping up my glass with champagne and telling me about the best places to ski. The Italian Alps, I seem to remember, was his destination of choice.

All it took was a quick fumble in the bathroom and a carefully worded email and we reached an agreement. I joined the next intake and he avoided difficult conversations with his wife and employer. Win-win. I'd been slogging away for six months with practice interviews and online tutorials and there I was with a job after one night. All it cost me was a hangover, and a little bit of my self-respect. I was willing to pay both.

I'm still smiling as I load my parcels into the van. There's only one delivery for Paradise Found. A large box for Mr S Winters. I'd have preferred to keep a low profile – in my experience, it's better not to rub people's noses in it – but I must admit, I'll enjoy seeing his face. I decide on Beyoncé for the drive. *Sing it loud, girlfriend.*

When I arrive at the green gate, I'm bopping in my seat. I've got through her solo material and moved on to Destiny's Child. I'd be dancing if I wasn't driving. I tap in the code and the gate opens, allowing me to roll inside and park up. The air seems cleaner here and the sun a touch warmer. For March it's excellent weather. I'm whistling 'Independent Women' as I approach the Winters' house with the box in my arms.

There's a buzz of activity as a handyman climbs a ladder at number five. I squint – is he installing a satellite dish? He's fixing something to the roof. He leans to one side and I see it's a pair of security cameras, one pointing to the door and the other towards the gate. I smile up at the cameras and press the new-fangled bell. *Cooee.*

No one comes. I stop whistling and listen, then press the bell again. There's a creak, but I'm unsure if it's from inside or just the wind. I check for a safe space but nothing is listed. I give the doorbell one last try and stare into the camera – *hello, Stanley, it's me* – before I complete the *'sorry we missed you'* form and go back to the van. I consider calling in on Patrick, but I return to my van, reasoning that now I have my route back, there's plenty of time for that.

I finish my route with Beyoncé and the girls and return home. I'd like to pick up a little something to celebrate but it feels wrong with Ramzan unwell. I settle on a nip from my flask once I've parked up. It's already dark and there are no signs of life at Ramzan's. The broken walkway light blinks.

I go into my flat and pour a glass of red. Sitting at my desk, I raise a toast to the photo of Sophie. I may not be any closer to finding her but I'm starting to take back control.

My phone pings. It's an email from Zippi with the subject *'Lockdown'*. It talks of *'pulling together'* and *'delivering essential services in the country's time of need'*. The world tilts as I read on, disbelief trickling through me like ice in my veins. I've been so focused on Paradise Found, I've missed something monumental. I don't have a TV but I open my laptop and go to the BBC website. There's a video of the Prime Minister advising that we avoid non-essential contact. Everyone who can is to work from home. People should only go out for exercise and essential items.

I imagine if this had been five years ago, what Dominic and I would have done. Would we have worked together or divided to conquer? I press my face into my palms for a moment. My isolation is so complete that 'lockdown' won't change that much for me. But it's strange to think that everyone will now be in the same boat. I lift my face and look out at the dark sky. I'm an outcast no longer. In fact, people need me more than ever. The realisation brings a rare, warm glow to my heart and I smile.

My glass of wine is already empty and I pour another, a large one this time. A coughing fit breaks out from next door, and I think about how the lockdown has come too late for some. I look up at Sophie. When you're looking for a needle in a haystack, perhaps the world being turned upside down is no bad thing.

Chapter Twenty-Two

I set off for the depot the next morning with a dull headache from the bottle of red I got through, listening to Mozart at low volume. Classical music is my dad's thing – he liked to open the back windows and blast it into the garden – and I always turn to swooping violins for a hit of nostalgia. It takes me back to the time before Dominic, before Sophie, when life was so much simpler.

I always assumed I'd never be a mother. It wasn't that I detested children, I just never felt the impulse some people describe, that biological pull that seems to trump all else. My work was my focus, and then I met Dominic and I fell in love. Although I took some persuading, having Sophie felt right, and I wouldn't take it back for a second. Not even now I see how low it's brought me.

As I roll out of the alleyway and turn onto Whitechapel Road, I feel a chill when I see that everyone is gone. It's a main artery into the city but there's almost no traffic and the pavements are deserted. A single-decker bus bombs by in the bus lane without slowing at the stop, as there's no one waiting. I drive past the McDonald's and the front window dazzles in the morning sun but I see there's no one inside.

At traffic lights I exchange raised eyebrows with the few other drivers. It's only cabs, vans and buses on the road. Along Euston Road I see a couple of police on foot in their high-visibility vests, talking to a lone homeless man. There is a flourish of strings and the piece ends. In the silence, the world feels emptied and I feel oddly disconnected. I inch down the window so I can feel the wind on my face and get some air.

It takes half the usual time to reach the depot, which is one good thing in all this. I collect the parcels via the automated process and find there are three for Paradise Found, one for Patrick, one for Evelyn and another for Stanley Winters. A message pops up on the app, telling me that there's a new protocol to record delivery. Instead of signatures, the parcels must be left on the doorstep and a photo must be taken once the door is open. There's a new photo upload feature to use.

The surrealness continues as I go about my route. The streets are empty and every recipient is at home, I don't fill in a single '*sorry we missed you*' form, but people are wary and no one stops to chat. Doors open and close rapidly and there's too much time to think. I find Simon edging into my thoughts again and I try to block him out. I may have needed him yesterday but I vowed long ago that he wouldn't be in my life. It's hardly like we can be friends and I've got Patrick now, unless I've already messed that one up. It's only mid-morning when I reach Paradise Found. As the green gate glides open, I feel a weight lift. I need a touch of normality. It's like I can finally breathe. Like I'm home.

I park in my usual spot in the loading bay and hop out into the fresh breeze, closing my eyes in pleasure as it plays on my face. Spring is well and truly in the air. Outside Evelyn's there are three new plant pots that weren't there yesterday, two cut back but one blooming with yellow tulips.

The street is quiet, but it's odd knowing everyone is at home, stuck inside their houses, and I'm their connection to the outside world. Essentials can be bought from shops but anything non-essential must be delivered – there's a whole array of things people might want that fall into that category. I stand straighter as I unload the two boxes, pulling up my spine and lifting my eyes to the sky. They need me more than ever and I won't let them down.

Deciding to leave Stanley's delivery to last, I begin at Evelyn's house where I follow the new protocol to a T, leaning her small box against the doorstep and leaping back once I've pressed the bell. I make sure I'm two metres away as the door opens, but it's Evelyn's daughter who answers. She's small like her mother, mid-thirties I'd guess, with pink-streaked hair piled on top of her head and a nose ring. They both remind me of birds, except Evelyn's a crow while her daughter's a sparrow. I wonder what she's doing here.

'Thanks.' She picks up the box and goes to close the door.

'Wait,' I call out. Her presence has wrong-footed me and I haven't got the camera ready. 'I need to get a photo of the package with the door open, to record delivery. You can place it on the ground if you prefer not to be captured.'

She rolls her eyes and puts the box back on the step. 'So now you're taking it seriously. Mum said you made her sign for the last package.'

I school my face into politeness. 'It was company policy at the time. Mr Williams at number one signed for her.' I get the camera ready, then have an idea. Since Evelyn's daughter can't see my screen, I pull back so I have her framed in the doorway.

She folds her arms and I snap a few pictures, my heart thumping.

'Nice flowers,' I say, keeping my voice casual. 'Did they come with you?'

'Yep. I drove up from Brighton last night. Thought I should be with Mum over lockdown.'

'That's good.' I hoist Patrick's box under my arm. 'I'm Laurel, by the way.'

A small frown creases her forehead but she flashes a brief smile and murmurs, 'Polly. See you around.'

The door closes and I turn and head for Patrick's, contemplating Polly. It's nice to have a new face on the street that isn't Stanley Winters. I've seen her before, of course, on her visits to her mum, but she's always been aloof and I've had the feeling that her mind is elsewhere. Now she's living here, I can't help but think there might be potential there. It's nice to make a new friend on the street.

I push Patrick's bell and he opens the door before I'm in position. There's a wildness to his eyes, as if he's had too much caffeine but he grins and I hope he's happy to see me.

'Laurel, hi. How are you? What do you make of all this then?'

I shrug. 'It's strange.'

'What's it like out there?' He gestures to the gate.

'Quiet.'

'Not a good sign for our third date.' He lets out an awkward laugh.

I laugh too but I'm pleased he's mentioned another date since it's been three weeks since the first one. Our relationship seems to have stalled since we slept together and a little voice – possibly my mum's – whispers that perhaps he got what he wanted. I shake my head and see he's still looking at me with a slight smile of bemusement and I realise I'm still holding his package. Placing it on the ground, I step back.

'I just need to take a photo.'

'Of course.' He leaps back and goes to shut the door.

'I need the door open, actually. It's the new proof-of-delivery instead of signatures.'

'I did see an email.' Patrick opens the door and stands in the frame, smiling bashfully.

I don't need him in the photo but I snap a few anyway to add to my collection. Completing the form on the app slowly, I try desperately to think of a reason to stay longer but nothing comes to mind. I give him one last bright smile. 'See you tomorrow.'

'I guess.' Patrick sounds dejected. 'Back to me on my lonesome, then.'

He doesn't close the door until I reach the van; though I make a concerted effort not to look back at him, I hear the slam behind me as I go to the back to retrieve Stanley's parcel. Glancing back at the row of houses, I see it's quiet again. No one is around. Only the cameras at number five watch me and I look away quickly.

As I carry the box towards the front door I tell myself I'm being paranoid but each step feels heavier than the last. I'm bound to see Stanley since everyone is at home and I don't expect him to be thrilled to see me.

I push his fancy bell and my eyes dart to the camera. Licking my dry lips, I stare straight ahead, my body tense as I wait. Through the door I hear footsteps thudding on the stairs. Is he running? I crouch to position the parcel on the step and lean closer to the damp wood to listen.

There's a loud bang and silence. I stand slowly and press the bell again, then I move back so I'm two metres away. Finally, I hear three locks unclick, then a fourth, and Stanley opens the door. He's in navy woollen loungewear that looks expensive and his hair is slicked into its side parting.

He frowns. 'What are you doing here?'

'You ordered something.' I'm surprised by how together I sound. Stanley's frown deepens and there's a long silence but he doesn't break my gaze. Eventually, he says, 'My wife, actually, but I see we're going to have to cut back.'

I try a smile. 'I'm sure I'll be here a lot since people are going to need a lot of deliveries during lockdown.' This makes him scowl so I say quickly, 'And will you be working from home?'

'Yes,' he says with gritted teeth.

'Then we should be seeing a lot of each other.' I give him one last sparkling smile. 'Can I get a photo, please?'

'Photo?'

'It's company policy to take a photo at delivery. You don't need to be in it.'

His face flickers and for a moment I think he's going to shout at me, but then he jerks back the door, muttering, 'Bloody breach of privacy.'

He's only left a sliver of a gap and all I can see is a ribbon of black. My pulse quickens as I realise that perhaps I can use my position to see more. 'Can you open it a little further, please?' I call out. 'It needs to be visibly open to prove delivery.'

He grunts in complaint but pulls the door inward another couple of inches so I can see the pale wood flooring and his bare, brown toes. Someone looks like they got some winter sun. I lift the phone to take the photo when I see a flicker of movement in the gap. A surge of excitement makes my fingers fumble but I think I manage to snap quickly and catch whatever it was.

'Thank you, Stan,' I call out, instantly regretting shortening his name but my mind was still on the photo.

He slams the door without another word.

Back at home, I sit at my desk and open the app. I haven't sent my daily report so the entries can still be edited. I go to the Paradise Found deliveries and open the new feature, scrolling through the photos first of Polly, then Patrick, saving the Winters' house until the end.

In these uncertain times, it's comforting to have something new to occupy my mind. I take a screenshot of each image and email it to myself, then close the Zippi app and open them on my laptop, and gasp at the quality of them on the bigger screen. It's like entering a hidden world. I make out a small anchor tattoo on the underside of Polly's wrist. Her baggy T-shirt has ridden up at her side and there's a sliver of pale skin on show. I run my fingertip over it, thinking how only a few years ago I used to dress in a way that showed more skin. But there's something comfortingly anonymous about a Zippi fleece, and of course, it's comfortable.

Patrick has nothing as exciting as a tattoo but for once, his shirt appears to have been recently ironed. Looking closer, I see a flash of pink sock beneath the cuff of his corduroy trousers and a gold watch on his wrist. I wonder if he bought it with the proceeds of his first novel or perhaps it's a family heirloom. He seems the type to have expensive trinkets. Simon is more new money, the type who prefers sports cars to thoroughbred horses, but I must admit I always got a thrill out of spending it too.

Polly kept the door positioned so I couldn't see inside but behind Patrick I can make out the frames on the wall, but not their contents. I spend half an hour zooming into each one but the image is too blurry. If memory serves me, they were mostly movie posters and prints of book covers anyway, nothing personal, though it's nice to have a reminder of going inside. Who knows if I'll be invited in again?

I turn to the photos I took at Stanley's with a shiver of anticipation. What was it that I saw? Perhaps it was only a twitch of his leg but it could have been a cat or dog or even the child. My fingers drum on the mouse as the pixels take a moment to come into focus. The gap is a fuzzy strip of black and I slump back in my seat as I can't make anything out, disappointed beyond measure.

I try again, squinting, and as my eyes travel down to his feet, I gasp. Just above his foot is the side view of a child-sized hand, clutching a stuffed toy of some sort. I double-click to bring it to the middle of the screen and realise that it's a llama. My heart squeezes in my chest. I look closer still and see a blanket with a llama's head stitched to it and around its neck is a pink gingham bow.

Sweat prickles my skin and tears flood my eyes. It's the same blanket that Sophie had with her in the car seat. The one she held to her face every night to send her to sleep. We bought the blanket from a small boutique around the corner from our old flat. There was a rabbit I liked, but Dominic insisted on the llama because, if memory serves me, it was limited edition, made exclusively for that store.

Jumping up, I pace a few steps then rush back to the screen to check again. I'm certain it's the same one; she took that blanket with her everywhere. What are the chances? It feels like I've found something. I've imagined this moment but I never dared believe it would really happen. Could the girl really be her? My body feels strange. I'm hot and cold, and excitement is rising in my stomach. I look up at the photos of Sophie and a tear escapes and makes its way down my cheek.

Going through into the kitchen, I splash some whisky into a glass, then add some more. My hands are shaking and the back of my throat burns as I knock it back. I close my eyes. Why would the Winters have my daughter? It doesn't make sense. I give my whole body a little shake and return to the desk. There must be a reasonable explanation so I google the shop and call the number, hoping for clues. The phone rings out but an automated message tells me to check the website so I scour the pages for information on the blanket. It doesn't take long to find the brand – a French make – and I scroll their snuggle blankets but I don't find the llama.

I don't speak French so I send an email to the manufacturer asking where I can get hold of a llama snuggle blanket, then I take my whisky and go outside for some air. It's still blowy but it's a mild evening and the sky is the colour of a pigeon's wing, with a streak of golden light behind the tall buildings. The estate is unusually quiet. People are taking the 'stay inside' dictum literally. As I look out at the sky, I take deep breaths, trying to make sense of the jumble of thoughts in my head, when there's a noise behind me that makes me jump.

'Laurel?' Ramzan's voice is hoarse.

I turn and see him standing in his doorway, the door part open, wearing a surgical mask and a tatty towelling robe. His hair is greasy and there are heavy bags beneath his eyes. Instinctively, I step towards him with my arms outstretched but he rasps, 'Stay back.'

'Are you okay?' I ask, wishing I could put my arm around him.

'I just need to talk to someone, man. I'm going crazy in here.'

'Come out.'

He shakes his head. 'I've still got the virus.'

'Just come out. I'll stay over here and you sit on your chair. The fresh air will be good for you, and you've got to see this sky.'

He hesitates, but I can see from the gleam in his eye that he wants to.

'Ramzan, come on. There's only me here. Just keep your mask on.'

He disappears for a moment and returns with his red puffa. He looks even skinnier than before and it looks almost comically big as he throws it over his narrow shoulders. He eases himself into his deckchair and tips his head back, taking in the view. His breaths sound laboured through the mask.

'It's so good to be outside.'

I sip my whisky and say suddenly, 'You want a drink?'

He shakes his head and starts coughing.

'No, of course you don't.' My face flushes and it takes him a minute to stop.

'I couldn't taste it anyway. Wouldn't want to waste your stash. So, what've you been up to?'

I open my mouth to tell him about Sophie but I can't quite find the words. It would require too much explanation and I'm not sure I could bear it if he didn't believe me. Instead, I peer at him. 'How are you feeling?'

He pushes the heels of his hands into his eyes. 'I'm over the worst of it and Rashida got it but she hasn't had it bad, but now my dad is sick.' He drops his hands and I see his eyes are bloodshot.

'How are the kids?'

'Fine.' His eyes go to the sky. 'How are you?'

In the face of his distress, I don't want to admit the lockdown suits me so far. I prefer the quiet, there's no traffic and it may even have led to me finding Sophie. It's not fair that Ramzan is suffering.

'I'm fine,' I say breezily. 'What can I do to help?'

'Nothing, man. Just talk to me. Tell me how it's going with your guy.'

I hesitate. I don't want to admit that things aren't going well with Patrick.

'Not much to report,' I say lightly, 'but let me tell you about this one customer I had – a total nightmare. All I did was try to help out by checking he wasn't being burgled and he reported me to Zippi. I nearly lost my job . . .'

Ramzan gasps and shakes his head and soon we're comparing our worst customers and he almost looks like himself again.

Chapter Twenty-Three

In the cold, morning light, my excitement is gone and I feel drained. There's no reply from the blanket's manufacturer but I reason that I can't expect to have heard back from them overnight, and in the meantime there's a simple solution: I need to see the girl. It's been five years but surely all it will take is one look at her face? I am her mother, after all.

Driving to the depot, I feel a grim determination that doesn't sit right with the bright blue sky and unseasonal warmth. There's only one package for Patrick. My relationship with him, whatever state that may be in, now seems trivial. When I arrive, he's sitting outside on one of his kitchen chairs in a patch of sun. Next to him, two metres away, Polly perches on a small stool in stone-washed dungarees that are splattered with paint. Patrick's coffee pot is between them on an upturned flowerpot. They're both laughing at something but I'm too distracted by number five to dwell on my pang of jealousy for long.

As I retrieve the box from the back, I check the windows and doors but they're all closed and with the sun dazzling on the glass it's impossible to glimpse inside.

'Hi, Laurel,' Patrick says, sounding pleased to see me. 'Will you join us for a coffee?'

I glance again at the Winters' place and nod. 'I do have a few minutes.'

'Great. Let me pull up a pew for you.'

He rushes inside and I faff with the box, placing it on the floor this time on the far left-hand side of the step. I may as well get a different angle. Patrick returns carrying a second wooden chair by the legs, and almost trips over the package.

'Whoops!' He wobbles and puts the chair down. 'My mistake. I forgot about this new delivery method.'

He's not the only one. Half my morning deliveries have tried to take the box from my arms and I've had to remind them of the rules. Some have taken it personally, as if I've accused them of purposefully spreading disease. Others hide behind their open doors, not wanting to be in the photos. I take three of Patrick – well, of the box but with Patrick front and centre – before he positions the chair outside.

'I'll just get you a mug.'

He darts back inside and Polly glances at me, looking bemused, and I smile politely back at her. I can see she's wondering why I'm joining them and I sit up a little straighter. He returns with a mug and pours me the dregs of the coffee and we sit in a line with the sun on our faces. I feel a flush of pleasure that Patrick remembers how I take it. Most men seem to forget little details like that but Patrick pays attention. For the moment, I can't see any sign of Stanley and Sophie, so I just allow myself to feel like I'm one of them.

'Can you believe that rationing is back?' Patrick says. 'The lead character in my new novel is just entering

World War Two so I feel a strange circularity. I never thought we'd see anything like it again.'

'People are idiots,' Polly says. 'Who needs that much loo roll?'

I don't say anything. People are scared. Who knows what they need? I crane my head to try to see the other houses, but it's not a good angle.

'Did you grow up here, Polly?' I ask.

I know full well she didn't. Evelyn bought the house a decade ago and Polly must be mid-thirties.

'No, but I lived here for a year after a break-up. That's when I decided to leave London. It's so claustrophobic.'

A two-million-pound house not big enough for you? I think savagely. 'Brighton must be lovely.'

She frowns as if she's forgotten she told me where she lives just yesterday. 'It's great to be by the sea and there's a real creative culture.'

'What do you do?'

'I'm an accountant.'

There's a pause and then yelling from somewhere followed by cheering.

'Stephanie's kids,' Patrick explains. 'School is closed so they've been out in the garden. Noisy buggers.'

'What a nightmare for their parents,' Polly says.

'I always wanted a big family,' Patrick says.

There's an awkward silence as if neither of us know what to say. I remember his revelation about his ex-wife's miscarriage and feel a swell of empathy. The chasm of loss I feel without Sophie is almost overwhelming. Sometimes I wonder if I'd have been a better parent if I'd given up work. Perhaps things might have worked out differently if only I'd been more present. The mug slips in my hand and I realise my palms are drenched in sweat.

'How are the Cohens?' I ask, grasping at something to say. 'I haven't seen them around for a while.'

'Didn't you know they've gone?' Patrick says. My anxiety hasn't fully subsided and I feel another hit as he says this. 'They packed everything up on Friday and on Saturday morning they drove down to the south of France. Harry has a place there. Lucky bugger.'

'Selfish bugger more like,' Polly says. 'People aren't supposed to travel, especially not to second homes. Imagine all these rural places being descended on by Londoners, taking their germs with them.'

'I think they left before the announcement was made.'

'Still.'

'You came here,' I say, and they both turn towards me, looking taken aback. I realise then that it sounds more accusatory than I intended, but I'm rattled and I can't cope with any more changes. I've already lost the Bateses and now the Cohens are gone too. Polly fiddles with the front of her dungarees.

'That's not the same thing. I came to look after my mum.'

'Sorry, of course not,' I say, trying to smooth things over before changing the subject quickly. 'What about number five? Have you met the Winters?'

'I met *Stan*,' Polly says. The emphasis she puts on his name sounds like they didn't see eye to eye. 'He was keen to remind me this is a private street until I told him I actually live here.'

Patrick frowns at her sympathetically.

Polly drops her voice and wrinkles her nose. 'Mum says the new neighbours are bankers.'

The talk of it being a private street makes me aware I'm here for deliveries only. I don't want to outstay my welcome.

'I ought to be getting on.' I stand and put the coffee mug on the chair. 'Thanks for the coffee.'

Patrick gets up and follows me to the van but keeps his distance. Behind, I see Polly watching us, squinting into the afternoon sun.

'Laurel?' he says tentatively, and I turn to meet his eye. 'I just wanted to say that I was really enjoying getting to know you.'

I feel my face growing warmer, but I'm pleased. He seems to notice and smiles, moving from foot to foot as he says, 'Would it be okay if I give you a ring sometime?'

My smile matches his. 'I'd like that.'

I'm happy he's asked but I also feel a rush of relief that creeps up on me. Perhaps I haven't been totally honest with myself about how much I've put into the relationship. Resisting Simon's advances was a big step for me. Patrick remains standing in the turning circle as I drive away and I watch him in the mirror as he smiles and waves until I turn the corner.

That evening, I sit at my desk and open a bottle of red. Nips of spirits perk you up, but there's something luxuriant about opening a Merlot and letting it breathe. I like to decant mine into an extra-large mug that Sophie gave me our last Christmas together. Of course, it was Dominic who took her to the paint 'n' bake place and painted the wavy pattern with her sitting on his knee – she hadn't turned two yet. He bought it and wrapped it and put it under the tree. She didn't give him anything that Christmas, I remember now.

I push away the guilt and check my emails but there's still nothing from the blanket manufacturer. There are several from Zippi in their peppy tone, reminding all drivers to '*stay safe*' in these tough times. They tell me they are creating a forum for drivers to share their experiences and '*have someone to lean on*' during lockdown. My username and password arrive in a separate email that I delete without opening.

There's also an email from Elaine at Missing Mums; it seems that although I've been barred from going, I'm still on the mailing list. Tuesday meetings can no longer take place in person but fear not, support is still here. Elaine is setting up a Zoom meeting so we can continue to meet virtually. She signs off her message with an e-hug. I take a big gulp of wine straight from the mug. I had intended to pour it into a glass but it's much more efficient this way. And anyway, who is there to see?

It's easy to find information online on Stanley Winters since he's a senior investment banker with a profile. Starting with a straightforward Google search, I find a couple of dull pieces on him in the *FT* and press photos of him in sharp suits and pressed shirts – always blue to bring out his eyes – and headshots where he's looking to camera through tortoiseshell glasses. His image could be his weakness; he clearly thinks a lot of himself.

There's one photo that I find of him at an event with his wife by his side. She's almost the archetype blonde, but not quite. Fair and thin but with a too-long face and high forehead. She's chewing her lower lip in the photo and the pink tips of her ears are poking through her thin hair. Everyone else in the line-up is staring down the barrel of the camera, while her gaze is off to one side. Confidence may be invisible but a lack of it is impossible to miss.

Next, I try social media and it doesn't take long to find his Twitter feed but after a quick scroll it's clear he uses it for professional purposes only. I can't find an account on Instagram but on Facebook I discover an account with an old profile photo that has public privacy settings. I'm smiling as I go to his photos, scrolling right down to begin with his university days, to prolong the anticipation. There's Stanley with his rugby team out at a club, him on a ski trip, him on a boat in Croatia with a lovely tan. I keep scrolling until I get to his wedding photos – they're one of those couples where the groom outshone the bride – before reaching the sparser collection from recent times.

I swig my red wine as I scan the latest photos that he's been tagged in. A couple are from weddings of friends and there's one of him at Twickenham drinking a pint. My smile fades as I realise that there are no photos of his daughter. Not one. Dominic was one of those dads who posted daily about family life. There was Sophie with bedhead, Sophie with a Cheerio stuck to her nose, Sophie's tiny shoes next to his big ones, and so on. Stanley must be a different type of father. Or else . . .

I drain the rest of the wine and cradle the mug against my chest when I hear my phone ringing. Could it be

Patrick already? Or perhaps Simon, trying to track me down again? I unzip my fleece pocket and see it's my parents' number, and feel a swoop of surprise tinged with dread. Their calls are rare and never easy.

'Hello?' I say.

'Laurel, it's Dad.'

My mouth gapes in surprise. I'd been expecting Mum's voice; Dad hasn't been able to speak to me properly since my life fell apart. He never did like failure. We used to chat regularly about nothing really – quiz programmes, cricket, the financial news – but email became easier than arguing.

'Is everything okay?' I say with a tight feeling of panic in my chest.

'Fine, yes, we're fine. Your mother wanted me to ring with everything that's going on. With this virus, we wanted to check you're all right on your own.'

'Dad, I'm a forty-year-old woman.'

'I know. She just – well, we just wanted to let you know that your old room is free. This could be a chance for you to have a fresh start. Come and stay for a while and maybe when it's all over you can get a new job.'

I try to make my voice calm and reasonable. 'Dad, I've got a job. People are counting on me.'

He snorts down the line but I force myself to stay in control.

'Thank you for the offer but this is the most positive I've felt in years. I've stopped going to my support group and I've met someone. He lives in this lovely community that I'm becoming part of. Things are really turning around.'

There's an uneasy pause and then he says, 'I'm glad.' He sounds doubtful.

'And—' I take a deep breath '—I finally have a new lead on Sophie.'

I don't know if I'm expecting joy or surprise but all that comes down the line is silence. The photo isn't enough, I know that, but it's something; it's a start. Desperate to fill the void, I start wittering, 'If I'm honest, I'd almost given up, but I've seen something on my route that's got me thinking.'

The silence continues.

'Dad?'

'Laurel, it's Mum.' Her voice is gentle and she must have been listening this whole time. 'Your father has gone to get some air.'

'Right,' I say flatly. Everything I do annoys him. If it's not his way then he can't abide it.

'He just wants what's best for you. We both do.'

'I know.'

She clears her throat. 'Laurel, we both think it's time to stop this nonsense. It's time for you to move on, like we are doing.'

It's like she's slapped me. I expect it of Dad, but not her. 'Move on? How can you say that? You're a mother.'

'I'm saying it as a mother – *your* mother. This has gone on long enough. Your father and I, we can't keep going on with this charade. It hurts too much. All we want is for you to get help.'

'The only help I need is with finding Sophie.'

Mum sighs. I hear Dad's voice in the background and the sound of a scuffle.

'Let me try one more time,' I hear Mum hiss.

'Laurel, it's Mum again.'

'Hi.'

'Listen, darling, there's no nice way to say this but your dad and I need a break.'

'A break from what?'

'This.' It takes me a moment to realise that she means me. A giggle bursts out of me at the absurdity of it all. My parents are divorcing me just when I'm about to find Sophie. I slurp my wine. 'You're asking me to choose between you and Sophie?'

'No. That's not how it is.'

'That's exactly how it is.' There's no hint of laughter in my voice now.

'Laurel, it's been five years and—'

'I will never give up.' I look into the eyes of my daughter's photo on the wall. I may not be the best mother in the world but I'm still her mum. 'I choose Sophie.'

Chapter Twenty-Four

I wake in my chair and discover I've knocked over one of the bottles of red and the dregs are seeping across the desktop and onto my Paradise Found notebooks. I panic for a moment that all my research will be ruined, but only the covers are a little damp and I dry them off carefully.

I check my phone, and when I see I have two missed calls hope surges through me that it's Mum or Dad ringing to apologise, but I feel silly when I see that they're both from Simon. He's left a voicemail. My finger hovers over the delete button but something stops me pressing it. Every fibre of my being wants to avoid getting dragged back but he did keep his word – that's more than most people – and he was happy to see me. I can't deny that felt good.

I press play and his voice comes down the phone, sounding breathy, as if he's holding it too close. 'Laurel, it's me. Simon. I just wanted to say it was so good to see you again. I've missed—' He stops talking and there's a muffled sound. In the background I hear a noise that sounds like a child crying.

I press the delete button without listening to the rest. Simon must be at home, ensconced in family life, yet he still snuck away to call me. Our relationship was always conducted in the shadows; snatched conversations and stolen moments that left me on edge, aware that I was playing with fire. Going back to him would be madness; I've had my fingers burnt once already. More than that, my whole life burst into flames and was razed to the ground.

Setting off for work, I see the roads are empty again as I sail to the depot and even the homeless are gone from the pavements. I drive with my mouth open in disbelief as my head swivels from closed shop to abandoned bus stop. A shiver runs through me and I switch on some seventies disco hits and turn up the volume to try to feel some life around me.

I collect my packages from the depot without seeing another person. Nerves tingle in my fingers as I wait for the delivery log to pop up on my phone and I scan it quickly. When I see Stanley's name I squeeze my fist in excitement. I've been given another chance, and this time I'm going to make the most of it. Running over the rest of the list, I see that there are also four parcels for the Addo-Smyths. I haven't seen Stephanie since I confided in her but any worries I had about what she might think have evaporated. It seems totally irrelevant now I'm so close to finding Sophie.

It's not as sunny today and when I arrive at the gate a few spots of rain fleck the windscreen. I open the window so I can punch in the key code. A cold breeze ruffles my hair and I shiver, sensing the rain moments before it lands in a scattered shower. I put up my umbrella and decide to deliver the four small boxes to the Addo-Smyths first, balancing the packages on the step and ringing the bell. Stephanie answers and from behind her I hear raised voices. She's in her usual athleisure gear but there's a stain on her T-shirt and she looks pissed off, but when she sees it's me her face lifts into what looks like a genuine smile.

'Hi, Laurel, nice to see you.' She looks up at the sky. 'Sorry about the weather.'

'Hardly your fault. How's it going?' We both wince at the racket going on behind her.

She rolls her eyes. 'Terribly. I've been trying to get the kids to make a volcano out of papier mâché, but all they want to do is stare at their phones.'

I try to give a supportive smile but at that moment there's a loud bang from the kitchen and Stephanie rushes inside. One of the children is yelling and I'm torn between running in and offering my help and waiting on the doorstep, but before I can act, Stephanie quickly reappears, leading one of the boys by the arm, her face tight with anger. It's hard to tell which son it is because his face and hair are coated in thick, red paint.

'I did tell you not to touch the reactive agents,' she says as she pushes him towards the stairs. 'Shower. Now.'

She returns to the door and I try for a supportive smile but the boy's face pops into my head and I have to smother a smile. I catch her eye and we both break down into giggles.

'Sorry—' I try to stop but a second wave takes over me. Stephanie puts her hands on her knees and bends over, her shoulders shaking silently. I know I shouldn't laugh at her efforts but something about seeing a fault line in her perfection and my nerves about knocking on Stanley's door have left me feeling on the edge.

Stephanie wipes her eyes. 'I needed that. The volcano looks like a dung heap anyway.'

This sets me off again and it takes another minute before Stephanie pulls herself upright. 'I shouldn't complain. It's lovely to do something together. And how are you?'

'I'm fine.' The thought of them all working on it together as a family unit sobers me quickly and all trace of laughter is gone from my voice. 'It's nice that there's no traffic on the roads.'

'Of course, that must be a relief.'

From the way her brow puckers I can see she's thinking about the accident I told her about, though that's not what I meant. I distract from the sticky moment by putting the boxes just inside the door out of the rain.

'I need to take a photo as proof of delivery.'

'Okay, I—' Then we hear another crash from somewhere inside the house, and Stephanie's head whips around, her face thunderous. 'Shit. Sorry, Laurel, back in a second.'

She disappears and I hear her raised voice. '*If I have to tell you one more time . . .*'

I take the opportunity to nudge the door with my foot. It swings open and I get a full view of the hallway. The door to the kitchen is open and I see the kids at the table with their books open and the ruined volcano on the floor by their feet. Stephanie has her back to me but I can tell from the tension in her neck and shoulders she is telling them off. In the hall on the wall is a framed photo of the family, all six of them dressed in white with bare feet. I open my app and snap as many photos as I can.

'All done,' I call out, and leave before she returns, hoping she'll think the wind blew the door open.

The rain turns up a notch as I return to the van for Stanley's parcel and carry it carefully beneath the umbrella, my nerves squirming with every step. He'll be looking for a speck of rain on the box or a smidgen of damage – any excuse to complain – and I don't want any distractions. I need to focus on Sophie. My hands shake as I push his smart bell and stare into the camera – could this be the moment I see Sophie again? – before crouching to position the parcel on the step.

The footsteps that approach are slow and purposeful and I brace myself for Stanley before the door opens and I see his quizzical face. As his eyes meet mine, his nostrils flare as if he smells something bad.

'You again.'

'This is—' My voice falters and I cough and try again. 'This is my route.'

He folds his arms and I take in the breadth of his chest and the muscles beneath his black turtleneck. I try to peer around him but he moves closer, blocking my view.

'I just need to take a photo.' I try to keep my tone bright and professional but there's a tremor that I can't hide.

Stanley simply smiles and closes the door, leaving only the faintest sliver of a gap, not enough to see inside, but it would be hard to argue that it's not open. It looks like he's been reading up on the Zippi rules. I take the picture and wait for him to collect the parcel, biting the inside of my cheek. He takes his time and when the door opens again, he glares at me.

'You're still here.'

He bends over to pick up the package and I move a step closer to try to see over his head, but the small hallway is empty.

'Keep your distance,' he warns.

I'm starting to panic but I force myself to speak before I can chicken out. 'I just wanted to ask, how's your daughter?'

He straightens up and I see a tinge of fear in those blue eyes. 'My daughter?'

He's not so cocky now, and as we stare at each other doubt clouds his features. A triumphant feeling spreads through me.

'You do have a daughter, don't you?'

'I don't see what business that is of yours.'

I tap the side of my nose. It's a gesture I haven't done since school, but it works. Stanley looks rattled. I must be on the right track – why else would he react this way?

'Leave my daughter out of this.'

There's nothing more to say so I walk backwards a few paces, watching him the whole way. Droplets of rain drum on my umbrella and I feel a sudden urge to feel them on my skin, something to match my inner feeling of being alive. I put down the umbrella and let the rain fall on my head, gasping with pleasure as the droplets wash my face and drip from my chin, and I'm quickly soaked. Stanley looks both unnerved and alarmed, like a gazelle eyeing an approaching lion. I hold his gaze until he blinks first.

'See you next time,' I say.

★

The rain slows and as I arrive back home, the sun breaks through, gold shafts piercing the clouds like divine intervention. I stop off at the Tesco on the high street and pick up a bag of shopping for Ramzan, but when I knock on his door, there's no answer. I leave the food outside, take a seat in his deckchair and open the scotch.

Taking small swigs from the bottle, I replay my victory over Stanley in my head. He's clearly hiding something about his daughter. Running through the possibilities, I keep coming back to the blanket. Could it really be her? I shake my head and try to suppress my excitement, but before I know it, half the scotch has gone and I'm planning my future with Sophie. We'll need somewhere to live – she can't live here – and perhaps I'll call Priya about that job. I wonder if Patrick would make a good dad? He said he wants kids so that's in his favour.

As the whisky starts to sing, I decide on my next move: I'm going to give his daughter a gift. A big box is sure to bring her outside. Even if it's not her, I reason, what child doesn't like presents? Plus, she deserves something nice after being cooped up with a man like that. Even though I keep telling myself that it might not be her, I can't help but browse with Sophie in mind. She was only two when she was taken but she loved her Duplo building blocks and the little pram that she'd push her dolly in. Of course, she also had the llama snuggle blanket that Dominic bought her as a baby. But those things don't help me buy a gift for a seven-year-old and I want it to be perfect.

I wish again that Ramzan was here. His boy is getting close to that age so he'd know what to get. I'd also kill for a cigarette. The heat from the whisky has settled in my stomach and is pulsating. I've reached my limit. Any more and I'll be throwing up, and I don't want that. It is an expensive bottle and I can't afford a hangover, not when I'm so close to finding Sophie.

The sun has faded while I've been lost in thought and the blinking light on the walkway has come on. Glancing down, I see goose bumps speckling my arms, and shiver. I go inside and sit at my desk. The computer is open from my research on Stanley, and I open a new browser window. I search for 'gifts for kids' and scroll through reams of colourful plastic impatiently, but they're not what I'm looking for. I find a classy website where the toys are made out of wood in pastel colours but they look a little too young. Another website lets me filter by age and price. Sending a mental 'thank you' to their website design team, I select the top price bracket and 'Age 7–8'.

A couple of hours later my eyes are stinging with staring at the screen and I'm about to give up – and that's when I see it: a pink castle complete with drawbridge and moat that can be filled with water. It's a metre tall and I imagine the huge box arriving at the Winters'. I remember Sophie squealing with delight at Christmas and birthdays. She always loved to unwrap things, the bigger the better and it gave us so much pleasure to watch her. It didn't matter if all that was inside was a mass of bubble wrap and a disappointing toy, tearing off the paper was the thrill. I feel a frisson of excitement as I think about how excited she'll be and annoying Stanley is a price I'm willing to pay.

Adding the gift wrap option, I get it sent direct to 'Miss Winters' without a message. What could I say? Let her think she has a fairy godmother watching over her. I smile and wave the bottle of scotch like a wand, pointing it towards the corners of the rooms with a 'zing!', then I catch myself and put it down gently. I've definitely had enough. I'm drifting off to sleep in my chair when my phone rings. I wonder if it might be Patrick but the hope that flares is crushed when I see Simon's name on the screen. Squeezing the phone in my hand, I weigh up whether to answer; it would be nice to talk to someone but with Simon I'm on dangerous ground. Taking a deep breath, I accept the call. 'Hello?'

'Hi, you.' There's a whooshing that makes it sound like he's outside.

'What do you want?' I ask.

'Can't we just chat?'

'No, we can't.'

'Laurel, I miss you,' Simon wheedles. 'We were good together, right?'

I close my eyes. 'We tore a hole in each other's lives.'

'But—'

'I've met someone else,' I say – the one thing Simon might listen to.

There's another silence and I hear the wind whistling down the phone. I picture him walking through woodland near his Cambridgeshire home while his wife and their kids are tucked up in bed. The scotch swirls in my stomach and I feel suddenly sick.

When Simon speaks again, his voice is low but firm. 'Laurel, I've seen the way you live, how you are. It doesn't seem like anyone is looking after you.'

Anger flares. 'I don't need anyone to look after me.'

'Don't you?'

I glance around the room and see the grime in the corners, the remnants of the spilled wine on the table, my notebook collection, and shame creeps across my chest.

'Things with Patrick are good,' I say, with as much conviction as I can muster.

'If you say so. Just remember that I'm here for you and you need me.'

He hangs up and I'm left alone in the dark, trying to convince myself that he's wrong, I don't need anyone.

Chapter Twenty-Five

The box arrives at the depot three days later, and I know what it is instantly as it's the biggest package I've delivered in weeks. The feeling of treading water is blasted away and replaced with a tingling excitement.

I turn on the *Frozen* soundtrack and sing along with Elsa. It *is* funny how some distance makes everything seem small. I used to hate the song. The first note would set my teeth on edge and I'd be rubbing my temples as Dominic danced Sophie around the room, her bare feet on his. But what I wouldn't give now to see them waltzing together, laughing.

Today it's the perfect accompaniment to my delivery, and I hit repeat on the big number. Elsa and I are in full flow as I punch in the code. The gate opens and, feeling rebellious, I keep the music up and the window down. Struggling to sit still, I bounce in time with the beat, and see two of the Addo-Smyth kids, the younger ones, are out front with their scooters. They stare at me until I cut the engine and the music stops, leaving an expectant silence.

Issy puts her arm around her brother and whispers something. They laugh and I join in because that's the mood I'm in. She frowns and runs inside, dragging him by the arm. They've left their scooters on the ground so I move them to safety against the wall of the house before opening the back door and unloading the box. I need my parcel trolley for this one.

I get a strange satisfaction from manoeuvring the box just so until I can tip back the trolley and wheel it straight to the door. It's amazingly easy when the balance is right. As I shift the box onto the pavement, I sense I'm being watched. I look up at the Winters' house but only the cameras are trained on me. Glancing over my shoulder, I see the Addo-Smyth family – all six of them – are out on the steps, jostling for the best view.

'That's a big box,' calls Stephanie.

My heart thuds in my chest as I realise that there's no going back now, but I'm pleased that there'll be witnesses. Stanley will be forced to behave himself. I trundle the trolley over to number five and push the bell, gripping tightly to stop my hands from shaking. It's a couple of minutes until I hear the locks, and even through my excitement, I can't help but wonder why it always seems to take them so long. Most people on my route have been answering immediately, grateful for a break in their day and someone new to talk to. The door clicks and Stanley's face appears in the gap.

'Wrong address,' he says flatly and starts to shut the door.

'Is this not number five, Paradise Found?' I ask innocently.

He scowls at me. 'We haven't ordered anything.' He's in his woollen suit again and his neck is an angry red.

'It's for a *Miss* Winters.' I didn't know her name. 'Your daughter, I presume.'

'Impossible.' Stanley tries to close the door again.

'That's what it says. See.'

I point at the sticker and he pokes his head out to read it. His eyes bulge slightly as he sees that I'm telling the truth.

'It's a mistake,' he blusters, but then his eyes travel over to the Addo-Smyths who are all watching, agog.

'Looks exciting,' Stephanie calls when he catches her eye. 'Clearly we don't get out much these days.' She gives a tinkling laugh that carries along the street.

Stanley tries to join in, but his jaw is clenched.

'It's not for us,' he growls.

The door opens at the end of the row and Patrick comes out with his newspaper under his arm.

He does a double take before waving at us. 'Looks like I'm missing all the fun out here.'

'For fuck's sake,' I hear Stanley mutter under his breath.

I look him in the eye. 'Is your daughter at home?'

'No.' He tugs at the neck of his sweater and I notice the sheen of sweat on his forehead.

I press on. 'She's not at home? But we're in lockdown.'

He blanches. 'I mean yes, she is at home, but she's busy.'

'Busy?'

One of the Addo-Smyth children has crept closer and yells back to the others, 'It's toys! I told you it was toys. It's got a *Toy Warehouse* sticker.'

Both Stanley and I crane our necks to see the orange sticker on the side, and I keep my face carefully blank. Stanley scowls and the boy runs back to his parents.

'I think you had better take it back,' he says.

Disappointment hits me like a punch in the gut. I try one last time and there's a note of pleading in my voice, 'Are you sure you don't just want to call her?'

'Just do it,' he says through clenched teeth.

'That's a shame.' I try to keep my tone light even though it feels like the ground has given way beneath me and I'm in free fall as I open the app and begin the rejection process, taking my time. 'Kids do love to unbox things. Even if it's a mistake, she could always open it and—'

Stanley frowns at me and his tone changes. 'Is this your doing?'

Heat begins to rise in my face but I hold his gaze and say plainly, 'I did *bring* it here. It's my job – I'm a courier.'

'You know what I mean.'

'No, sir.'

'If I find out—'

'Everything all right over there?' Patrick cups his hands around his mouth and shouts from his front step and I feel a rush of gratitude towards him.

Stanley raises his arm and forces a smile. 'Everything's fine, thanks, Paddy.' Through gritted teeth, he says to me, 'Just take it back.'

I process the rejection on the app.

Are you sure this item is not being accepted by the recipient?

My finger hovers as something makes me hesitate. If I hit '*yes*' the item will be returned to the depot and Zippi will send it back to the seller. Stanley is watching me but he can't see the screen. I hit '*no*' and grin.

'All done.'

★

Patrick calls that evening when I'm out on Ramzan's deckchair, drinking a six-pack of beer, and seeing his name lifts me from the dark mood I've been in since I got home. It's been hard to accept that the castle didn't work. I felt a strange need to see it assembled so I put it together and I'm soaking my feet in the moat, which I filled with water from the kettle.

'Laurel, how are you?' he asks.

'I'm fine,' I lie.

'What was all that about today at the Winters'?'

'Just a wrong address. These things happen.' I wish I was more engaging but my brain feels sluggish. We fall silent. Patrick clears his throat.

'Have I done something to upset you?' he says tentatively.

'No, of course not,' I say quickly. 'It's just been a tough time with everything that's going on.'

'Of course it has, for all of us. I'm going crazy wandering the house. You should hear me talking to myself.'

'At least you've got Polly.' My jealousy seeps out and the words sound bitter. Patrick gives a strained laugh.

'Yes, it is nice to have a neighbour to chat to but you know that's all she is to me. I don't have designs on anything more.'

I sip my beer with a small smile on my face.

'Not like I do with someone else we both know.'

My smile grows.

'Someone else?' I ask lightly.

'Yes, I must say Stanley Winters is exactly my type. All that pent-up aggression.' We both laugh and Patrick drops his voice. 'No, seriously, you know I mean you, don't you?'

My face hurts from smiling so wide and I swig my beer to rein it in.

'I was hoping we could be lockdown buddies?' he asks. 'Be a friendly voice on the phone if the other person needs it. Make sure our heads are in the right place. What do you say?'

I glance at Ramzan's dark windows. His absence has left a hole in my days and I feel a gnawing worry whenever I think of him.

'That would be great.'

'But one rule . . .'

'Go on.'

'No talking about the virus.'

I crack open another beer. 'Fine by me.'

'Where shall we start?' Patrick says. 'Why don't you tell me about your first kiss.'

'You first.'

'If you insist. You won't be surprised to hear that it was rather odd. I was fourteen and we were doing a school performance of *Romeo and Juliet*. I played the nurse.'

I snort with laughter. 'Does the nurse even kiss anyone?'

'We were teenage boys doing an experimental performance. *Everyone* kissed someone.'

I laugh and we drift from jokes to our childhoods to neighbourhood gossip, which is my favourite. I'm pleasantly surprised by how easy Patrick is to talk to. Of course, we've been out a few times and have had sex, but that's always been fuelled by drink. Now we're actually talking it catches me off guard how much of a good time I'm having. He seems to be genuinely interested in all the little details of my life and I find I enjoy sharing, only editing out the parts that make me look bad.

Half an hour later, Patrick is still talking when a sound close by makes me tense. Was that footsteps? My pulse quickens and I grip the neck of the beer. I move the phone away from my ear and listen but there's only silence. It sounded like someone on the stairs.

'Hello?' I call out.

It's too quiet and I shiver, only realising now that the water around my feet has grown cold. It's dark and this section of the walkway is in shadow because of the broken light overhead and I have the odd sensation that someone is watching me. I make a mental note to fix the light tomorrow as I return the phone to my ear and interrupt Patrick. 'I'm sorry. I've got to go.'

'Of course. Listen to me, jabbering on.'

'I've really enjoyed chatting. It's nice to feel connected to someone.'

'Me too,' he says. 'See you tomorrow, I hope.'

We hang up and I listen again. There's another scuffling sound on the stairwell and my heart leaps in my chest.

'Is someone there?' I hate the tremor of fear in my voice. 'Simon?'

There's no response and I lift my feet from the water – the skin is a bluish grey like fish skin – and go inside, locking the door behind me and hurrying over to my desk. My hands shake as I rummage in the crate below and lift out a bottle of red. I'm not thirsty anymore but I sit in my chair, watching the door, clutching the bottle like it's a bat and wondering who could be watching me now.

Chapter Twenty-Six

The estate remains quiet and after some time I manage to convince myself that it must have been a cat. Opening the bottle, I pour myself a glass of red and turn my attention to browsing for gifts for the girl. Just because the castle didn't work doesn't mean I will give up – I just need to be cleverer. I can't let Stanley Winters outsmart me and I won't stop until I know for sure whether the child is Sophie.

And what if she is? Just thinking it fills me with nervous energy and makes it hard to concentrate, but the alcohol helps settle me as I browse. There must be something that will bring her to the door and that's my best shot. Delivering parcels is my job, after all. I look at cute clothes online but what child enjoys a new outfit? I toy with an electric train set but I worry it's too young and maybe she'll be into girly things. After a couple of hours of searching, I feel close to tears of frustration. It shouldn't be this hard but then I realise I have the perfect gift already. Leaping up, I go through into my bedroom and clear the boxes of notebooks from in front of the wardrobe. The doors are floor-to-ceiling mirrors that reflect back the grubby state of the room. The bare bulb overhead doesn't provide much light but it doesn't matter, I know exactly what I'm looking for.

The bag from this year is a large purple gift bag covered in emojis, since I guessed seven was too old for unicorns and fairies. Inside, the presents are wrapped in matching paper. There's a card with '*Sophie*' written on the front but I take it off as I'm not certain enough to give it to the Winters girl yet. What if I'm wrong? I push that thought deep inside and lift out the parcels. It took me ages to choose the sparkly notebook with the two-way sequins – a heart one way and a smiley face the other – and the matching pen and pencil case. There's also a silver necklace with her birthstone, and I'll just have to hope the Winters girl was born the same month.

I don't open the wrapping paper because I don't want to ruin it, but I feel each one in turn, pressing them to my chest. All I need is for the girl to spot the bag and she'll be too intrigued not to insist upon opening it – what child can resist presents?

I collect my parcels the next morning with the purple bag on the passenger seat. The delivery log spits out a route, but I make straight for Paradise Found. Nothing matters to me anymore other than Sophie; Stanley may have come to expect me at lunchtime so I plan to mix it up today.

The Winters haven't ordered anything since Stanley vowed to stop shopping with retailers that use Zippi but there's another box for the Addo-Smyths, who are on daily deliveries since lockdown began, and a heavy box for Patrick. It's the same size, shape and weight as a pair of dumbbells I've delivered to several households this week and I recognise the brand as a company Dominic used to order equipment from for his PT clients. I smile at the notion of Patrick getting in shape for me as I load the van. My delivery log is longer than usual; people are ordering more these days, maybe through necessity but I suspect more through fear and boredom.

When I pull through the gate at Paradise Found, I spot Patrick and Polly outside again, deep in conversation with a pot of coffee between them. Her hair now has orange streaks at the ends and I notice she's wearing eyeliner. How has she managed to change her hair during lockdown? Patrick seems pleased with his new friend and I can't help but feel another pang of jealousy in the midst of my emotional turmoil. She is pretty and confident, the kind of woman I can easily imagine Patrick with, but he did say last night he wasn't interested. That has to count for something.

I hop out and unload the boxes from the back, deciding to begin with the Addo-Smyths' delivery to settle my nerves. It's still unseasonably warm for March again and the short pavement that runs in front of the houses is a suntrap. Where Patrick and Polly are sitting does look pleasant and I give them a wave as I walk to the door of number three and push the bell.

The younger teenage boy answers the door. 'It's the Zippi driver,' he yells over his shoulder.

'Laurel,' I say. 'My name is Laurel.'

There's a commotion behind him as I put the box on the step but I've already got several photos of their interiors so I'm not too worried about how I position the parcel. I'm just straightening up when the rest of the kids appear with Stephanie at their heels. They rush forward and crowd the door, while Stephanie tries to restore order.

'We made this for you,' Issy says, producing a large card from behind her back with 'thank you' written in glitter glue on the front. She puts it on the ground between us, beaming. All of the kids are staring at me and I feel the sudden pressure of tears. Covering my mouth with my hand, I hold back on speaking until I'm sure I won't cry.

'Thank you,' I say, my voice husky with emotion. 'This is so kind.'

'And we got a little something for you.' Stephanie puts a bottle of red next to the card. 'We wanted to thank you for continuing to provide your services. I'm sure there are lots of vulnerable people relying on you.'

I shake my head because it's really not necessary but my eyes are filled with tears and I know I can't speak. Stephanie meets my eye and gives me a grateful smile. 'Thank you,' she mouths.

They have been keeping me busy with daily orders; the parents on my route really have upped their ordering with supplies for home-schooling, but I never expected any thanks.

'Such a lovely surprise,' I say when I can.

The kids drift away back to their schoolwork and Stephanie waits by the door as I pick up the bottle and card. They've drawn a picture of my van on the front with a superhero mask over the headlights. It gives me a fuzzy feeling and I hold it carefully with my fingertips.

'How are you getting on?' Stephanie asks.

'Okay, thank you, but it's busy. People seem to need more now they're at home.'

She ducks her chin. 'Sorry. we must be the worst offenders. I tell Oliver we need to cut back—'

'No, don't do that. I'm happy to help. It's the one thing I can do. It must be a nightmare keeping the kids busy.'

'I'm so worried about their schoolwork,' she sighs. 'They've got worksheets from school but it's hard to motivate them. I don't know if I'm supposed to be a teacher, policeman or mum, and it's impossible to teach them all.' She leans in conspiratorially. 'I barely understand most of what Raff is doing for his maths A level.'

Raff is the eldest. It crosses my mind that I could offer to tutor him, but would that be a step too far?

'You have a little girl, right?' she asks and I frown, trying to remember what I told her. 'When we had that drink, you mentioned you were taking her to nursery, when . . .' She tails off, clearly not wanting to mention the accident with the cyclist again.

I force myself to smile and nod, 'Sophie.'

'How are you finding it?' she asks. 'Must be tough with your job, being out of the house all day.'

I open my mouth but I'm not sure what to say. I don't want to lie to her.

'It's always a juggle,' I settle on.

'I think you said she's seven?' It's all I can do to nod. 'That's a great age. They're just gaining a bit of independence but still can be persuaded for a cuddle.'

My mind reels backward to the last time I held Sophie in my arms. It was that morning, on the way to nursery, when

I strapped her into the car seat. Why didn't I hold her more tenderly? My tears return and I blink them away. Returning to the present, I realise my cheeks are aching from holding the smile, and Stephanie is peering at me in concern.

'Thank you so much for this.' I gesture to the wine. 'I'd better take the photo.'

'Of course. I'll just check on the kids.'

Stephanie leaves the door open but I've got photos of their interiors already so I just take one shot for Zippi. It's the Winters' house I need to see, and the child. It's only then that I realise it's been weeks and I've still only seen Stanley. It's as if he's a guard dog, always prowling. I know in my gut that I'm not imagining his odd behaviour, and I need to get to the bottom of it.

Collecting the parcel for Patrick and hooking the purple bag over my elbow, I walk back towards number one, where Patrick and Polly are sitting. I know Patrick is a writer, but don't accountants ever have to work? I'm being catty, but I can't help it, I'm on edge. I glance over at the Winters' house but there's nothing to see from the outside. Of course, it's very unlikely that it's actually Sophie, I tell myself. There must be tens of thousands of seven-year-olds in London. Just because this one has the same blanket, dark hair and is hidden away by her parents . . . But they *have* behaved oddly. And then there's all the security. My heart skips. It's impossible not to get my hopes up.

'Howdy,' Patrick says. 'I wasn't expecting you until later.'

'Change of route today,' I say. 'Here's your parcel.'

I heave the weighty box onto the step. 'Getting fit?'

There's a flash of what looks like panic in Patrick's eyes before he frowns in confusion, 'Not me. Just something new for the kitchen.'

His reaction tells me not to push it but I'm sure inside is a set of dumbbells. It weighs enough for one thing and the company name may be obscure but I definitely know it from Dominic's work. I wonder why Patrick is concealing something so mundane; it seems like every other household on my route is having exercise equipment delivered at the moment. To cover the awkwardness, I take the photo and upload it to the app.

'Would you like to join us for a coffee?' Patrick asks.

I glance over and see there's still no sign of life at the Winters' place and I'm grateful for the opportunity to delay since I'm not relishing another confrontation with Stanley. 'That would be great,' I say with a smile.

Patrick disappears inside to get me a chair and a coffee while Polly busies herself dead-heading a pot plant.

'Quite a garden you've got there.' A number of tubs have appeared on the pavement between their houses since Polly arrived. She doesn't look up and a small frown creases her brow before she smiles.

'It's the perfect spot – really catches the sun. Patrick and I are having a sunflower competition seeing who can grow the tallest one over lockdown.'

I look around and see two black pots side by side containing weedy sunflowers.

'Is that one Patrick's?' I point to the one that's struggling to open.

'Yes. He insists on feeding it coffee.'

We both laugh as Patrick returns.

'Here you go. This one's Bolivian.' Patrick hands me a mug. 'What am I missing?' Polly and I exchange a smile. I wouldn't say I'm warming to her but I feel a slight thaw.

'How's your mother?' I ask.

This is clearly the right question and Polly delivers a monologue on Evelyn's health complaints. As if I'm not well aware. Patrick and I make concerned sounds in the right places, and all the while I keep one eye on the Winters'. When she runs out of steam, I jump in. 'I'm sorry to hear that. And how's the situation with the neighbours? You mentioned you'd had a run-in with Stanley.'

It's a direct question but I'm desperate to know as much as I can about the Winters. A small frown creases Polly's brow and I realise I'm holding my breath.

'He's been a real shit, actually.'

'There's a lot of tension with the virus and everyone at home,' Patrick says in a placatory voice. 'Especially for them moving in so recently.'

Polly sighs. 'It's not like they're harming anyone. I don't see how anyone could find them offensive.'

I blink at her stupidly, wondering what on earth she's on about. Then I realise from the way she's stroking their leaves that she's still talking about her stupid plants.

'He's asked Polly to put them in the back garden,' Patrick says out of the side of his mouth.

'Where there's no sun,' she says scornfully.

'So we're growing our sunflowers in protest.'

'Patrick's backing me.' Polly gives him a watery smile.

I feel a burning flare of anger that we're talking about something as mundane as a few pot plants. I wish I could tell them that there's something odd – potentially *criminal* – going on right under their noses.

'Have you even seen the rest of the family?' I ask.

Polly gives me a sharp look. 'Yes. They're around.'

'Don't you find it strange that it's always Stanley answering the door?'

They look at each other.

'Is it?' Patrick says. 'I had a nice little chat with Cassie just yesterday in fact.'

I frown, feeling a little silly. 'Cassie?'

'Stan's wife.'

'She'd been out for a walk with her daughter—'

My heart thumps. 'You saw the daughter?'

They both look at me, startled by the sharpness of my voice. Polly's hands stop caressing the plant.

'Yes,' Patrick says, clearly baffled. 'She's not a prisoner.'

I begin to feel a bit hot in the sun. I gulp my coffee and stand up. 'I should be getting on.'

'What's in the bag?' Polly says.

The purple is iridescent in the sunshine. I move it behind my back but it's too late. There's no address or postage and it doesn't even look like a delivery. I'm annoyed at myself but there's no way I can say it's for Stanley's daughter without them asking more questions.

'I'm dropping it off at a friend's. It's her daughter's birthday and she's so disappointed her party is cancelled because of lockdown.'

'How kind,' Patrick says, giving me an admiring smile.

'Bye, then.' I walk slowly back to the van.

*

I return to Paradise Found later in the afternoon, driving through the gate with Rihanna blasting. It's been impossible to stay away knowing Sophie may be so close and a grim determination drives me forward. The gentle heat of the sun has gone and Patrick is outside, alone this time and reading a newspaper, bundled up in his maroon jumper. His eyes follow me as I edge as close as I can to the Winters' house but I just give him a brisk wave and hop out, determinedly ignoring him as I push the bell with the purple bag at my feet. I'll just have to come up with an explanation later.

It takes the usual couple of minutes for the locks to open, and yet again I am struck by the unusual amount of security they've had installed. It crosses my mind that Stanley may not be trying to keep people out but keep them in, and a shiver runs down my spine. His face appears in the gap and it's clear at once he's not happy to see me.

'What do you want?'

'Good afternoon,' I say with a smile, trying to lift the mood.

'What the hell is that?' He narrows his eyes at the bag. It's a bit of a giveaway that it's not in a box and doesn't have a postage label.

'A gift.'

'That better not be for anyone here, you fucking psycho.'

I wince but only allow my smile to disappear for a moment.

'I'm dropping it to Great Ormond Street Hospital after this. It's for children who are too sick to be discharged during lockdown.'

He sags, then restores himself and I have to suppress a smile. One-nil to me.

'What is it you want then?'

'Is your wife in?' I crane my head but the hall is dark behind him.

'I don't see what business that is of yours.'

'I'd like to speak to both of you.'

The vein on his forehead throbs. He should part his hair on the other side. The way it is now only highlights his stress.

'You can speak to me,' he growls.

'It really would be better—'

He slams his hand against the doorframe. 'Just get on with it.'

My tongue feels too big for my mouth as I trip over my words. 'Mr Winters, as a valued customer of Zippi, I'd like to express the company's sincere apologies for the recent delivery mix-up.'

'We'll never buy anything from a shop that uses Zippi again.'

'I'm sorry you feel that way.'

'Do you really think . . .' He exhales and his shoulders drop as he massages his temples with his fingertips. 'It's not worth it. Just stop coming to the house or I'll call the police.'

My smile is gone and I'm tense but I'm sure that's an empty threat. I may call them myself once I see the girl.

'I don't think that will be happening.' I keep my tone light but feeling confident I'm onto something.

'What?' he says sharply.

'Any of that. I won't be stopping and you won't be calling the police, now, will you?'

Stanley's hand darts forward and he grabs my wrist. For a fleeting moment his bare skin is on mine and he squeezes. At first I think he's joking but as his fingers tighten and twist my skin, I let out a yelp and bend backward to try to stop the pain.

'You're hurting me,' I gasp.

He pulls me close and says in a low voice by my ear, 'I don't know what's wrong with you and, to be frank, I don't care. This is your last chance to walk away from here. Stop, just stop.'

'Are you threatening me?' My voice is high and tight, but I feel triumphant. His anger only confirms to me that I'm touching a nerve.

Stanley squeezes once more then releases my arm so that I stumble back a step. 'Fuck off.' He disappears inside and slams the door, leaving me gasping for breath and clutching my arm. I duck my head and breathe slowly until I feel back under control, then I give myself a mental shake and return to the van. Patrick is watching over his newspaper, shading his eyes against the low afternoon sun.

'Everything okay?' he calls out.

I lift my hand and waggle my fingers but I don't trust myself to speak to him. Miming a phone, I put the purple bag back into the front seat and set off for home, wondering just how I'm going to get past Stanley and see the girl. A panicky feeling rises up but I force it back down and tell myself there must be a way.

Patrick rings my mobile half an hour later, just after I've parked the van and am making my way up to my flat.

Stopping on the stairwell, I lean against the wall and answer.

'Hello,' I say.

'*Hola*. I know it's early but I was worried. What was going on between you and Stan? It looked heated.'

I keep my voice casual, trying to downplay it. 'He's a tightly wound guy. I went to apologise after the mix-up the other day – it's company policy – and he lost the plot.'

'I knew it. I saw him grabbing you and was just about to come to your rescue when he let go. That's totally unacceptable; you should report him. How in God's name he works in a high-intensity job, I don't know. It must be like working with a pressure cooker – any moment and the lid might blow.'

'Do you think he's like that with his family?' I let this thought percolate.

'Come to think of it, Cassie does seem to come out of her shell when he's not around.'

I stand up straighter at the mention of her name but I keep my voice level. 'I've never met her. I know you've seen her but it's always Stanley who answers the door to me.'

'Maybe he just works closest to the door?'

I make a noncommittal sound, hoping Patrick will come to the conclusion that something more sinister is happening on his own. It can't be something so trivial.

'He does go out for his daily exercise though.'

The phone almost slips from my hand as excitement whirs in my body.

'That's when I chat to Cassie. She stretches her legs while the girl scoots up and down. I never realised how

perfect the street is for scooters. Perhaps I'll get one myself. It must be good exercise and I'm sure I could pull it
off. What do you think?'

'When does Stan run?' The intensity in my voice is
impossible to hide and I feel a rush of something like love
towards Patrick.

'He's a late afternoon jogger. Five o'clock. I know because that's when I take my tea. I suppose we're all crea-
tures of habit.'

My eyes go to the sky where a flock of birds is circling.
I feel like jumping up and down or kissing Patrick, but I
just cough and say, 'Thanks. I better get going as I've just
got home. Call me later?'

'Later.' We hang up and I run up the final two flights
of stairs and burst out on my walkway with a grin on my
face to see a small boy balanced on an upturned bucket
with his hands cupped against the glass as if he's just
been peering inside. His head is turned to me and his
liquid, dark eyes are round with terror.

'What are you doing?' I demand.

The boy half leaps and half tumbles from the bucket.
He's slight, with a cap of dark hair – I think I've seen him
around the estate.

'There's nothing worth stealing in there,' I say.

He scowls and then rushes towards me, leaving me
with no option other than to press myself against the
stone wall and let him bound down the stairs like a startled fawn.

When he's gone, I carry on to the walkway, looking
around warily. Nothing is out of place. The pink castle
sparkles in the sunlight and I see the tiles are scattered

with glitter. Maybe that's what drew the boy? It does look enticing. I'm not afraid of the kids on the estate but I still wish Ramzan was around. It's exhausting dealing with everything alone.

Chapter Twenty-Seven

The next afternoon, I park near to the gate, close enough to see the comings and goings at Paradise Found but far enough away to avoid raising Stanley's suspicions. My body is humming with adrenaline and I barely slept last night. It feels like I have Stanley hooked and I'm about to reel him in.

It's bang on five when the gate glides open and Stanley bounds out in shorts and a running vest. A slow grin spreads across my face. *Thank you, Patrick.* Stanley's body is on display and it's impossible not to admire his smooth, golden chest on show beneath the wide straps of his vest, though I prefer men to be more manly and rough round the edges, like Patrick. As he jogs along the pavement, I watch his taut back disappear in my mirrors, the muscles and sinew contracting and moving like a textbook example of a runner.

When he rounds the corner, I hop down and collect the purple bag from the passenger side. My fingers are shaking and my mouth is dry, but I shove the plastic handles over my arm and slip inside the gate as it's closing. There have been so many wrong moves, so many failures – I need to get this right. Patrick is out front with his mug of tea, bent over one of the plants, examining the leaves but he doesn't see me. I don't call out; I just keep my gaze fixed on the Winters' front door and keep putting one foot in front of the other. I swallow hard; it's now or never.

Lifting my hand, I take a deep breath and rap on the wood instead of pressing the fancy bell. The cameras are recording anyway but the bell sends a notification when rung and there's no need to give Stanley any extra help. All I can hear is a low rumble of traffic from the main road close by and the cry of a bird overhead. I listen for footsteps but none come. The seconds tick by.

'Laurel?' Patrick's questioning voice calls across the street.

I turn and force a smile. 'I'll be over in a moment.'

Patrick folds his arms as I knock again. How long is an average run? Stanley looks fit but I have no idea of his routines – he could be back any minute. I don't wait long before I start banging on the door with the flat of my hand.

'Mrs Winters, I know you're in there,' I call out.

There's a sound behind me and I glance back to see that Polly has joined Patrick on the front step. They're standing closer than two metres apart – breaking the social distancing rules – and muttering to each other. Polly is shading her eyes to the low afternoon sun and Patrick is blinking behind his glasses. Desperation rises inside me and I turn back to the door, banging with the side of my hand. 'Mrs Winters!'

My hand hurts and I'm about to yell again when the locks begin to turn. A rush of relief and nerves make me suddenly light-headed. The door opens and Mrs Winters peers through the crack. She looks like she does in the photos I saw on Facebook, only paler, and she isn't wearing any make-up. Her blonde hair is greasy and pulled back from her face. I freeze. I've been so focused on speaking to her that I haven't planned what to say.

'Yes?' She seems confused as if she's just woken up or been drugged.

'I work for Zippi, the delivery company.'

'Okay?'

'I'm sorry for the intrusion. I understand you have a daughter?'

She frowns and opens her mouth but I go on. 'Well, good news. You've been selected at random to receive one of our gift bags to keep kids entertained over lockdown.' I lift my arm to show her the bag, but she doesn't smile. Her pale grey eyes don't leave my face and I start to feel sticky in my fleece.

'Here.' I try to hand her the bag but she doesn't move. 'Is your daughter home?'

'What business is that of yours?' Her voice is suddenly steely.

'I . . . um.' I'm sweating now and a droplet tickles my back.

'My husband told me about you.' She lifts her hand and jabs her finger at my chest. 'You've been sticking your nose in where it's not wanted.'

The handles of the bag begin to slip from my grip. I open my mouth to try to rescue the situation, but have no idea what to say and just close it again. I glance back at Polly and Patrick and see that Stephanie has joined them. The whole street is out. Heat rises up my neck and I have the urge to run, but I resist. From the way Mrs Winters is behaving, all I can think is she must be in on it too.

'I'll just leave it here.' My voice comes out shaky. I put the bag on the ground and take out my phone. Of course it's not a real delivery but out of habit I open the camera to record acceptance. I snap a photo.

'What are you doing?' She sounds panicked.

'Recording delivery.' I take a couple more pictures and move back to get a wider view of the house.

'Stop that!'

'It's company policy,' I say but I lower my phone.

'Have you seen this?' Mrs Winters shouts to the neighbours. 'This woman is taking photos of our house.'

I take a few more steps backward to put some distance between us.

'She's with Zippi,' Patrick says as if that explains everything and I flash him a small, appreciative smile.

Mrs Winters steps over the purple bag and comes towards me with one finger outstretched, jabbing at the air. 'She is here without permission. This is not company business. We haven't even ordered anything.'

'Like I said, it's a contest . . .' I try to speak calmly but panic is squeezing my chest. It's all going wrong. 'You won a prize.'

'We never entered any contest.'

I take another step backward. In the house behind Mrs Winters, movement catches my eye and I almost cry out. The girl has crept into the doorway and is bent over the bag of presents. I can see the white line of her parting and a tumble of dark curls. Without another word, I raise my hand and take another photo.

'What the . . . ?' Mrs Winters yells.

Someone grabs my upper arm and spins me around but I keep snapping photos. I'm face to face with Stanley, who is breathing hard. Heat is coming off his body like a winning racehorse at the finishing line. He must have sprinted the whole way here.

'What did I tell you?' he growls.

Tears spring to my eyes. His grip is so tight I know there will be a bruise. He starts walking to the gate but he doesn't let go, and I have to run to keep up.

'I'm sorry,' I say.

'Hold on a tick,' Patrick says, sounding shaken and hurrying after us. 'I think we're all a little worked up.'

'Stay out of it,' Stanley snaps.

Patrick stops a few feet away and pushes his glasses up the bridge of his nose. He glances back at Polly and Stephanie, as if checking he has witnesses.

'Now, Stan, I don't think that's quite on.' He reaches for Stanley's arm but Stanley shoves him with his free hand. Patrick's deck shoes catch on the edge of the kerb and he lands hard on the grass. Stanley doesn't even slow. We reach the gate and Stanley hits the 'exit' button. He pushes me through the gap.

'You need to stay away from here, and don't you ever come near my family again. Do you understand?'

I don't reply, just run to the van and lock the door behind me. I try to slow my breathing and gulp back my sobs. My arm throbs. I blink and hot tears fall down my cheeks. My hands are shaking but I take out my phone and open the latest photo. I've caught the top of the girl's head and her mum's snarl of anger. I check every photo but none have a view of her face. A wail builds in my chest.

Three hard raps on the window make me lift my head. Patrick is outside. He gestures for me to lower the window and takes a deliberate step back. I suck in the pain and wipe my eyes.

'Are you okay?' he says.

Despair is sucking me into a downward spiral and I can feel blood pulsating in my arm where Stanley grabbed me, but I nod blindly.

'That family.' Patrick checks over his shoulder, shaking his head. 'I don't know what's wrong with them. They seem to think that they're above the rest of us. I saw how he had hold of you. He shouldn't treat anyone like that.'

'I'm okay.' My voice is small but I give Patrick a weak smile. 'How about you? Thank you for coming to my rescue.'

The one lift of pleasure I feel is that Patrick tried to help.

'It was nothing, really.' There's a shift as he stands straighter. 'Anyone would have stepped in.'

I smile wider. 'You're my hero. I think I'd better get home.'

'Are you okay to drive?'

I start the engine, thankful that Patrick doesn't know the half of it since I've driven in much worse states than this.

'I'll be fine.'

I don't go straight home. Instead, I drive into central London, passing through Covent Garden and into Leicester Square where the usually crowded streets are devoid of people. It's impossible not to think of a disaster movie, as if I've landed in a post-apocalyptic world, matching my mood.

A solitary man shuffles along the pavement. Pigeons flock and flutter onto the grass having to resort to worms rather than litter. I consider stopping at a police station – they must be still open – but what would I say? The Winters are a respectable family and I can't prove anything. All I have is a photo of the top of a girl's head and my word, and I know that won't go very far. Not anymore.

There's no reason to be out and nowhere else to go, so I make my way home and stop on the way at a Tesco Metro for a couple of bottles of the white that I remember Ramzan liked. I know we're only supposed to be out for essential reasons, but personally, I think the definition of essential depends on your perspective. When I make it back to the flat, I see he's still not at home, and I try not to feel uneasy about him. I fill a mug with tepid wine and put the rest in the fridge, then sit down at my desk and stare at my phone.

I could ring Patrick but I don't want to talk about the Winters or what happened today. I check my emails and there's one from the blanket manufacturer in French. I run the message through Google Translate and discover that only one batch of a hundred blankets was made. They didn't sell well apparently. My heart races and I gulp my wine. My fingers are shaking as I click on the next email, a reminder from Elaine that the Missing Mums meeting is being held online tonight. My mouse hovers over it wistfully. I know I'm not supposed to join but I could really do with the support right now. Without thinking it through, I click the link and see that all you need is to set up a Zoom account with an email address. That shouldn't be too tricky.

It only takes a few minutes to create a new email address with a fake name and I settle on Sophie Winters since she's all I can think of. I take a big gulp of wine and log in to the meeting where a black screen tells me that

I am waiting for the host. While I wait, I create a profile using a photo of Stanley's wife that I found on Facebook, and I sip my wine. There's no law against me returning to group, I tell myself. Denise isn't even in charge so her banning me may not even have been valid.

The black screen disappears and is replaced by a video of Elaine sitting at a desk in front of a bookcase.

'Hi, everyone. I hope you can hear me.' She tucks her hair behind her ears and nibbles her lip awkwardly. Leaning closer to the screen, I scan the titles on her bookshelf and see she's a romance fan. There's also a framed photo of what must be her son on her desk. 'I see a few of you nodding. I know this is a bit different, but we can't let the virus stop us meeting. There's no pressure to speak or turn on your video, but it's just good to be together.'

While Elaine shuffles some papers in front of her, I change my view so I can see little tiles of each member. Of course, I keep my camera off but I get a thrill as I check out each of the other members in turn. Denise has a red scarf tied around her hair and is wearing gold hoop earrings.

'I've got some ideas here of things we can discuss, but first I see there's a new member.' My heart thuds in my chest. 'Sophie, I'd like to extend a warm Missing Mums welcome to you.'

The little tiles of people all start waving. I raise my wine too though of course they can't see me and I pray Elaine will move on quickly.

'Typically new members listen in for a while and when they feel ready, they share their story with the group. Does that sound okay to you?'

Panic hits me as I wonder what to do but then I spot a chat box and I post a 'thumbs up'.

'Excellent,' says Elaine. 'Let's start with my first exercise. Would anyone like to share something they have found difficult this week?'

Audrey offers to go first and talks about how lonely she is. The others all nod along and I find myself nodding too. It *is* a difficult time, especially when you're alone. As she talks, I study the walls behind her and see several degree certificates in frames. It takes a minute or so to decipher them but I discover Audrey has a Masters and a PhD in neuroscience and I fear I may have misjudged her.

Hello, Sophie. A private message pops up from Denise. *I wanted to say welcome.*

I bring Denise into full screen and study her home. She's at a desk with a mug of tea that says 'Number-One Grandma' on the side. My fingers hover on the keyboard before I type, *Hi.*

How did you find us?

A friend told me about the group.

Who?

I feel a niggle of irritation that Denise thinks even she's entitled to interrogate new members. She can't know it's me. I check the tiles to see who hasn't logged on so she can't check my answer and see that Sharon hasn't joined.

Sharon.

Lovely Sharon!

I frown at Denise's fake enthusiasm but post a smiley face. Audrey is still talking about finding solace in television and recommends a programme about a man who breeds tigers and builds his own zoo when a new tile appears.

'Hi, everyone, sorry I'm late.' It's Sharon who interrupts Audrey, sounding slightly breathless.

The others smile and wave as panic floods through me and I move my mouse over to the 'leave meeting' button but something makes me stay.

'Welcome, Sharon,' Denise says. 'It's great that you brought a new friend.'

Sharon is on her sofa in a pink velour suit with a large glass of white in her hand and she's made the effort to put on make-up. Her face crumples in confusion.

'Sorry, what do you mean?' Sharon says.

'You invited a new member along,' Denise prompts but Sharon shakes her head.

'Sophie?' Denise says, acting surprised, but I'm sure she's figured it out.

Elaine and Denise speak at once while Sharon just blinks at the screen. I enjoy the moment of confusion before I turn on my camera.

'Surprise.' I grin and lift both hands, waggling my fingers, realising I've got through quite a lot of the wine.

Their reactions are priceless. Elaine begins typing madly, Denise simply stares, and Audrey, bless her, smiles and waves.

'Shall I go?' I say. 'Something I have found difficult this week . . .'

I drain the couple of inches of wine left in my glass.

'There is one thing. Now, I can't be sure, but I *think* I have found my daughter.'

Zoom really adds to the drama – we should always do group here. I see all of their expressions change at once. The little tiles transform into shock, doubt, joy – it's like looking at the seven dwarfs. Most people put their hands to their mouths. Elaine half stands and then slumps down in her chair as if she's been shot. The only move Denise makes is to put her mug on her desk with a clunk.

'Laurel, I can't in good conscience sit back and do nothing,' Denise says. 'We both know that's not possible.'

I frown. 'Which part?'

'You being reconciled with your daughter. I've spoken to the police. They told me what happened.'

I scowl at her little picture on the screen. 'The police have been useless. I've tracked her down on my own and I'm going to take her back.'

Denise leans forward so her face looms. 'Listen to me, Laurel. You can't just take a child.'

'Someone took mine.' It sounds churlish but I'm past caring. They cut me loose when I needed them most.

'This is very serious,' Denise says. 'You are telling us that you are planning to abduct a child. I'm afraid I'm going to have to report it to the police.'

I narrow my eyes. My crow's feet are deeper than I re-member – it's disconcerting watching yourself on screen.

'You're meant to be on my side.'

My phone starts to ring, and I see that it's Patrick.

'I've got to take this.' I hold up the phone. 'I want to wish all of you good luck with your searches and let my story be a lesson – there's always hope.'

'Laurel, wait—' Denise cries out, but I click on 'leave meeting' and slosh some more wine into my glass before picking up the phone.

'Hello, hello.' Patrick sounds excited and I wonder if he's been drinking too. 'I've been thinking about what happened this afternoon, all that animosity, and I've had an idea.'

'Go on.'

'We're going to have a street party.'

I frown, feeling confused. 'What about lockdown?'

'That's the beauty. Everyone will stay in their own front garden and have their own food and drink but we'll be outside together. The government can't ban chatting. I've already checked with Polly and Stephanie and they think it's a brilliant idea. People can barbecue or bring their own food out and we can have drinks and play music. It will be like a proper party.'

I make a noise at the back of my throat, playing for time while I think. It sounds like the perfect opportunity to see the child and not just that, it sounds nice, but I have no reason to be there. I don't want to admit that I'm jealous.

'You will come won't you?' Patrick says quickly and the tight feeling in my chest eases. 'I know it's not strictly allowed but you can sit at the edge of the group and wave to everyone like the queen.'

I snigger at this just after I'd taken a sip, and wine comes out of my nose.

'Is that a yes?'

When I've stopped coughing I say, 'Stanley won't like it.'

'He doesn't have to. We'll be in our own little area and there's nothing he can do about it.'

'Then yes, I'd love to come.'

Patrick continues planning the event with only the occasional murmur required from me. He wants to organise what he terms a 'sing-song' and wonders aloud whether anyone plays the keyboard. Somehow, I can't see Stanley joining in. While he's talking I polish off the second bottle so my head is swimming nicely. All I can think of is that in less than a week I will finally see Sophie again.

Chapter Twenty-Eight

The day of Patrick's barbecue is sunny and surprising-ly warm for March. Children are playing outside in the estate and their screams and squeals cut right through me. I've called in sick at work since the incident with the Winters, beyond caring about my route since I found Sophie, and it's been a difficult few days of waiting but today I feel lighter than I have done in years. Today is the day I'm going to see Sophie again.

Getting ready carefully, I wash and dry my hair and apply the make-up I ordered from Amazon. I dress in bright, happy clothes: a yellow blouse I found in the back of my wardrobe and a white skirt that I must have bought when drunk but I decide I like. I want to be as Sophie remembers me. Well not exactly as she remembers – a brighter, shinier version of me.

Patrick has called a few times and kept me up to date with his plans for every little detail of the day. He's sent around recipes for food so the residents can eat the same things, provided everyone with drinks ideas, he's even compiled a playlist that he shared for requests. I've been supportive but kept my suggestions to a minimum; it's Patrick's party and I have my own objective.

Since it's such a nice day, I leave the van at home and walk. The streets are silent but for the occasional jogger and the air is fresh without any traffic on the road. London is much more pleasant in lockdown, take away ten million people and it's the perfect place. I stop at the Little Waitrose and buy a bottle of champagne and a family pack of crisps. If this isn't a day for celebration then what is?

At Paradise Found, blue and orange bunting is strung across the bars of the gate. Patrick told me he made it himself from a couple of old shirts and a pair of chopped-up braces. He learned to sew at school, apparently. I'm discovering new gems about him all the time and I really feel like we're getting closer. A cluster of balloons that are tied to the gate gently sag as I go through and see Patrick is the first one outside, setting up his garden table on the patch of grass.

'Laurel, you made it.' He grins at me but he's holding a portable record player in his arms and I notice his biceps bulging. The exercise regime must be going well. 'I'm just finding a spot for this.' The table is already loaded with salads wrapped in cling film, and a big bowl of what looks like punch. Patrick edges the record player onto a clear space.

'Have a seat.' He gestures to the table where there are two chairs.

I take the one at the far side, where I can sit in the shade of the house, with a clear view of the Winters' house at the end of the street but behind the table so it would be hard for them to see me.

'I've put out cutlery for you to use and here's your glass. Help yourself to some punch.'

I peer into the bowl. The liquid is a ferocious orange.

'What is it?' I wrinkle my nose.

'My own recipe based on Negroni, only not quite so lethal.'

I pour a ladle into a glass and take a sip, then cough lightly and gasp involuntarily.

'Good?' he asks.

'Delicious but quite strong.'

Patrick waves his hand dismissively. 'It's mostly soda water.'

Taking another sip, I enjoy the way it settles my nerves. 'Are all the neighbours coming today?'

'Polly and Stephanie are part of the organising committee so they can't let me down. Stanley on the other hand . . .' His face darkens and I feel my insides plummeting.

'Are they not coming then?'

'He said he'll see how busy he is with work.'

Patrick grimaces and I take another sip, keeping my hand near my mouth and nibbling my thumbnail. I try to think of a way to force the Winters outside while Patrick sets a record going and positions the speakers so one is facing the other houses. He's chosen Vera Lynn songs for a wartime vibe that feels a bit sad to me.

'Hello,' Polly calls, coming out of her front door with a deckchair in each hand. Her hair is streaked with purple and she's in a vintage tea dress, and when she spots me, she fixes me with a stare and stops in the doorway. Her smile falters but she recovers and says, 'Hello, you two. Laurel, I wasn't expecting to see you today, what a nice surprise.' The tone of her voice says it was anything but.

She drags the chairs outside and erects one either side of their front door using more force than appears necessary.

'I know this is bending the rules, but would you like to try some of my punch?' Patrick asks.

'Go on then. Quick, before my mum comes,' Polly hisses.

Patrick pours her a plastic glass and tries to catch her eye but she refuses to look at him as she drains half in one go and smacks her lips. 'I needed that.'

Further down the row, the front door at the Addo-Smyths' opens and Stephanie comes out. Her hair is clipped up and she's in a pair of white jeans and a pale linen top. When she spots me she smiles and waves. 'The kids are going to play in the back but Oliver will be out in a minute with the barbecue.'

'Drink?' Patrick gestures to the punch with his ladle.

'We've got our own, thank you.'

She leans against the wall while her husband and one of her teenage sons appear, carrying the barbecue between them. The boy is as tall as his dad and seems to be managing his side much better as Oliver Addo-Smyth staggers under the barbecue's weight. Stephanie disappears and returns with two glasses. From the back garden, we hear the rhythmic ping of the trampoline begin and the bubbling laughter of the children. Closing my eyes for a moment, I let the sound wash over me and try to relax.

'Cheers everyone.' Stephanie raises her glass. 'What a lovely day for it and great you could join us, Laurel.' Her smile appears to be genuine.

She sips her drink while her husband bends over and begins scrubbing the barbecue with a sponge. The top of his head is balding and the pale, freckled skin glints in the sunshine. The record finishes and there's a strange, uncomfortable silence.

'Any requests?' Patrick says just as there's a flurry of activity and two of the Addo-Smyth children bundle out through the front door. Issy is crying and her mother wraps her arms around her, rubbing circles on her back. Issy's tears are soon dry and as she rushes back inside, Stephanie glances up and catches my eye. Her eyes twinkle as she smiles.

I feel Patrick's eyes on me and I turn to him. He gives me a supportive smile. 'You okay? It must be hard seeing other mothers and their kids. I know I sometimes feel a pang when I see dads at the park and I realise what I'm missing out on.'

I return his sympathetic smile. 'I'm fine.'

'Can I ask, have there been any leads?'

I sit up straighter. 'There have actually.'

Patrick's eyebrows shoot up.

'I think I've found her.'

I see Patrick is torn between doubt and joy. He settles on a big smile and squeezes my hand.

'I'm sorry, I know touching isn't allowed, but that is just such fantastic news.'

Taking a deep breath, I put my empty glass on the table. 'Thank you, Patrick.'

'Where is she?'

I help myself to a crisp and crunch.

'I'd rather not say. Not until I'm certain.'

'Absolutely. Just let me know if there's anything I can do.'

Patrick tops up my glass and busies himself with lighting the barbecue and I get a hit of the heady smell of firelighters before the ashy smoke rises. He should have cleaned it first. Soon the Addo-Smyths' is going too and two columns of smoke rise over the roof line. Polly is vegan so she and Evelyn are grilling vegetables inside.

The barbecue gives off a pleasant heat and the weak sun is nice, but I start to wish I brought something warmer to put on. A bird caws from somewhere and I close my eyes. It's the lack of background noise that makes London feel eerie. No traffic, no planes overhead, no sirens.

'You know beef is the worst for carbon production?' Polly asks snottily.

I open my eyes and Patrick gives me a wink. 'I thought it was intensive avocado farming?'

She and Patrick enter into a heated discussion about whether meat substitutes could ever replace meat. I smile and nod but I'm barely listening. All I can think of is the Winters. Patrick is just putting the meat on when I hear a noise from number five and I look up to see the front door opening. It's all I can do to remain seated and quiet.

'Finally,' Patrick mutters, then calls out, 'Hey, Stan? Is that you?'

Both Polly and Patrick stand up and I shrink back in my seat, positioning myself behind the barbecue, hoping the Winters won't notice me from that angle. Stanley comes out first, wearing a black roll-neck despite the weather, his blonde hair perfectly combed into its side parting.

'Neighbours.' He waves. 'Since it's such a nice day, we thought we'd join you.'

Supercilious prick.

'Glad you could make it,' Patrick says mildly.

'Ask if his family are joining him?' I say.

Patrick frowns but calls over. 'Will the family be coming?'

'Well I'm not barbecuing alone, Paddy.'

His sarcastic response makes me want to punch the air but I need to remain inconspicuous so I simply smile and help myself to more punch. I begin to feel a slight softening as the alcohol circulates and it helps me relax. All I have to do is be patient and I'll see the girl. Patrick hands me a plate of grilled lamb chops and chicken skewers but I can only nibble the blackened edges. Oliver Addo-Smyth has finally got the barbecue going and rows of fat sausages sizzle and pop. Evelyn and Polly sit with their heads together, eating salads, and occasionally throw me a look as if they're talking about me but I don't care.

Laughter and shouting carries over from the Addo-Smyth kids as they come barrelling outside and begin playing piggy-in-the-middle in the turning circle. Issy, the youngest, seems to be the piggy more often than most. A misjudged throw bounces over all of their heads and lands in Evelyn's flower bed.

'Watch my hydrangeas,' she yells from her deckchair.

The game resumes. Overhead the sky is an untouched blue. There's a soft breeze. Patrick pops the bottle of champagne I brought and splashes some into my glass. He offers it to Polly and Evelyn but they both refuse.

Stanley remains alone, grilling two steaks on the barbecue, and I begin to wonder if the daughter is a figment of my imagination.

'We've got our own,' Stephanie says, waving a bottle with a yellow label.

'What about the Winters?' Patrick shouts across. 'I hope they're well-watered.'

Stan says something to Stephanie and she turns back to us and pulls a face.

'He has to work this afternoon.'

'Spoilsport,' Patrick says under his breath.

The ball bounds free of the game once more and hits one of the back windows of the Cohens' house – it's lucky they are in France. A few minutes later, it thuds against the glass harder this time and bounces towards the Winters' house, almost landing on the barbecue. Stanley starts to say something to the kids and Patrick chooses this moment to switch off the music, walk into the middle of the road, and clink a spoon against his glass.

'I'd just like to say a few words.'

Polly and Evelyn remain seated and the Addo-Smyths cluster together by their front door. At the far end, Stanley yells over his shoulder and his wife appears in the doorway. I feel a surge of hope but I can't see the girl anywhere.

'It's a strange old time,' Patrick says, 'and I'm proud that we have come together to support one another. If we can take one thing from all this, let it be a renewed sense of neighbourhood. My door is always open – or I should say, my chair outside is always open – for anyone who wants to have a socially distanced natter. To old friends—' he glances at me and smiles '—and new. Cheers.'

There's a murmur of 'cheers' and I knock back the rest of my champagne as the ball squirms free from the gaggle of kids and bounces towards the Winters' house again. Movement catches my eye as the girl appears from behind her mum and skips forward to catch it. I grip the arms of the chair and it's all I can do to remain seated. With the orange ball in her hands, she straightens up and her thin arms go over her head to throw it back.

My breath catches and I feel dizzy. It's Sophie. I'd know that face anywhere. It looks as if she's wearing make-up because her eyelashes are so thick. Her dark eyebrows are straight and then there's the mass of curly hair falling down her back, much longer of course but the same unruly hair. Dominic used to watch YouTube videos for hours until he could plait it into intricate styles.

'Sophie!' I call out but she's lobbed the ball back and is already turning around.

I try to stand but I stumble back. My arms and legs won't do as they're told. I sit heavily and hear Evelyn say archly to Polly, 'The courier is in a state.'

Suddenly I sense the others falling quiet and faces turning my way. I try to keep my eyes on Sophie but when Stanley spots me he hustles her inside with a look of pure fury on his face. Patrick is kneeling by Polly's chair and they're speaking in hushed voices, but when I try to shout again, he comes over and crouches by my chair.

He gently takes the glass from my hand. 'Laurel, I think you've had enough.'

I frown and try to resist but my arms won't obey. Have I drunk all that much?

'I know we're supposed to stay apart but I think I ought to take you inside. Is that okay?'

Testing my legs on the floor, they feel like jelly.

'Help me,' I try to say but it comes out as a moan.

'Is she all right?' Polly says. She's frowning and I notice the green sparkles on her eyelids. My own make-up must be a mess and as my hands go to my face I catch a string of saliva hanging from my mouth to my sleeve. My head bows and the world spins.

'She just needs to lie down,' Patrick says.

I feel his hands under my armpits as he lifts me, and I go limp. I have no idea what's happening to me and tears of frustration catch in my throat as the back of my shoes drag on the pavement as Patrick carries me inside. I manage to open my eyes before we go in. The sky is a relentless blue and the Addo-Smyth children are lined up against the wall, watching me with open mouths but I don't care. I've found her.

Chapter Twenty-Nine

Waking feels like trying to swim up from the bottom of a lake. I begin to stir but I feel myself going in and out until I manage to take a big gulp of air and open my eyes.

'Laurel, it's Patrick.' His voice is close by but I can't bring him into focus. I try to sit up but his arms are pinning me to the bed and panic adds to the swirl of confusion I'm feeling.

'You've had a bad dream,' Patrick says as his arms gently lift and I relax my head onto the pillow.

'Where am I?' My voice is hoarse, as though I've smoked a packet of cigarettes.

'You're at my house.'

Glancing down, I see the navy sheets are pulled up to my chin and I'm fully clothed, which I'm grateful for. The curtains are part way open and fingers of sunlight are pushing their way into the gap. Snippets from the barbecue flash in my mind and I sit bolt upright as I'm hit by the memory of Sophie's face and a wave of panic.

'Sophie!'

'Shhh, calm yourself.' Patrick lays a cool hand on my forehead. 'You've been calling out in your sleep.'

I need to get to Sophie. I try to get up but my head spins and the edge of my vision turns black, forcing me to remain prone. Rubbing my face with my hands, I let out a low moan.

'What happened to me?'

'You had a bit too much to drink.' His voice is gentle but my whole body suddenly feels too hot as I cringe with embarrassment. There was punch and then the champagne but it hadn't felt like too much; I'm certainly used to much more, and it wasn't like I was drinking to forget.

'What was in the punch?' I ask.

'Campari, soda, apple juice and a dash of whisky, but it wasn't that strong. I drank it all afternoon myself.'

I try to count the number of drinks I had but I can only remember two. That can't be right. It crosses my mind that I must have been drugged but the only person who might want to drug me is Stanley and he never got close to my glass.

'You were really going for it.' Patrick coughs and looks away, pinching the bridge of his nose with his fingers. 'I wasn't sure if I should tell you but you've been saying some pretty crazy stuff.'

Our eyes meet and I feel a hit of terror as I wonder how much of myself I've revealed.

'About the Winters' daughter,' he says uncertainly.

The girl's face is seared into my memory and the second I saw it, I knew – a mother always knows – it was her. My Sophie. Her toddler's softness replaced by a longer, leaner little girl, and big front teeth where tiny white pearls were, but the same eyes. Of course, there are a thousand questions like how and why, but all I know is I've found her. Before I know it, tears are coursing down my cheeks.

Patrick pulls a white handkerchief from his pocket. 'Here.'

I blow my nose.

'I've found Sophie,' I whisper, testing the words, and Patrick bends forwards from his perch at the edge of the bed, locking his hands together, the knuckles turning white.

'Laurel, please, think about what you're saying. Stanley Winters is a successful man and they're a respectable family. The girl is their daughter.'

'She's mine.'

'How could that possibly be?' There's a touch of exasperation in his voice and I see in his eyes that I'm disappointing him. He takes my hand and holds it to his lips. There's sadness etched in his face and it's clear that he thinks I'm the one who's sick. I pull my hand away.

'Patrick, listen to me. I've found my daughter. I don't know how or why but I know it's her. That's why they've been keeping her hidden.'

'This is madness.' He raises his voice. 'She hasn't been hidden. I've seen her out on her scooter, in her school uniform, at the shops. Your mind is playing tricks on you.'

There's a silence as we both stare at each other with open hostility before Patrick shakes his head.

'Come on, let's go downstairs and have some breakfast. You need to get some food back into your stomach and you'll feel much better.'

Back? Was I sick? Heat rises to my cheeks as I lick my chapped lips and taste something sour.

'Patrick, I'm so sorry.'

'Come now.' He rubs my legs through the duvet. 'We've all been there and you've clearly got a lot on your mind. I'm going to give you the number of a friend of mine, lovely chap. He was at university with me and went into the talk therapy profession.'

'No,' I say sharply before realising how ungrateful it sounds. 'No, thank you. I've tried it and it's not for me. Besides, I know my problem. My problem is that my daughter was taken and now I've found her.'

Patrick lets out a groan of frustration. 'Laurel, listen to yourself.'

I push back the duvet and swing my legs around. It's an effort but I manage to stay upright.

'I need to go to my daughter.'

He runs his hands through his hair and tugs at his collar as if he needs air.

'What do you think is going to happen if you go to the Winters' house and ring the doorbell?'

A heavy feeling settles in my stomach.

'Do you think they're going to hand over their child to you?'

I say nothing.

'They're going to call the police and you will be arrested. Is that what you want?'

'No, they won't.' But even as I protest, of course I know he's right. I can't convince Patrick she is my daughter, let alone the police, and it would be my word against Stanley's.

'Just come down and let's have some toast. You'll feel better.'

Food is the last thing on my mind but I nod and let Patrick haul me from the bed. I lean on him and he helps me downstairs and into the kitchen. When I see the mess inside, I stop suddenly, my hand going to my mouth in horror. It looks like a wine glass has been knocked from the table and smashed on the floor, a bowl of salad appears to have been hurled across the room, and plates and mugs are overturned on the table.

'I had a bit of a job getting you to stay inside.'

Shame prickles my skin and I feel shaky once more. 'I'm sorry, Patrick.'

'Don't worry, let's just sit you down.' He eases me onto one of the wooden chairs and gets to work clearing up. I massage my temples and try to pull on the loose threads of my memory but nothing comes. I remember the barbecue and seeing Sophie of course; I was outside and then in bed with only a blank in between. Why can't I remember? When I've had blackouts before I've drunk a lot more. All I can think is that the punch must have been much stronger than it tasted.

I stay slumped at the table, while Patrick sweeps up the broken glass, puts the dirty plates in the sink and cracks eggs in a pan. The smells of fried oil and singed toast fill the air. The kettle rattles and he fills a cafetière. It's hard to see a way forward, the Winters are on their guard and they must be expecting me. I know that if I confront Stanley, he will win. Who would believe me?

Squeezing my eyes shut, I try to think of another way. Sophie may remember me but she was only two when it happened. Surely a mother's love is imprinted on her child, but perhaps I wasn't a good enough mother. It was

Dominic who looked after her and put her to bed every night.

'Eat up.' Patrick puts a plate of fried eggs and toast in front of me. Butter glistens on the bread and my stomach churns.

'I'm sorry.' I push the plate away. 'I don't think I'm ready yet.'

'Start with a coffee.' Patrick's answer to everything. He smiles and hands me a mug of strong black.

I manage a sip but it makes me gag. It's hard to think of the woman I was – a respected professional, a high-flyer even – and now I have zero credibility. What must the neighbours think of me? I don't want to lose Paradise Found, but if I'm honest with myself, it feels already lost.

'You're right,' I say.

Patrick looks up from his eggs, frowning. A speck of orange yolk glistens on his chin. 'About what?'

'I've got carried away.'

He takes my hand and massages my fingers. 'You've been through a lot.'

'Do you think I can go back to bed?'

He laughs. 'Of course. I want you to know I'm here for you. We all have our demons.'

'Thank you, Patrick.'

He doesn't kiss me but he rubs a small circle on the back of my hand with his thumb. I put my mug down and he helps me back upstairs into bed. It's a relief to sink into the pillow. The bed smells of Patrick but it's not warm and cinnamon-y like I imagined. There's a clean-ness that belies him – the sharp, citrus note of bleach.

★

I lie in bed with my eyes closed, but I'm not asleep. Patrick is by my side and has been there over an hour. I appreciate his concern but I'd like him to leave so I breathe deep and slow, hoping he'll think I'm asleep. He is silent. I wonder if he's dropped off but I can't open my eyes.

Eventually, there's a creak. Patrick must be easing himself out of the chair. I hear a shuffling – his footsteps on the carpet as he moves to the door. He waits and I count to a hundred before he pads along to the bathroom. The silence stretches until there's a clank of the shower being turned on. The water thuds against the glass door and then the sound softens; Patrick must have stepped inside.

Now's my chance. I throw back the duvet and hurry down the stairs. My need to see Sophie is physical. It pushes me out of the front door and into the street even though I'm not wearing any shoes. It's another nice day and I blink into the sun. My head is killing me. I rub my face with my hands and rake my fingers through my hair. I start walking towards number five, putting one bare foot in front of the other, unsure of what I'm going to do or say but just knowing I need to try.

As I lift my hand to ring the bell, something makes me pause. I don't feel strong enough to face Stanley but I need to find a way to get Sophie outside, to speak to her alone. I take a couple of steps back and look up at the upstairs windows, searching for Sophie's room. A flesh-coloured smudge in the corner of the furthest window startles me. Squinting and moving to a better angle, I see it's a person with their head in their hands. Is that

Sophie? My heart starts hammering but then they look up and our eyes meet. It's Cassie, not Sophie, and she's sobbing as if her world has broken in two.

For a moment, neither of us moves, then she disappears and I feel a rush of fear that she's on her way here. My arms and legs feel too weak to make it back to number one.

'Laurel?' Patrick's voice rings across the cul-de-sac and I almost crumple in relief.

Turning slowly, I see him striding towards me in only a tatty bathrobe that's gaping at the waist, displaying his pale soft stomach. I open my mouth but no sound comes out. Patrick's arm goes around my waist. His skin is damp and he smells of lemons.

'Come on, let's get you back.'

My mind and body go slack as Patrick leads me away. My fight is gone. Why was Cassie crying? Perhaps she knows how close I am to taking Sophie back. Whatever it is, it's more evidence that something is very wrong at the Winters' house.

We make it through Patrick's front door and I sink down and sit on the bottom stair. Patrick squeezes in next to me and puts his hand on my knee.

'You need to be careful. Last night, you weren't in your right mind. You were shouting and screaming all sorts of things and Stanley was furious. It took an hour for me to convince him not to call the police.'

I put my head in my hands. 'I'm sorry, Patrick. I'll get out of your hair.'

'You're very welcome—'

'No, you've done enough. Where are my shoes?'

Patrick goes into the kitchen and comes back with my ugly shoes. He kneels down and puts them on my feet and tears prick in the corners of my eyes at his kindness. I push my fingers against the ducts to stop them falling down.

'Let me at least call you a cab,' Patrick says and I smile weakly, feeling unsure that I'd make it without his help.

He rings a local cab company from his mobile, and thankfully they can send a car within ten minutes. While we wait, I lean my head against the bannister and Patrick sits by my feet, resting his head on my knee and I run my fingers through his thick thatch of hair. From this position, the locked door is almost in touching distance and I can't hold in my curiosity any longer with it so close, looking right at us.

'Patrick?'

'Yes?'

'What's in that room?'

There's a long pause during which our eyes meet and I feel a strange sense of unease. But then he lets out an embarrassed laugh. 'Before Maria left she was using it as her studio and she ended up sleeping in there when things got so bad between us. Instead of sorting it out and doing a charity shop run, I just locked the door. I know I need to clean it up. Ridiculous really, to waste all that space.'

Smiling to myself at the mundanity and my own over-active imagination, I squeeze his shoulder. I know all about hiding from things. It does make me wonder how bad things got with Maria but I know about relationship breakdowns too. His phone rings and it's the cab driver letting us know he is at the gate.

'She'll be out in a minute,' Patrick says. I use the bannister to heave myself up but Patrick's hand on my shoulder stops me.

'Before you go, Laurel, I want to say that you mean a lot to me. You know that, don't you? There's no shame in it but it seems that you could do with some support right now and I want to help you. I've been thinking, I know it's crazy but I'm just going to say it. Why don't you move in?'

'Here?' I can't keep the surprise out of my voice.

'I know it's soon but we need to stick together. We could keep each other company. Just until things return to normal, if you like.'

My surprise turns into something that feels like a bubble of hope rising inside me. It does sound nice, not ever having to leave and Paradise Found being home. Sophie would be right along the street until I find a way of getting her back. It's more than I ever dreamed of when I first fell in love with this place. I must have had a sixth sense that Sophie was nearby.

'I know it's probably a bit much right now, but just promise me you'll think about it.' He pulls me up.

'Thank you, Patrick, I will. And sorry again about last night.'

'I won't hear another word.'

He wraps me in a big hug and I fold myself against him, feeling safe, but then he lets me go and I'm on my own again. Outside, the car is waiting just beyond the gate and it's breezy. Shivering, I get in the back and lean my head against the window so I can watch the sky. As we make our way east, the fluffy clouds begin to blur. The driver has Classic FM on and Beethoven's Fifth begins – my dad used to blast it into the back garden while he did the weeding – and it sounds like fate knocking.

He drops me at the estate and I make my way up to my flat. My body feels disconnected from my brain and it's a challenge to move my arms and legs at the right time. It takes me twenty minutes to reach the fourth floor and there's no sign of life at Ramzan's. Where is he? I sit heavily on his chair feeling despair engulf me. I needed to see a friendly face or hear the happy voices of his kids.

I suddenly really want to hear my mum's voice and I take out my phone and call my parents' house.

'Anne speaking.'

'Mum, it's me.'

There's a pause. I hear the soft snick of a door closing and Mum speaks again in a quieter voice. 'Your father won't be happy you're calling, but how are you?'

'I found Sophie.'

She sighs heavily. 'Darling, don't start all that again.'

'Didn't you hear me? I found her.'

'Laurel . . .' Mum's voice cracks. She begins to sob gently down the line. 'I don't want to talk about Sophie.'

'But, Mum, this time—'

'No. After what you did; everything we've been through.' She sniffs hard. 'Don't you ever think how hard this is for us? Your dad is right. We've got to draw a line under everything that happened. It's not good for any of us to keep coming back to it.'

'Just stop. Listen to me. I have found Sophie.'

'This is ridiculous. Laurel, please, you need to get on with your life too.'

'What's going on, Anne?' I hear Dad's voice in the background. 'Who's that on the phone?'

'Tell him it's me. Tell him I've found Sophie.'

Mum speaks away from the phone. 'It's just the local assistance co-ordinator checking whether we are self-isolating and if there's anything we need.'

'Tell them to bugger off,' Dad says.

Mum comes back on. 'We have everything we need, thank you.'

I wait for her to get rid of Dad and return to the call but she hangs up and I'm left staring at the screen, convinced she will ring back, but she doesn't. The minutes tick by and I feel hollow inside. I scroll again but there's only one other person I can think of to call: Simon. What we had wasn't perfect but it was an important relationship in my life. I lost everything because of him so maybe it's time he was there for me.

I take a deep breath and press 'call'. A cold wind whips through the estate and I shiver as I listen to it ring. Eventually, the automated message cuts in and I hang up, wrapping my arms around my chest and rocking in my seat. I feel all at sea apart from the sudden spikes of pain reminding me that my hangover is still raging. A friend is what I need, someone who knows what I've been through. I try Simon again and I'm about to give up when he answers.

'Hi, Dan, how are you?' His voice has a false note of brightness.

He must be with his family. Five years ago, he used to call me 'Dave' in these situations. I wonder when I changed identity and whether there have been any other 'Toms' or 'Charlies' or 'Robs' between then and now. Knowing Simon, I'm sure there have been, but instead of jealousy I feel bitterness at how little his life has changed. 'It's Laurel. Can you talk?'

'Yes, I know, such strange times. Of course, it'll be in my emails. I'll just go and check for you.'

Away from the receiver Simon says, 'Darling, I'll be right back. I just need to ping over an email.'

I don't hear her words, but her tone sounds tetchy. Simon takes the time to murmur something else and there's a moment where I imagine him massaging her shoulders or nuzzling her neck. Next there's the sound of his heavy footsteps tramping through his house and a door closing before he comes back on the line.

'Hi.' He sounds strained. 'Anything wrong?'

I try to think of how to articulate what's been going on but it's hard to find the words. Almost everything seems to be wrong.

Simon cuts into the quiet. 'Look, I'm sorry, but whatever is going on, I can't help you today. It's Jasper's birthday and we're really trying to make a fuss of him since his party has been cancelled. You know how much of a big deal these things are at that age.'

Still, I don't say anything. Jasper must be thirteen now so really I don't know since Sophie is stuck at two in my mind.

'Shit, Laurel, sorry, I wasn't thinking.' Simon sighs. 'I'll tell you what, why don't I give you a call in a couple of days when things have settled down? We'll chat.'

'Simon.' I rasp and cough. My head feels about to implode; I need someone to understand about Sophie.

At his end, I hear a woman's voice yelling and Simon calls back, 'Almost finished.' Down the line he says, 'Yes, Dan, got it. Why don't you have a read and we can discuss. I'll call you tomorrow.'

'Simon? Wait,' I say desperately. 'I need to tell you something . . .'

'Great, catch up then.'

'I found Sophie,' I say, but he's already gone.

A wave of anger washes over me and I feel like screaming over the rooftops but I simply sit and breathe deeply, wondering where to turn, and then I text Patrick, reasoning that there'll be plenty of space at his house once he clears out the locked room. I can help him.

If the offer is still open, I'll bring my things tomorrow afternoon?

I only have to wait three minutes for his reply. *Great! See you then.*

Chapter Thirty

It takes me most of the night to get the flat sorted out since I don't plan on coming back. The landlord hasn't exactly gone out of his way to provide me with a comfortable home, but I will leave it as I found it, no better but no worse.

First, I pack a suitcase with the things I am keeping. I wear my jeans and a jumper, pack my work uniform, and add a handful of tops, underwear and socks. It's not much but it's a start. I'll need a whole new wardrobe when I finally get Sophie back and I can be the fun mum I always wished I was – some colour for sure. Maybe I'll stop working for Zippi and get in touch with Priya since Sophie and I will need some money for our new life. We can't rely on Patrick forever.

From the living room, I take down my photos of Sophie and place them carefully into the bag's front pocket. The desk and the chair will have to stay and there's nothing else that I want. Back in the bedroom, I lift out the cardboard box from the bottom of the wardrobe – it hasn't been touched since I moved in. Sitting on the bed, I open the flaps and reveal all that is left of my old life. On top is a framed photo of the three of us on a beach, Dominic is shirtless and tanned, holding a toddler Sophie on his hip with his other arm around my waist and his hand resting on the knot of my leop-ard-print sarong.

We spent a week in Dubai six months before the ac-cident, staying in one of those complexes. I remember sneaking off to phone Simon twice a day while Domi-nic and Sophie splashed in the pools and ate ice cream. But there were happy moments – Sophie squealing with delight as her toes wriggled in the sand; Dominic and I drinking wine on our balcony after Sophie went to bed. I'd felt trapped but I wish I'd known then how precious those moments were.

The box is filled with Sophie's clothes and toys and I get a waft of her sweet, milky smell but when I lift her pink jacket with ears on the hood and press it to my face, it's gone and all that's left is the musty damp that per-meates everything in the flat. I feel like crying but I force myself to keep sorting. My wedding rings are loose in the bottom of the box and I slide them on. They're plain silver bands and the engagement ring has a single soli-taire. Simon used to laugh at the size of the diamond but Dominic bought it with his savings – he worked hard for that ring. I hold my hand out but the diamond is dull and doesn't catch the light from the bare bulb overhead.

I pack the rings, photo frame and pink jacket into the suitcase. The rest of the clothes go in the bin and toys I put aside for Ramzan's kids. I add to that pile the pre-sents I collected for Sophie's third, fourth, fifth and sixth birthdays – all wrapped in bags in the wardrobe. It's a wrench to give them away because for so long they were my only link to her but I tell myself that Ramzan's chil-dren will enjoy. Sophie's too old now, anyway.

Next, I locate a roll of black bin liners and bag up everything else. My notebooks are hard work – I tear out the pages first in handfuls to recycle and chuck away the covers. People deserve to have the small details of their lives I've recorded disposed of properly. It takes a dozen trips to the refuse room but when I'm done, the flat is empty. The peeling wallpaper in the living room and black mould in the bathroom look worse without my stuff.

I leave the pink castle and the gifts for the kids on the walkway and sit in Ramzan's deckchair with a page torn from a notebook to leave a note. I put his name at the top but then get stuck. There are things I'd like to tell him but the words won't come. The early morning noise on the estate is muffled. I hear the footsteps on the stairs a few floors away and my body tenses as I strain to hear. Are they coming this way? The soles slap up a flight then stop for a break before continuing.

As they grow closer, I watch the stairwell. Whoever it is slows to a walk. I grip the arms of the chair, my uncertainty giving way to fear. I've sensed someone here a couple of times. Has someone been watching me? I run through possibilities – Simon, Denise, the police? Or perhaps Stanley has come to warn me off. The footsteps are close. I look around for something heavy to grab hold of but there's nothing.

I'm considering picking up the chair when Ramzan emerges and I'm flooded with relief but it's a shock to see his face. All of the condition is gone from his skin – he's gaunt and haggard – and any trace of youth has been drained. He looks older than me.

'I'm in your chair,' I say, forcing a smile.

'Take it easy.' His eyes seem to shimmer as if he's happy to see me or else glad to be home but he just leans against the balcony and takes out his cigarettes even though he's breathing hard. He offers me the packet and I accept one and we both light up.

'Should you be smoking?' I ask.

'Simple pleasures, man. I haven't had one in weeks. Rashida goes mad when I even think of cigarettes.' He points his trainer at the bags on the walkway. 'What's all this? Are you leaving?'

'Yes.' I raise an eyebrow. 'You timed your return well.'

He shrugs. 'Nah, my cousin, Bilal, lives one floor down. I asked him to keep an eye on you. He rang earlier and said you were either chopping up a body and hiding the parts in the bins, or moving out.'

I should be angry that he's been having me watched but I just laugh again. My emotions are all over the place because of my hangover.

'Where have you been?' I ask.

'At my parents'. We're going to move in for a while. It's been tough, Laurel.' Ramzan's thumb ring sparkles as his hand goes to his eyes. He pinches the bridge of his nose. 'My dad has been in hospital. It was touch and go.' My hands go to my mouth. 'God, I'm so sorry.'

He takes a long, hard drag of his cigarette.

'He's back at home now but my mum needs our help.'

'Is there anything I can do?' I ask, ashamed that I've been so focused on myself. Dominic always said I was selfish.

'No, man. We're getting through it and like Rashida says, the new baby will be a fresh start for us all.'

We exchange weak smiles.

'So what about you? Where are you going?' he asks.

'I'm moving in with that guy.'

Ramzan flicks his fingers three times.

'Just for the rest of lockdown. I know that's not strictly allowed . . .'

'When are you going to be needing that driver? I'll wear a suit and everything.'

'Let me have your number. I'll give you a call.'

I pass him my phone and he enters his contact details.

'Make sure you let me know about the baby. There's some bits here for the kids too,' I say.

He spots the wrapped presents. 'You didn't need to.'

I just wave my hand; I can't bring myself to explain. We finish our cigarettes looking out at the blustery sky filled with puffy white clouds and birds being buffeted by the wind. When Ramzan is done, he drops his cigarette and crunches it under the foam toe of his trainers.

'Careful, they look flammable,' I say with a smile.

Ramzan laughs and the heavy feeling in my chest lifts. He starts loading the bags onto his arms. 'Thanks for this. And, Laurel, you take care, yeah?'

'You too.'

He jogs down the stairs, faster on the way down than up, and I listen until his footsteps are gone.

Chapter Thirty-One

I wait until late afternoon before loading my meagre possessions into the van. My plan is simple: I'll wait at the gates for Stanley to go on his run and approach the mother. She'll be easier to handle alone.

On the drive over I listen to shouty rap music to psych myself up. Parking in my usual spot, I watch for Stanley, trying to remain still in my seat to avoid attracting attention, but bouncing up and down with nerves. I swig the bottle of red the Addo-Smyths gave me to try and calm down. It doesn't work so I turn on Radio 4 but I can't concentrate.

At 5pm on the dot, Stanley exits the gate and sets off along the street. My heart thrums in my chest. Five years I've waited for this moment. I'm so close. I watch the hands on the small clock on the dashboard jerk one minute, then two before I can't wait any longer. There's a mouthful or two left that I drain before shoving the empty bottle under the seat and hopping down.

As I approach, a shrill noise stops me in my tracks. It begins as a scream but ends as a shriek; a happy sound like Sophie's giggle. It *is* Sophie's giggle. Through the bars of the moss-green gate, I see the girl's back. She's outside on a turquoise scooter, racing along the pavement and completing a swooping turn at the end of the row. The door to the Winters' house is open and Mrs Winters is perched on the step, staring at her phone.

It's hard to be this close and hold back. She completes the turn and I see her face smiling broadly and my heart stutters in my chest. I feel the pull of Sophie almost stronger than gravity. All I can think is that I need to get rid of Mrs Winters and I rack my brains until an idea forms. I take out my phone and open the Zippi app. There's a notification asking me to complete my availability for the week but I ignore it. Instead, I open the delivery log and review the Winters' deliveries. It takes me five minutes to find an old one for Mrs Winters and I check the photo to see it was a small box that I recall had a GHD stamp on the side. I scroll through the delivery details until I have her mobile number.

Every action I've taken is against company policy and probably also against the law. I figure Zippi and I may be parting ways soon so I don't give it too much thought and tap the number into my phone, hitting 'call'. Mrs Winters frowns at the screen. Her hair *does* look straight. The Zippi handset is programmed to come up as an unknown number and I wonder if she will answer. She's pale and drawn and looks more miserable than she does in any of the photos online. It's hard to tell from this distance but her eyes seem slightly swollen as if she's been crying again.

I keep ringing. *Answer it.* She glances up at Sophie who is charging along the pavement, then slowly lifts the phone to her ear.

'Hello?' She sounds uncertain.

'Hi, is this Mrs Winters?' I put on a perky voice.

'Yes?'

'This is Amy from Zippi customer services. I'm contacting you about a delivery you received on 13th March. A pair of hair straighteners.'

'Okay.'

'We've been contacted by the merchant who has asked us to urgently request a return of the product.'

'Why?'

'Unfortunately there is a fire risk if the product is left plugged into the mains.'

'What?' Now I have her attention.

'It's rare but there have been instances of spontaneous combustion so the entire product line is being recalled. It's all covered by your manufacturer's warranty.'

'Combustion?' Her voice has gone up a notch.

'I'm afraid so but only if they are left plugged into the mains for an extended period.'

'So should I unplug them now?'

'Yes. The product should be unplugged and repacked into its original box if possible for collection. We will send someone.'

'I'd better go.' Mrs Winters scrambles up and calls to Sophie. 'I'll be right back.'

She rushes into the house and I tap the code into the keypad. The gate opens. The girl reaches the end of the path and turns. When she spots me she stamps on the back wheel and stops the scooter. My heart beats hard as we take each other in. I long to wrap my arms around her but I hold myself back: it has been five years.

'Hi,' I say.

She is so grown up. Her mass of dark curls is pulled into a high ponytail with a ribbon. Her button nose is wrinkled. My heart lifts in my chest and I feel a thousand feet tall. It's almost impossible to believe that it's her.

'Who are you?' Her voice is high and accusatory.

I feel a crushing disappointment and say softly, 'Don't you remember me?'

'I saw you at the barbecue. Daddy says you're a psychotic bitch.'

She says it without a wince. It's strange looking at her face. Her chin is square like Dominic's but she doesn't have his bone structure. Children do go through podgy phases. I walk towards her and she holds her ground. There's a round dented pockmark on her forehead that I don't remember. Had she already had chickenpox? My head swims.

'Sometimes even daddies get things wrong,' I say.

She frowns and her mouth falls open and I see her tongue working a loose tooth.

'He said you're dangerous and I should stay away from you.'

I grit my teeth. 'That man is a liar.'

The girl drops her head and when she speaks again her voice is small. 'He says he and Mummy are getting a divorce. Is that a lie?'

Mummy. The word is like a sword through my heart. I glance back at the open door. I'd like to reassure her and tell her everything will be okay but there isn't much time; Mrs Winters could reappear at any moment. I take a step closer and she shrinks back. She's long-limbed with a thick torso. It would be hard to lift her. Would she scream?

'Do you like hot chocolate?' I say.

She nods slowly.

'Would you like to get one now?'

Her head doesn't move but her eyes grow round.

'There's a Costa just around the corner. We can be there and back in five minutes.'

She glances back at the door.

'Your mummy won't even know that we're gone.'

She cocks her head to one side. Her tongue wobbles the tooth and I see she's thinking. The silence stretches and my nails dig into my palms until her frown lifts and she says, 'Can I get marshmallows?'

I smile, relaxing my fingers. 'And whipped cream.'

She lets her scooter fall and walks over to me, slipping her hand in mine. I can't speak anymore. I have to concentrate on walking without breaking down or falling over. Her hand is hot and small and I hold it gently like a baby bird. She skips every third step. We reach the gate and I press the 'exit' button. As it whirs open, a feeling of weightlessness takes over. I can't feel the ground beneath my feet as we walk the few steps to the van. I unlock the passenger door and the girl's expression changes. Her frown is back and her straight eyebrows knit in the middle.

'It will be quicker in the van,' I say.

I smile encouragingly but she tugs her arm away and as her fingers begin to slip from mine, I hold tighter.

'Let go!' Her voice is louder than I'd like.

'Come on, we'll be there and back in a few minutes.' I pull open the door and bundle the girl into the passenger seat. She starts to yell as I slam it and turn the key, locking her inside. My heart is pounding and I'm panting.

Our eyes meet and I see terror that makes me miss a step and stumble as I make my way to the driver's side. It isn't the reunion I pictured.

When I open the door, she starts to scream.

'Sophie, please . . .' My voice is half pleading, half desperation: the tone I often used with Sophie when I couldn't control her.

The screaming stops. 'I'm not Sophie.'

I feel a stab of pain that she doesn't remember as I get into the van and drop my keys on the dashboard. 'Please, can we just talk? Let me explain what's going on. It must be very confusing for you.'

'You're kidnapping me.' Her voice is high and panicked.

'No, I'm your mother. They kidnapped you.' I fling my arm at the gate. 'Those people. I know it's not a happy home and I'm here to take you away.'

I try to squeeze her knee but she flings her legs away from me and her toe connects with an empty wine bottle on the floor. It spins into view and we both watch it turn once until it lands with the neck pointing to me. She lifts her head and there's an understanding in her gaze that makes me cringe.

'Daddy said you drink too much.'

This time I don't call him a liar. 'That man isn't your daddy.'

The girl frowns and goes still. She's looking out of the window and seems to be searching for help but there's no one around. Cassie hasn't returned but I know it could be any second. I reach for the keys to start the engine. Her head turns as she watches my hand and her eyes widen, then her words come out quickly.

'My name is Lottie Winters. I live at five Paradise Found with my mummy and daddy.' She turns to look me full in the face. Her jaw wavers. 'I don't know you.'

Instead of starting the engine, I drop the keys in my lap and reach out to touch the pockmark on the girl's forehead. She shrinks back but a memory edges into my mind.

It was the Christmas party. The bank always held it in January to avoid stories of excess making the papers. Simon and I had booked a hotel for after. I told Dominic I had a client event the next morning and put on a black silk dress, stockings and suspenders especially. I was on my way to the venue when Dominic rang. Sophie had chickenpox. She was asking for me.

'*Bung her some Calpol and she'll be fine,*' I said.

Of course, I went to the party. Simon and I ended up staying two nights at the hotel and I fabricated a client emergency. The chickenpox was a bad case but when Sophie recovered there wasn't a mark on her.

'Please let me go,' Lottie says now. As I study her, I see more of Stanley in her features. They both have square chins and expressive frowns. Could I really have got all this wrong? Humiliation ripples through me but I tell myself I could be mistaken. There are still things about this girl that I don't understand. I stare out of the front window, watching the gate.

'Why is your dad angry all the time?'

'He says you're to blame. He *hates* you.' Her voice is hard with anger but then she sighs. 'But it's not really you.'

I think of the cameras and the locks and Cassie's tears. 'Is something else going on? Something at home?'

Some children would cry but Lottie juts her jaw forward. 'It's my mum he's cross with. She's got another boyfriend. We moved here for a fresh start but Daddy says she never really tried. He's been trying to convince her to stay but she won't. She says we won't be a family anymore but she still loves me.'

My head spins. I'd been so convinced it was Sophie, that Stanley was holding her prisoner, that I'd never considered they had their own problems. Tears run down Lottie's cheeks and I give myself a shake. What am I doing? The family are going through a divorce not committing a crime.

'Of course she still loves you. They both do.' I should know. You never stop loving your children.

'I have a daughter your age.'

'Sophie?' She stops crying and I smile.

'Yes, Sophie.' Up close it's impossible to confuse the two. They're nothing alike beyond their colouring.

'What happened to her?' Lottie says softly.

'She . . .' I think of her in the car. The suction handle on the cracked window. The empty car seat. I close my eyes and the words get stuck in my throat. Until a few minutes ago I thought this child was Sophie. I don't know what to believe anymore.

'She's . . .' I can't bring myself to say it. 'She's gone,' I settle on. 'Come on, let's get you home.'

I go round to her side and help her down from the van. My legs are shaky and her skin is clammy. As we're walking through the gate, Cassie bursts out of her house and lets out a curdled scream, 'Lottie!'

'Go.' I shove her gently towards the gate as it begins to whir. When it's open wide enough, Lottie slips inside and I see Cassie charging towards us. Her face is contorted with emotion; her phone is to her ear. She spots Lottie and the phone slips from her grip and clatters onto the ground as she throws her arms around her child and buries her face in Lottie's hair.

I know I should probably leave but I can't make my feet move. Their embrace is everything I crave. All I want is Sophie back in my arms but it's not her. It's never her.

Chapter Thirty-Two

It's like the world is crashing down around me as I trudge back to my van. I can no longer picture Sophie. All I can see is the empty car seat and the cracked window. I let out a low moan, clutching my head when a voice calls out from behind me. 'Stop!' It's Cassie. I keep walking.

'Hey!' I almost reach the door but she grabs my arms and spins me around. 'What did you do to my daughter?'

After Sophie was born, I lay in bed with Dominic, her in the bassinet on his side of the bed since I was a heavy sleeper back then, and he said, 'Do you feel it?'

'What?'

'The terror. It's like I've been handed a huge glass vase that I need to look after for the rest of my life. One wrong move and it will smash into a zillion pieces. Only I am the glass vase so if it breaks, I break.'

'I think you need some sleep,' I said with a laugh.

Parenthood didn't change me instantly like it did Dominic. It was only after the incident that I understood what I'd lost. Cassie has the same look Dominic did – a glimmer of something wild, almost feral. All her polish is gone.

'I'm sorry,' I say.

'Did you just call my mobile?' She's making leaps, putting it all together.

'I'm not sure—'

'Did you?' She grabs my shoulders and shakes me hard. My head snaps forward and back. I don't defend myself. How can I?

'What is wrong with you?' She shakes me again.

What I did is hitting home. My energy is gone. I want to slide to the ground and curl into a ball. My neck hurts but I don't have the energy to fight back and I deserve what I get. From somewhere behind, I hear Lottie crying. Her sharp little sobs cut through me.

'Cassie?' Another voice interrupts us and Mrs Winters lets me go.

I rub my neck as Stephanie comes into focus. She's in her running gear, approaching the gate, with a shocked look on her face. She gets between us and touches my arm. I don't deserve her sympathy.

'What the hell is going on?' she asks Cassie.

'This freak was harassing Lottie again. She tried to take her somewhere. It's the final straw, Steph.' Cassie's face is a greyish white beneath her make-up and Stephanie turns to me with horror in her eyes.

'Laurel, is that true?'

I lower my eyes, feeling a burn of shame. 'I got confused.'

'I'm calling the police,' Cassie says and looks around for her phone.

'Lottie, can you pick that up for me?' The girl slips away to retrieve the phone and I'm relieved to see her tears have stopped.

Before she returns, Stephanie puts her hand on Cassie's arm. 'Can we just get off the street and talk this over?'

'I'm sorry, I really am,' I say quietly, biting back tears.

Cassie shakes her head. 'You've terrorised us since the day we moved in here. I'm hardly sleeping. Stan is stressed beyond belief. Look what you've done to Lottie.'

Lottie walks towards us and we all look at her tear-streaked face but I drop my gaze quickly. It's too much.

'Mum, I'm okay,' Lottie says in her determined little voice. 'I don't think she meant to hurt me.'

A single tear escapes my eyes but I brush it away with the back of my hand.

'She kept calling me Sophie.'

Stephanie moves closer to Cassie and they speak in quiet voices while Lottie watches me with serious eyes. Cassie bites her cuticles and mutters sharp responses until her anger spills over again. 'I can't have this anymore, Steph.'

'It was a mistake,' I say.

Cassie's arm darts forward and she grabs the front of my fleece, twisting the material and pulling me towards her. 'Too right it was a fucking mistake,' she spits.

'Mum!' Lottie tugs at her arm. 'Please can we just go back home.'

Stephanie intervenes again. 'Cassie, calm down. I know how upset you are and rightly so, but I don't think Laurel is dangerous.'

Cassie turns her pale grey eyes on Stephanie. 'You'll vouch for her?'

Stephanie looks at me. Her face clouds over and I bow my head. I don't even trust myself.

'Laurel, you'll need to stop delivering parcels to Paradise Found, understood?'

I nod.

'And stay away from the Winters.'

'Yes,' I whisper.

'Louder!' Cassie demands.

'Yes,' I say louder.

'And you must never so much as look at Lottie again,' Cassie adds.

'Of course.' I keep my eyes on the ground.

'One wrong move . . .' Cassie warns, and she puts her arm around Lottie and leads the child back in through the gate.

My last semblance of control slips and tears spill over. I feel a rush of gratitude towards Stephanie but it's all I can do to stay upright as sobs judder my shoulders. Cassie would have been well within her rights to call the police and they wouldn't have been happy to see me again. It might have meant a return to prison and I can't bear to go back there again. I shudder and Stephanie touches my arm.

'Come on, let's go inside and have a cup of tea.'

I nod blankly and let her take my arm. It's all I can do to put one foot in front of the other and follow her back into Paradise Found to number three. She unlocks the door and leads me into her front room that's decorated in bright colours with African art on the wall – carved wooden masks and oil paintings with swirls of reds, yellows and burnt oranges – and to a yellow sofa that looks out onto the garden. 'Have a seat.'

I sag down as she leaves the room and when she's gone I pick up a tasselled cushion and hold it over my face, stifling a scream. I'm no closer to finding Sophie after all and I just can't compute it. It feels like I'm unravelling. When I feel back in control, I lower the cushion and clutch it to my chest. There are signs of the Addo-Smyths children all over the room. The coffee table in front of me has homework open – someone is studying the periodic table. Underneath is a wicker basket full of toys that must belong to one of the younger ones – it's filled with tiny dolls in clip-on dresses and boots.

On the wall is a framed photo of the family – they are highly photogenic other than Oliver who is a pale, washed-out man with a prominent Adam's apple. I study the youngest girl, Issy. She must be nine or ten, older than Sophie and of course, mixed race. It's a relief that there is no possibility of confusion. I can look at her without wondering.

Stephanie returns with two mugs of tea, closing the door behind her. 'Here.' She sits beside me. 'Do you want to tell me what's going on?'

I wrap my fingers around the mug but can't drink. I stare at Issy's easy smile, her single dimple and corkscrew curls. I miss Sophie so much it hurts.

'It might help to talk about it,' Stephanie says gently.

I take a sip of the hot, sweet tea and it reminds me that I haven't eaten in a long time. I imagine looking at myself through Stephanie's eyes, seeing the mess I'm in, smelling the wine on my breath, and I slump further into the seat, ashamed that I've let myself fall to these depths.

As if sensing what I'm thinking, Stephanie says, 'I won't judge.'

I shut my eyes and rub my face. I've been running from the truth for too long but it's hard to tell someone like Stephanie, sitting here surrounded by her beautiful furniture and mementoes of her happy children. Admitting what I did feels impossible. It's hard enough to admit it to myself.

I clear my throat. 'You know I told you about the car accident, the cyclist who died?' My voice is barely above a whisper.

'Yes,' Stephanie says.

'Well that wasn't the end of the story.'

She waits. I struggle to find the words.

'Is it to do with your daughter?'

I try to remember what I told her.

'You said she's seven,' she prompts.

I nod.

'Did something happen to her?'

I nod again. We sit, side by side, looking out onto the garden filled with the detritus of children – a punctured football, a discarded tennis racket, one trainer. I try to speak but no words come. All of the children run through my mind. The little girls who were not her but of course, they never could be. Because I know exactly what happened to her, if I'm honest with myself.

'Later that day, I was too shaken to drive so I asked my husband to collect the car and drive Sophie home.'

Stephanie turns to me, her brown eyes glistening in anticipation. Emotion chokes my throat but I keep going. 'They were in an accident on the way home. A lorry hit them head-on. They both . . . They were both . . .'

Stephanie takes my hand. Tears drip from my eyes and roll down my cheeks. Finally I manage to say, 'They died.'

The world doesn't shatter when I say it.

'It was my fault. If only I'd driven as planned. I should never have—'

'You can't think like that.'

The doorbell rings and Stephanie gives my hand a squeeze before jumping up. 'Sorry, let me just get that.'

She wipes her eyes as she leaves the room and I let my head fall forwards. The truth has felt like a shifting, cunning thing that I've struggled to grasp over the years. When something you did hurts your own child, it's hard to admit and it becomes something to run from, as fast as you can, never slowing and never looking back.

From the hallway, I hear the door open and Patrick's voice say, 'Is Laurel here? Stan's been looking for her.'

All I hear of Stephanie's reply is a hissing but Patrick's tone shifts. He becomes defensive and they bat back and forth with me only catching the odd word.

'. . . just tell her I'm outside,' he says.

The door closes and Stephanie returns. Through my despair, I wonder why she didn't let him in or encourage me to leave. I'm sure she'd rather I was gone given all the trouble I've caused. There must be a quizzical look on my face because as Stephanie sits down she says, 'We don't have much time. There's something else I want to talk to you about.'

I see the sorrow has gone from her eyes and her mouth is set.

'How well do you know Patrick?'

'Why?'

'Just . . . how well do you know him?'

Frowning, I try to work out where she's coming from. If I didn't know any better, I'd say she was scared But Patrick is one of those polite, bumbling men who bakes his own bread – surely there's nothing to worry about with him?

'We've been seeing each other and he's been really great. He's asked me to move in with him.'

Stephanie's eyebrows shoot up and I realise that perhaps it is a little soon. 'It's only temporary,' I say defensively.

'I know it's not my place but I don't think you should trust him.'

Now it's my turn to raise my eyebrows. 'Why not?'

'You should ask Polly. They got so close and then . . . Have you noticed how they're not growing sunflowers anymore?'

I shake my head.

'I saw her hacking at them with scissors after the barbecue and she said Patrick wasn't the person she thought he was. Reading between the lines, I think she felt like he'd been acting as if they were more than friends and then you turned up . . .'

I shrug. 'Perhaps Polly misread the situation.'

'I'm not so sure. I've seen them together, acting cosy. And then there's all that business with his sister-in-law.'

'Clara?'

Stephanie blinks and I add, 'He told me all about her.'

'Did he tell you she's been round here making a scene? Making all sorts of accusations . . .'

'He told me she asked him for money.'

The doorbell rings again, and this time whoever it is doesn't let up.

'We're coming!' Stephanie shouts but she takes my hand again. 'Laurel, please, just ask yourself, why is Patrick always in the middle of these difficult situations? It's like he enjoys them. He seems to fan the flames. I don't trust him and I don't think you should either.'

The doorbell is still going and we hear footsteps stomp down the stairs. Stephanie leaps up but the door opens and after a moment Patrick barges in with Issy on his heels.

'Mum, I couldn't stop him.' Her hair is in two bunches on the top of her head that look like mouse ears and her brown eyes are wide.

'It's okay, darling.' Stephanie holds out her hand for her daughter and Issy slips into the space beneath her mother's arm. I feel a tug of sadness as I think of the hollow in me where Sophie should be.

'Laurel, there you are.' Patrick strides over and hugs me before turning to Stephanie. 'I'm sorry for barging in like this but I've been worried sick. Stanley told me what happened and he's apoplectic.'

I just nod as Patrick looks from me to Stephanie.

'Is everything okay?' he asks.

312

'It will be.' Stephanie says it with conviction. I want to believe her. She squeezes my fingers once more then drops my hand.

'Shall we go home?' Patrick asks.

I hesitate, looking from Stephanie and Issy to Patrick. He rubs his stubble and smiles. I nod once and hang my head. Where else could I go?

Chapter Thirty-Three

We make it back to number one and Patrick says, 'Straight into bed with you and time to rest. Doctor's orders.'

I'm suddenly exhausted as the emotion drains from my body. I feel numb. I told Stephanie that Sophie is dead and she still wanted to help me. This gives me a lift and I manage to haul myself upstairs with Patrick's help. We make it into his room and I collapse onto the bed.

'Under the covers,' he says as he tucks me in. I let my head fall back on the pillow.

'Rest now,' he says, kissing the top of my head.

My eyelids flutter shut and quickly I drift into sleep. A while later, Patrick brings me a tray with a bowl of chicken soup, a hunk of home-made bread and a glass of red wine. He lies beside me and takes my hand, putting an episode of *Blackadder* on his laptop. My dad used to watch it and the familiar jokes wash over me in a soothing way. I manage a few spoonfuls of soup. My eyes are heavy but I fumble for my phone.

'What are you looking for?'

'My phone.'

Patrick props himself up on his elbow. 'Don't worry about that now. You need to rest.'

I feel a flicker of panic, remembering Stephanie's warning. 'Where's my fleece?' I ask.

He sighs but goes downstairs and returns with the fleece. My phone is in the pocket and when it's in my hand, I realise how stupid I'm being. Stephanie is wrong; Patrick is the only person who's there for me. And who would I call? My parents? Simon? Denise? None of them are speaking to me. What about Priya to arrange a return to finance? This thought almost makes me laugh. Of course that won't be happening; that dream is dead.

'Put that down,' Patrick says, taking my phone and putting it on the bedside table. 'Relax.'

He hands me the wine glass and I have a few sips. It's a bitter Sangiovese – not my favourite but it's soporific. A new episode of *Blackadder* begins and the familiar theme tune plays. I can't keep my eyes open.

The chime of the doorbell drags me back from sleep where I'm dreaming of the suction handle on the glass. I'm drenched in sweat and my body feels heavy. For a moment I wonder if it's Stanley coming to hurt me but then I hear a woman's voice. She and Patrick talk for a couple of minutes and her pitch escalates until it's clear she's furious. Pushing myself up to sitting, I frown and listen. It doesn't sound like Polly, or Stephanie. I wonder if it's someone Patrick's been seeing as well as me, but then I catch a couple of words of Spanish.

I swing my legs out of bed and stand up. My co-ordination is shot and I have to use the wall for balance as I walk as quietly as I can to the top of the stairs. Patrick has his back to me and is speaking in a raised voice in fluid Spanish to a young woman with dark hair and a slash of red lipstick, carrying a huge backpack, the kind you see on students at airports. Neither of them spot me, so I sink onto the top step, leaning my pounding head against the bannister, and watch the exchange, unable to translate but certain they don't like each other very much.

The woman raises her arms and begins grabbing at Patrick's shirt, her voice dropping to a low, pleading tone. I'm certain it's Clara, his sister-in-law, but then it crosses my mind that this could be Maria and I can't help but feel a pang of jealousy. The woman is beautiful even with her face contorted with fury and despair. They look good together, like the type of couple who should live at Paradise Found. The argument seems to reach a conclusion and Patrick pulls himself free of her grasp and goes to shut the door but she rushes into the gap, blocking him. Her eyes travel upwards and rest on me.

'*Señora.*' She reaches out. Her eyes are wet and desperate.

'Go back to bed, Laurel,' Patrick says firmly but I can't ignore her pain. Leaning heavily on the bannister, I walk down the stairs and join them in the hallway.

'Laurel, please, this is a family matter.'

The woman reaches out and grabs my arm. 'You girlfriend?'

I glance at Patrick and he says, '*Si.*' Despite everything that's going on, I feel a flutter of pleasure like a butterfly inside me, lifting and swirling. 'Laurel, this is my sister-in-law, Clara.' Patrick sounds weary. I give a tentative smile but she heaves the bag from her back onto the floor, and takes out a leather-bound book from the front pocket that she shoves into my hands. It's a photo album

316

and inside the plastic sleeves are images of a beautiful woman similar to Clara, only her features are more regular. A straighter nose, fuller lips, skin unlined by age or worry.

'Maria.' She jabs her finger.

I pour over the photos hungrily; so this is the ex-wife. In the first few she's a teenager in Argentina: long-limbed, smiling shyly in a way that shows she hasn't grown into her teeth, and wearing sexy clothes she can't quite pull off yet. There's one of her on the back of a scooter. Another at a barbecue holding a beer. Her family have been cropped from view but their arms and legs are there, hugging her and holding her close.

I turn the pages until I reach one of Maria with Patrick. She looks only around twenty and he's a decade or so older, but he's handsome in his sharp suit. His hair is longer, almost girlishly so, and he must be wearing contact lenses because his eyes are definitely not that piercing in real life. Maria has a daisy chain threaded through her dark waves. Their heads are tipped back, laughing, and his arm is snaked around her waist. She's wearing a red dress but it's clearly their wedding day.

I glance up and see disgust on Clara's face.

'You ask him where is Maria,' she spits.

I frown, recalling that Patrick told me she was travelling but I turn to him. 'Where is Maria?'

Patrick sighs again. 'How should I know? Bangkok probably.'

Clara slaps her thigh and shakes her head furiously. 'She last in Londres. Patrick last person who see her.'

I'm confused. 'When?'

Clara says the number in Spanish and I look at Patrick to translate.

'Clara hasn't seen Maria since 2013 but as I've told her many times, I can't help with that. She always was a free spirit.' He says something back to Clara in Spanish and I watch the sorrow etch on her face.

'Liar,' she hisses.

'Now you must go.' Patrick begins to push her from the house but I put my hand on his arm and look into her eyes. If what she says is true then Maria has been missing longer than Sophie has been gone. I glance at the photo again, trying to see the truth behind it. Patrick seems happy and Maria is young and beautiful. It's easy to imagine how she might have grown bored by his life. Perhaps she did jump on a flight to Bangkok or Bali, as Patrick said. Why would he lie? Clara must be mistaken but I can't let him push her onto the street.

'Please, Patrick. Can we help her?'

Clara bows her head and I see her anger is thin and beneath is a mass of hurt and pain.

'What do you need?' I ask her.

'A ticket. I need go home.'

We both look at Patrick. He shifts uncomfortably and tugs at the collar of his rugby shirt before throwing up his hands. 'You win. I'll see what I have.'

He goes into the kitchen, opens and closes a drawer and returns with a brown envelope that he hands to Clara. She tries to take it but he keeps hold and says something in Spanish to which she nods.

'The last time,' he says for my benefit.

She snatches the envelope and opens the top and I see a flash of banknotes. My eyes grow wider but I don't let Patrick see my surprise. Clara shoves the money and the photo album into her bag and turns to go but before she leaves, she squeezes my wrist.

'Stay away. He monster.'

We watch her shoulder the huge bag and stride away. Patrick closes the door and lets out a sound of exasperation. 'That woman.' He shakes his head. 'Come on, let's get you back to bed.'

I can't think of what else to do and everything aches, so I let him take me back upstairs and get under the covers where I shiver, trying to get warm.

'Cup of tea?' Patrick says and I nod. He goes downstairs, and I try to make sense of it all. Something isn't quite right; Stephanie doesn't trust Patrick and Clara despises him. And why would he give her so much cash if he's done nothing wrong? I feel a frisson of fear as I hear his footsteps on the stairs but he enters the room with a grin, a cup of tea and a plate of cookies.

'Freshly baked,' he says.

I help myself to a cookie and slurp the hot tea which is heavily sugared.

'You'll feel better once you've got something inside your stomach,' he says. I manage half while he hovers beside me. When I lower the mug, he takes it from me and sits on the edge of the bed. 'You probably have some questions.'

Nodding, I try to order my thoughts but I find the harder I try, the slacker they become. I manage a word or two before black creeps into the edges of my vision and I slide into sleep.

★

I wake to the smell of bacon frying. It reaches into my dreams and pulls me out but I have a hard time surfacing. I struggle and slip back into unconsciousness several times before I manage to push myself up onto my forearms. My head still hurts. Blood pounds in my temples and there's a dull pain at the base of my skull. I'm still in Patrick's bed, alone. The navy sheets are tucked tightly across me and the curtains are open, letting morning sun stream inside. It takes me a moment to process that I must have slept soundly all night and I wonder whether Patrick was beside me.

I wriggle free of the bedclothes, testing my toe on the carpet, but when I put weight on my leg it buckles and I fall head first, landing with a loud thud. It's soft enough that only my pride is bruised and I sit for a moment, trying to work out what's wrong with me. Glancing down, I see I'm wearing Patrick's button-down pyjamas. When did I change? I rest my head in my hands, wondering if I've had a stroke before I tell myself not to be silly. It must just be the events of yesterday catching up with me.

From downstairs, the smell of burnt toast mingles with the bacon. Getting onto my knees, I realise I'm not ready to stand so I use my arms to crawl along the carpet to the door and out onto the landing. I pray Patrick doesn't see me like this. As I listen, voices drift up the stairs. First Patrick's plummy tones, then another man's voice that's quieter but familiar somehow. Who's down there? The bannister helps me drag myself to sitting position and I bump down the stairs on my bottom, the way Sophie used to.

'So how many repetitions would you advise on this set?' Patrick asks, his voice clearer from here.

'Let's start with ten and we can increase as you get stronger.' I know that voice. I'm grateful to be sitting or else I'd surely have fallen over. My body convulses with panic and I launch myself at the door but as I push it open, I feel a flicker of doubt. Surely it can't be.

The kitchen door swings and I see Patrick sitting at the table with his back to me, his laptop in front of him, and on the screen is a man standing in a white room in exercise clothes, demonstrating a lunge. I stagger across the flagstone floor and grab the back of the chair.

'Dominic?' I gasp.

The man's head snaps to the screen. His soft, dark curls fall across his forehead. His square jaw tightens. My ex-husband looks at me like I'm a sea monster rising from the deep. 'What the fuck is this?' he says.

I reach out but my fingers hit the screen; of course, I can't touch him. His face is all fury but five years have been kind to him and he's in great shape – his forearms and calves are muscled and tanned and the deep frown lines I remember are gone. I finger-comb my hair but my hands get stuck in the tangles and I feel a burning shame imagining what I must look like. Dominic always said I was at my most beautiful without make-up but I'm sure he will be shocked to see me like this. Or he would have been, before I shattered any illusion he had of me.

Patrick is the only one of us who is calm and I feel a squirm of worry as he looks from Dominic to me, theatrically.

'Do you two *know* each other?'

'Is this some sort of sick joke?' Dominic says.

'Unless you find my physique a joke, which would be perfectly understandable . . .'

'Shut up, Patrick,' I say. I reach over and pick up the laptop.

'Dominic, it's me. Please, don't hang up.'

He lifts his eyes to the screen. We stare at each other and suddenly I'm back looking at him through the empty car window. The abandoned car seat between us. My throat tightens and it's becoming harder to breathe. Why can't I remember the good times? It's like that single moment obliterated everything else between us. His tanned face is drained of colour and twisted with anguish.

'I'm sorry,' I gasp.

'Don't say that,' he yells. 'Don't you dare say that. If you were sorry you would have changed.'

I wish I could say I have. 'I can't,' I say softly.

He doesn't reply but his shoulders slump as if the anger is gone from his body. We just stare at each other until Patrick takes the laptop from my hands and puts it back on the table. He steers me to a seat.

'Your ex-husband?' He says it like a question but I can tell he already knows the answer.

I nod. What else can I do?

'I seem to recall you said he was dead.' His tone is strangely light as if he's enjoying this.

I put my head in my hands, trying to remember exactly what I told Patrick. It's hard to keep track of the lies but the truth is too painful to admit.

'Hello,' Patrick says brightly and waves at the screen. 'I'm a new friend of Laurel's. Sorry about this. What are the chances? We'll let you get on with your day, then.'

His hand goes to the power button and the screen goes black. I yell in anguish and scrabble for the button but Patrick closes the laptop.

'Why did you lie to me?' he says sternly.

I may have lied to Patrick but he is the one doing Zoom calls with my ex-husband. I think back to when I saw him doing his fitness regime in the kitchen. Was he talking to Dominic then? My eyes narrow. How much does Patrick know?

'I thought we were here for each other,' he says.

'We are.' My voice wavers. I wish I were back in my flat with my notebooks and a bottle of red. Or two. Patrick's kitchen doesn't feel like home; it's full of his things not mine. And I realise I don't know him at all.

'I'll go.' I use my arms to push myself up but Patrick grabs me and pulls me down.

'Sit.' It's not an invitation.

Our eyes meet. There's fury blazing in the hazel and his fingers dig into my arm. 'You owe me the truth.'

I hang my head. I've told so many stories – to Patrick, to Stephanie, to myself – that I'm not sure where to begin.

Patrick fixes me with a stare. 'Just don't lie to me this time.'

So I don't.

Chapter Thirty-Four

Three hours I was with Simon in the hotel room and after, I strode into the office feeling sky-high. My hangover was gone. My head was clear. I made it to our bank of desks but didn't get my handbag off my shoulder before Alison – the team PA – intercepted me, looking at me down her nose.

'Dominic has been trying to reach you,' she said in her nasal voice and gave me a look like she knew what I'd been up to.

'Client meeting,' I breezed. 'Must have left my phone in the car. I'll call him back.'

'He's rung ten times.'

My heart gave a flip and I told myself that it must be an exaggeration. I reached for the desk phone but my hand stopped mid-air. Had I . . . ? No, impossible. But then again . . .

My fingers went to my mouth. 'Sophie!'

Alison was saying something in her whiny voice but I pushed her aside and ran. Heads turned. People dodged out of my way. One of the summer interns didn't move in time and his coffee went up into the air and down onto his shirt. There must have been chaos behind me but I didn't look back.

My heels squeaked on the tiled floor of the lobby. The security guard rose from his stool but before he could intercept me, I slammed my pass on the plastic gate and flew out of the fire exit onto the street. The early lunch crowd was out and the pavement was busy. I pulled off my shoes and tossed them into the gutter. A layer of grime crunched beneath my bare feet.

I found speed I never knew I had. My skirt tore up the seam but I didn't slow down. I lost one little toenail but I only realised much later. The sun was blazing white directly overhead. I tried not to think about how hot it had got. Sirens blared in the distance and grew louder as they came closer. A long, rolling wail. A short chirrup. Too many to count.

I reached the parking lot and took the stairwell. The door slammed against the wall then banged behind me as I sprinted upward. It was quiet apart from my ragged breaths and the slap of my feet on the cold concrete. Up I went, counting the floors, until I reached the final door and burst out onto the rooftop.

Blue filled my vision – the dazzling light, the sky, and the emergency vehicles crowded around our car, all I could see was blue. There was a fire engine, two police cars and an ambulance, and a knot of people blocking my view. I'd been expecting movement and noise but it was silent and still – that was much worse.

I crossed the concourse and barged through the group. Hands grabbed at my arms, my clothes, but I threw them off. The car was parked where I left it but the back window had been removed and discarded on the floor, whole but cracked. A suction handle was attached to the glass.

'Get her back,' someone yelled.

I surged the final few feet like a basketball player leaping for the hoop. A hand grabbed a fistful of my shirt, but I made it close enough to see into the empty window socket. There was her car seat and the frayed straps where they'd been slashed.

Sophie was gone.

I turned on the spot. A blank face shouted at me. I couldn't grasp what was happening. The sun beat down, catching on the windows and dazzling me. I shaded my eyes, scanning the parking lot for any sign of Sophie.

'Are you the mother?' a female voice said in my ear.

I must have said yes because I felt hands on my arms, steering me towards a small group of people gathered at the back of the ambulance. It was then that I saw Dominic. Still in his workout clothes – shorts and a black T-shirt – only there was a foil blanket around his shoulders like he'd run a marathon. His usual tanned face was devoid of colour. He looked up at me from under a curl of dark hair but his eyes slid off me onto the ground.

'Dominic?' He didn't react. 'Dominic!'

'Your husband is being treated for shock,' the voice said. 'Let the paramedics do their job.'

I saw the officer for the first time. She was young and blonde in full uniform including the funny little hat with the upturned brim. Her mascara wasn't smudged – that gave me some hope.

'What's going on? Where is my daughter?'

'The detectives want to speak to you.'

'Just tell me.'

She clutched my arm with strong fingers and thrust me into the path of a young, black man and an older, white woman, both wearing suits. Names were given but it was all just noise to me.

'Where is Sophie?'

I directed my question to the man. He was handsome and I was suddenly conscious that I was breathing hard. My bare feet were stinging and the toes on my right foot were bloodied, leaving a red-brown trail on the pale concrete. I fanned the neck of my blouse. A waft of my perfume mingled with sweat and a distinct note of sex reached my nose. I dropped my hand, feeling a sudden rush of shame.

'When did you last see your daughter?' The woman stepped in. She was harder-looking with an efficient bob and no make-up.

'This morning. I drove her to nursery.'

'The nursery staff rang your husband after Sophie didn't arrive.'

I swallowed. My throat was dry and the rich eggs I'd had at breakfast were sitting heavily in my stomach.

'Have you got any water?' I gave the male detective a small smile.

'Let's concentrate on the questions for now,' the woman said. 'Did you drop off your daughter at nursery this morning?'

'Yes. No. I don't know.' The drive was seared into my brain. Sophie crying. The cyclist. We reached the parking lot and I remembered standing under the sky and feeling sweet relief – my head back, the sun on my face. And then?

'Let me help you. Sophie was not dropped off at nursery. How do you explain that?'

'I . . . I must have.' I couldn't bring myself to say it. 'I've had a lot on my plate.'

'Tell us where you last saw Sophie.'

Sweat ran from my hairline to my chin. There was no shade. I glanced over at Dominic. He was bent forwards with an oxygen mask attached to his face. Terror whooshed through me as if I'd been thrown off the edge of the building. Black spots floated in front of my eyes.

'Please, just tell me, is Sophie okay?'

I turned my eyes on the male detective, opening them wide, pleading.

'This is an active investigation,' his partner said. She muttered something to the uniformed officer and a bottle of water appeared. I gulped it but most of it ran down my chin and onto the front of my shirt. The wet fabric clung to my burning skin.

'Answer my question. When did you last see Sophie?'

'This morning. Around eight thirty.'

'And where was she?'

My eyes betrayed me. I glanced at the back of the car. The door was open and the frayed straps of the car seat were just visible. The cracked passenger window with the suction handle attached was on the floor and I knew I would never get that image out of my head. It was a thing of nightmares.

'Here.' It came out as a whisper.

'Can you repeat that?' She wanted to make me say it again.

I raised my voice. 'Here. I left her in the car.'

Tears weren't going to work on the female detective – that much I could tell. I wiped the sweat from my face and tried looking her in the eye, woman to woman. There was no trace of pity and her features didn't soften.

'Laurel Lovejoy, I'm arresting you on suspicion of child neglect and endangering the life of a child. You do not have to say anything but anything you do say may be used as evidence. Do you understand?'

Not murder.

'So she's alive?'

'Do you understand?' she repeated.

'Yes,' I croaked.

'She's alive. Just about.'

The detective turned away to speak to her colleague as I dropped to my knees and put my hands flat on the warm ground. My body felt wrung out. Tears just wouldn't come. I didn't think then of what might come next; the court case, prison and divorce were a long way from my mind. All I could do was stare at the ground, grit my teeth, and say to myself over and over, *She's alive*, until the knot in my stomach gradually eased.

Before you have a baby, no one tells you that birth is another type of death. A child is born. The person you were before you became a mother dies. You are no longer the top of the food chain – you need to make sure that your baby survives at all costs and if you fail? God help you.

Chapter Thirty-Five

Patrick listens but his expression is inscrutable as I lay my life bare. When I'm done, my heart is pounding and I feel oddly elated. I've spent so long hiding from the truth that it's a relief to say it aloud.

Patrick squeezes my hand. 'That wasn't so hard now was it?'

I shake my head. Suddenly I remember Dominic and my hand darts towards the laptop.

'Be my guest,' Patrick says.

I don't have time to wonder what his motivations are, I just snatch the laptop from him and return to Skype and dial the last number. My heart is in my mouth as the ring tone bleeps but then the call opens and Dominic appears, his dark eyebrows knitted together.

'What the hell is going on, Laurel?' he says.

I ignore the question. 'Dominic, is she there?'

'No. Laurel, no.'

I grip both sides of the screen. 'Please. I need to see her. I've been losing my mind.'

Patrick snorts but I block him out.

'I can't stop looking for her. Everywhere I go, there she is. It's impossible, knowing she's out there but not knowing where.'

I never expected to find it so hard. After everything that happened – the court case, my sentence, Dominic being awarded sole custody, I never fought it – even I could see it was in her best interests to stay away from me. I was a terrible mother but now I'm stuck seeing her in every child, wherever I go. Looking for her every time someone opens the door and I say 'delivery for you'.

Dominic shakes his head and sighs. 'I can't believe I'm saying this after what you did, but you could challenge the court order. We both know they look favourably on mothers . . .'

Even before he's finished I'm shaking my head and Dominic buries his face in his hands.

He doesn't understand; he never has. For him, having a child trumps all else and his whole purpose is to care for her. But I can't change who I am and I saw what I was doing to Sophie. She was a different child with me. A monster of my making. I only understood the expression 'if you love someone set them free' after I became a mother.

He spreads his fingers and one dark eye reappears. 'You never could put Sophie first.'

Heat and shame rise up my neck and I feel indignation. I've sent myself mad by staying away in order to protect Sophie. I'm doing my best for her. But before I can protest, a little, nagging doubt starts inside me. I've always known that to challenge the court order I'd need to prove that I'm capable of looking after a child. I'd need to be sober.

'I'm not a mother,' I say.

331

Dominic lowers his hands and shakes his head. I've disappointed him again.

I swallow and try a lighter tone. 'But my parents, they still want to be grandparents . . .'

'That's not the way it works. How can I explain to Sophie that you're out there living your life and you just don't want to see her? It's better for her to forget you ever existed and that includes seeing your parents. But don't put that on me. This is all your doing.'

The guilt creeps across my chest and I feel suddenly desperate for a drink. A sip of beer, a bottle of vodka, anything. I glance at Patrick but he is standing with his arms folded and eyes narrowed. We stare at each other before he breaks away and goes over to the sink to clear away the breakfast things.

I turn back to Dominic and see he is looking off screen. Hope flutters in my chest.

'Is she there?'

He doesn't answer but I see from the way he clenches his jaw that she is.

'Please, just let me see her. I'll turn off the screen and I won't say anything. Dominic, I'm begging you.'

A sob judders in my chest. He frowns and shakes his head but I know he'll say yes. Dominic's one of the good guys – that's why I trust him with Sophie.

'Screen off. Microphone off. If you say one word I will end the call.'

'Thank you.' Tears drip down my cheeks.

Dominic picks up the laptop. I turn off the video and hold my breath. We get a close-up of his face and the tiny freckles on his cheekbones that I used to kiss as he carries the laptop into another room. The camera jogs and the screen is filled with the black of his T-shirt – it must be pressed to his chest. I feel a rush of anticipation so strong that it's hard to breathe. Behind me, Patrick is humming under his breath and I hear the clink of the coffee pot and he puts a mug of black coffee on the table. I'd forgotten him but I nod my thanks and wrap my fingers around the hot mug to anchor myself.

The screen jostles and turns and suddenly there she is. Sophie. My heart soars. My blood sings. How could I ever have mistaken anyone else for her? She is so profoundly Sophie: the angle of her eyebrows, the upturned nose, and Dominic's freckles. Perfection.

'What are you doing, Dad?' she says and her voice is soft and light like music.

'Work stuff. You need some help?'

She is sitting at a table with what looks like schoolwork in front of her. Dominic positions the laptop so I can run my fingertip across her face and he sits beside her. She asks him a question and I'm amazed by her poise. Dominic tries to help but it's long division and he never was any good at numbers.

I open my mouth to explain the proper way to do the sum but I know I can't. It's my constant battle – to hold back when it damages me but protects Sophie. There have been times when I've lost my grip but I press my lips together. Sophie starts singing under her breath and my heart lifts. I remain perfectly still, drinking in the moment, wishing I could pause time and forget everything else. Looking at them, I can almost believe I could be a different person, a better mother, *sober*. Perhaps, I can change and we can be a family again. I take a deep breath, feeling a new resolve.

Suddenly, the screen goes black.

I feel as if I'm falling into the depths of the ocean and I realise how far from them I am. 'No!'

Patrick's finger is on the power button. I shove him away but it's too late.

'Sorry, were you not done?' There's an odd smile playing on his lips.

We stare at each other and it's like looking at a stranger. Patrick seems to be standing straighter and there's no doubt or confusion on his face. I begin to wonder how much of this was planned.

'Patrick, I don't understand.'

He lifts his hand like a surrender and sits beside me. 'Let's just drink our coffee and have a chat like civilised people. I think we've both been telling some little white lies and it's time to come clean.'

My mind whirs as I sip my coffee and try to think what he might mean. I think of Clara and wonder if Patrick is just as flawed as I am. Perhaps he holds guilt for something too and that's why we've been drawn to each other. I find this thought oddly soothing. It makes him knowing what I did easier. How can he judge me if he's made his own mistakes?

Taking another slurp of coffee, I wait for his confession but it doesn't come. I open my mouth to ask Patrick what is going on but I slump forward onto the table. My head suddenly feels too heavy for my neck. I frown but when I look at Patrick, I see he's smiling and I feel a chill of fear.

'Don't fight it,' he says.

A moan escapes my lips and Patrick presses his finger against them.

'It will be over soon.'

I panic. The mug slips from my grip and smashes onto the floor with a loud crack. Tiny pieces of white ceramic float in the brown liquid. I try to stand but I only manage to slide from my chair onto the mess on the flagstones. I stare up at the ceiling. Maria's face comes to mind and I wonder what Patrick has done to me. Running through my escape options, I think of Stephanie only two doors down, already suspicious.

'Stephanie?' Patrick says mockingly. I must have said her name out loud. 'You told Stephanie your daughter is dead. What is she going to think when I tell her the truth?'

Black presses at the edges of my vision. I've been running from the truth for years. I should have just told Stephanie what happened but I couldn't bear to see her impression of me crumble. How can I ever admit that I left my own daughter for dead? I forgot her so I could meet my boyfriend in a hotel for sex. Ten minutes longer and she would have died – that's what they said. It was such a hot day.

It's easier to say that she's dead, or missing. I don't want to play the victim but there's nowhere to go once I've admitted the truth. I discovered that back when I first served my sentence and I tried being honest with people. Friends stopped calling; men made up excuses. I realised it was easier to lie.

I look up at Patrick and bite down hard, tasting blood at the back of my throat. I know now that I went too far.

I lied so much that I began to believe it myself and now there's no one around me who knows the truth. Is there anyone who will even look for me?

My eyelids flutter. I return to consciousness in a whoosh but it takes a moment to remember.

'Patrick?' I croak.

Above me is a white ceiling with a fluorescent light strip. My head is heavy on a pillow. I manage to lift it and see pale green walls before my strength fails. Black returns to my vision and I feel myself being dragged down. I suck air in through my nose – there's a strong smell of disinfectant.

'Laurel?' Patrick says. 'Laurel?'

He's shaking my arm. I open my eyes and realise I'm in a hospital bed. The metal bars are raised and Patrick is bent over me. What's wrong with me? My pulse quickens but I feel his cool hand is on my forehead and I try to relax. I lift my legs but there's cold metal tight around my ankles. I try my arms and there's a rattle – I'm cuffed to the bed.

'Patrick, what's going on?'

His face is creased with concern but when I speak he smiles. 'There you are.'

As he looms, I can smell the coffee on his breath and see a gleam of what looks like excitement in his hazel eyes. He settles into a chair by my side and takes my hand. I try to pull my fingers away but he holds tight.

'Now you've told me your story, it's probably time I return the favour. No point holding anything back now. Do you remember that night I found you out at the bins?'

Blinking is all I can manage but of course I remember.

336

'You'd delivered packages here before but I suppose I'd never really looked at your face properly. That night, I did, and you'll never believe it, but I recognised you.'

My eyes open wider as questions tumble in my head. I try to speak but Patrick touches his finger to my lips.

'All in good time. You see, five years ago I was planning to write a crime novel and I spent an interesting couple of months sitting in the public gallery of courtrooms. The book didn't work out,' he sighs heavily, 'but I did observe a fascinating case of a mother who left her young daughter in her car seat on one of the hottest days of the year.'

I feel as if the blood is draining from my body and I'm glad to be lying down or else I might have fallen. My arms and legs go slack and the cuffs rattle. I try to think back but my memories of those days are sparse. I was concentrating so hard on holding myself together that there wasn't much room for anything else. All that really stands out were the eyes. There were lots of people staring and judging but I didn't notice Patrick among them.

'Not guilty was the plea. *Not guilty.*' Fury tightens his face. 'How could you say you weren't guilty when you were so careless?'

I close my eyes and shake my head. I've felt sick with guilt since it happened. Of course it was my fault but the lawyers advised me what to say. It wasn't in anyone's interests for me to get a long sentence, that's what they said. I'd made a mistake, not committed a crime. In the end, it didn't matter. The jury didn't agree.

'Some people don't deserve to be parents.' His face is flushed and his whole body seems to be trembling with emotion.

'Yes,' I gasp. That's one thing we agree on.

'Don't you realise that children are precious, longed-for things? They're special and not everyone gets to have them. It's a privilege to be a parent, an honour . . .'

As Patrick rants, my gaze slides from his face and I look around the room. I take in the pyjamas I'm wearing and the rough blanket over my legs. The room is large with the bed in the centre that is surrounded by medical equipment. The floor is wipeable lino and the walls are padded with some sort of rubber material. A cold ball of fear is beginning to set in my stomach.

'Maria didn't get it either.'

His words cut through me like a knife. 'Maria?' I repeat shakily.

'You remind me so much of her, caught up in your own little world and drinking like it's going out of fashion. Maria didn't even cut down when she found out she was pregnant. Not that she told me. No, I only found out when she lost the baby and it was too late. It all came out then. She said she'd been planning to leave me, go back to Argentina and have an abortion.' Patrick's nostrils flare and I can see the whites of his knuckles as he grips the bed rail.

'She said falling down the stairs was fate. Nothing to do with the two bottles of red she'd put away. And that was that. The baby was gone and Maria was pleased. She didn't even mind that she'd broken her leg, once she'd swallowed half a pack of painkillers.'

I look again at the room and the way it's set up: stark and clinical.

'We converted the dining room for her recovery. She wanted a doctor but I felt it best we looked after her at home, without any prying eyes. I had to do everything for her.' He says this with relish and I feel a strong sense of foreboding.

'What happened to her?'

Patrick stares over my head and refuses to meet my eye. There's a faraway look on his face before his mouth twists into a snarl.

'I loved her.'

'What did you do to her?'

He doesn't respond. My head aches and the black pushes into my vision once more but I bite hard on my lip to stay awake. 'Patrick!'

Shouting startles him and he drags his eyes to me. It takes an effort to meet his gaze and see the hard look of hatred reflected back. Fear chills my blood as I suspect what he might say but I force myself to ask again, 'Tell me, what did you do to her?'

He sighs. 'I looked after her, like I always have. But a part of me couldn't forget what she did. Her carelessness meant I wasn't going to be a dad and she was happy about that. Can you imagine how much it hurt?'

His eyes are bright and there are spots of colour on his cheeks. It's hard to see any sign of the Patrick I thought I knew. Thinking of Clara, I force myself to ask the question again, 'What did you do to her?'

He removes his glasses and pinches the bridge of his nose as if it hurts him to recall. 'Let's just say, I couldn't let her leave.'

The words hang in the air between us. I try to sit up but the cuffs hold me down. The rattle of metal on metal seems to get through to Patrick and he puts his glasses back on and looks up.

'And then I saw you again and I couldn't believe there you were, going about your business as if you didn't have a care in the world, after what you've done.'

I think of my little life; my horrible flat and the solitude. 'You know nothing about me.'

'I know that you sat in that courtroom with a smug look on your face and refused to acknowledge what you'd done. And I know that you don't keep in touch with your daughter. You don't even send her a birthday card. Dominic had a lot to say about you when I got him talking. Of course, he thought he was talking to a random PT client who found him on Facebook but he does like to vent.'

I close my eyes for a moment and the temptation to keep them shut is almost overwhelming. It clicks into place that the heaviness I feel inside isn't a coincidence. Patrick must have done something to the coffee. I wonder how long he's been drugging me. Perhaps since our very first date when I felt awful the next morning. The thought makes tears prick my eyes and a wave of hopelessness washes over me. Forcing myself to look at him once more, I say as calmly as I can, 'Patrick, I am more sorry than you can know about what happened. Please, just let me go and I promise you will never see me again. I won't ever come back to Paradise Found.'

Patrick snorts and shakes his head. 'I can't let you go, you must see that. You know far too much. Besides, I think you need to spend some time thinking about what you've done before we start upping your medication.'

I feel a rush of panic.

'What medication?'

Patrick smiles and pats my cheek.

'Just something I concocted for Maria that I think you'll enjoy. You both seem unable to process the guilt you should feel after how you treated your offspring and this should help open your mind, just watch out for the paranoia.'

My body writhes in fear as I try to pull my arms and legs free whilst Patrick crosses the room to a cupboard, humming to himself as he clinks something inside. I think of Maria and all of the things he might have done to her and I open my mouth wide and scream. Patrick's spine straightens but he continues fiddling inside the cupboard before closing the little doors and returning to the bed.

He bends and says in my ear, 'The padding stops the sound and besides, who is there to hear?'

My scream dies as I feel a sharp pain in my leg and see Patrick has injected me with something.

'Patrick?' I gasp.

'Just close your eyes.'

He leaves the room and locks the door behind him. I hear the soft click of a Yale and the turn of a deadbolt. I try to sit up but the cuffs will only let me raise my neck. At the foot of the bed is a window. The glass looks thick and there's an extra square of plastic on the inside so I couldn't touch it even if I could get up. My heart thuds. I don't need to look out anyway to know where I am.

I'm inside the locked room. On the other side of the window is Patrick's garden and behind that, there is the fence and if I look very closely, there'll be a small eyehole in the wood.

Acknowledgements

Firstly, thank you so much to my fantastic editors, Thorne and Beth, who gave me so many great ideas and so much nurturing support – of course, I couldn't have got here without you. And thank you to the rest of the Hodder team for your fantastic proofreading, copyediting, typesetting, designing and marketing skills, all so much appreciated.

Thank you to my agent, Daisy, for believing in me back when we first met and sticking with me over the years. I'm so happy we made it to publication together. And thank you to Jenny for being a fantastic stand-in agent at the start of this process – your advice was much valued.

Jodie, Isi, Katie and James, thank you for taking the time to read early drafts of this book. Your comments and ideas really shaped it. You're all amazing! I also want to thank everyone who has read and commented on my work previously, in particular, my friends and teachers from the City University writing course – that was such a great year and I had a blast.

I'd also like to thank my family and friends for loving and supporting me in this and everything else. Mum and Dad, Andy and Aurore, and Heifa, without you looking after the kids, I certainly couldn't have written this book so thank you! I'm not going to try to name everyone, but thank you to all of the Alexanders, all of the Downs, all of my wonderful friends, and of course, my loves: James, Cleo and Delilah.

And last but not least, thank you to Jodie, to whom this book is dedicated. You are the best friend anyone could wish for. The type of person who would lend you the shirt off their back whatever the weather. Without you asking about my writing, and listening to my ideas (which I fear is akin to having someone tell you about a dream they once had), I'd have given up years ago. You're the best.

In the best books, the ending often comes as a shock.
Not just because of that one last twist in the tale,
but because you have been so absorbed in their world,
that coming back to the harsh light of reality is a jolt.

If that describes you now, then perhaps you should track down
some new leads, and find new suspense in other worlds.

Join us at www.hodder.co.uk, or follow us on
Twitter @hodderbooks, and you can tap in to a
community of fellow thrill-seekers.

Whether you want to find out more about this book,
or a particular author, watch trailers and interviews, have
the chance to win early limited editions, or simply browse
our expert readers' selection of the very best books,
we think you'll find what you're looking for.

And if you don't, that's the place to tell us what's missing.

We love what we do, and we'd love you to be part of it.

www.hodder.co.uk

@hodderbooks

HodderBooks

HodderBooks